A Lover
and A Fighter

CJ George

Published by CJ George

Northern NSW, Australia

cjgeorgeauthor.wordpress.com

ISBN: 978-0-6487336-0-7

Luca was in the mood for trouble. He'd always had a knack for finding it, and today was no exception. As he perched precariously on the edge of the old wooden pier, contemplating diving off into the enormous, angry, pre cyclonic surf below, he recalled his father's attempted words of wisdom earlier that day.

"Whatever you do, don't go surfing… you'll kill yourself you moron!"

Luca had tried hard to shake his bad mood all day. But no matter what he did or where he went, it stuck to him like glue. A surf was what he needed. It always made him feel better. Alive. Free. As the surging, menacing waves smashed against the sturdy old pylons below him and the ice-cold wind whipped sand around him like confetti at a wedding, Luca thought back to the conversation he'd overheard earlier in the day. The one that had put him in this funk. Mrs Rodrigues, his mothers' best friend and neighbour for over 30 years had dropped in for a morning coffee and chat with his mother, as she'd done every morning for as long as he could remember. Luca, standing in the kitchen inhaling his bowl of cereal before his daily run to training, greeted her with his usual obligatory hug.

"Luca, you've gotten taller!" she declared, as she took her regular seat at the kitchen table.

"I'm 27 Mrs Rodrigues, I stopped getting taller a few years ago," Luca chuckled in between mouth fulls.

It never failed to surprise him how alike his mother and her best friend were. Like twin sisters, in looks and in behaviour. Both short in stature, with chestnut brown hair, olive skin, and almond eyes. Wise and knowing eyes. For as long as he could remember, and probably before then, both women had been important influences in his life. From cleaning his scraped knees when he was little and spent too many hours trying to climb trees and ride skateboards; to giving him stern lectures when he came home with ripped pants after jumping his bike off a neighbour's roof. From cleaning his bloody noses when he'd come home from school after scrapping with bigger kids; to cleaning his bloody noses after his father found out he'd skipped school again. And even now, at 27, his two favourite women were there for him after each of his professional fights. Bloody nosed or not. He felt very blessed to have them both in his corner.

"I'm off Mum, I'll be at training until lunchtime then I'm heading over to check out the venue for my fight this weekend. I should be home for dinner." Luca lent down and kissed his mother on the cheek as he walked past her and towards his room.

"See you tomorrow Mrs Rodrigues," he called, making his way into the hallway.

Turning into his bedroom, the same room he'd grown up in and the room he now shared with his two little boys when they came for a visit every second weekend, Luca began searching for his gym gear. As he rummaged through the mountain of clothing strewn hap hazardously across his bedroom floor- some clean, some not so clean, the voices of the two chatting women echoed down the hallway,

"The garden is so overgrown Mireya; I really don't know what I'm going to do about it. Jose never has any time to clean it up. He barely has time to sleep these days, what with working so many hours. I really worry about him sometimes."

Luca could hear the concern in the older ladies voice and knew he needed to help. After everything Mrs Rodrigues, Carmen, had done for him in his life, a little weekend gardening was a small price to pay. Walking to his bedroom door, about to call down the hallway and offer his assistance, Luca was instantly stopped in his tracks. In that split second his heart felt like it stopped beating. His palms became instantly sweaty. Had he heard her right? He couldn't have. It wasn't possible. Was it? Thoughts began racing around his head like a busy intersection with no traffic lights. Could it be true? After all this time, could it really be true? Was Emily coming home? Luca's phone began to ring loudly in his pocket.

"Hello" he snapped, answering the phone while random thoughts flew around in his mind, making him feel disorientated.

John, Luca's boxing coach took a deep breath, "Wow, did you get out of the wrong side of the bed today buddy? Where the hell are you? You were meant to be here training 20 minutes ago."

Luca glanced at his watch, not noticing what it read.

"Shit sorry… I'm… I'm on my way now," he insisted, as he pressed end on the call.

He made a quick grab for any training gear he could see, shoving it unceremoniously into his gym bag and racing out the back door, down the side of the house and onto the road where he started jogging in the direction of the gym. He couldn't have heard her right, he thought to himself as he ran down the long, straight road towards the centre of town. He dodged a couple of parked cars and a neighbourhood cat as he turned left and made his way onto the main road. He must be wrong. He must be. Luca felt confused. And a little irritated. He'd been having a great morning up until he'd overheard Carmen. Overheard what though, he thought to himself. Nothing? Or everything?

He took a deep breath as he picked up his pace. He loved to run. To feel the bitter, icy cold hands of the wind hitting his face as he pushed along the roadway. Damned if he was going to let this ruin his day, he told himself. For all he knew, he'd misheard her. Maybe she hadn't said that her daughter was returning home for good. Emily Rodrigues, the girl Luca had grown up with; spent the best part of his childhood with; who'd left town 10 years earlier to go to university and medical school. Not just visiting, but moving back to LA. After so many years away, so many years without any contact, she was coming home.

"Get a grip man," Luca muttered to himself, as he turned the final street corner.

In the distance he caught sight of the Inner City Boxing Gym. Known as one of Los Angeles best boxing training facilities, with its blue corrugated metal roof, large enough to land a jet, its brightly painted walls, and frosted glass front doors. It was Luca's home away from home. As he approached the building, slowing down to a light jog, he decided he needed to put the whole Emily thing out of his mind. He needed to concentrate on his upcoming fight on Saturday. He couldn't afford to let anything distract him so close to fight day. It meant too much.

"Hey man, where have you been?" John remarked, as Luca raced into the gym and threw his bag on the floor.

"I'm sorry… My watch was slow," Luca lied, unconvincingly.

John could pick a lie at a thousand paces. He'd spent his entire career reading and calling fighters on their bullshit. Attitudes, prejudices, entitlement… John had seen it and dealt with it all. He could tell straight away there was something going on with Luca today, but he didn't push. Luca was a grown man, he thought to himself. If he wants to talk, he'll talk.

"Your fight is this weekend Luc. I know how important this is to you; how hard you've worked for this. Don't let anything get you off track." John said, attempting to sound both stern and supportive.

"I know, I know. I'm fine." Luca replied.

"Then let's get into it my friend," John said, pointing to the boxing ring in the centre of the gym. "Warm up for 10, then we'll throw you a couple of guys to spar with. Nothing too hard… it's fight week."

Luca nodded and headed towards the ring.

"Luca," John called, as Luca turned to face him. "Smile brother, you're one step closer to the top."

Luca smiled. He was close. To all his dreams coming true. Everything he'd worked for, since he was 14 years old. He wasn't going to let anything get in his way. He put his head down and started pacing out his fight strategy.

Now, hours after training had finished, after he'd visited the arena he was fighting in that weekend, visited friends and shopped for a new suit, all the while trying to shake the feeling of unease in the pit of his stomach, he found himself sitting on the old wooden pier staring into the angry ocean. Metres above the earth, about to jump into the menacing, tumultuous water, Luca grappled with the realisation that he couldn't forget; he couldn't pretend. His life was unequivocally and without doubt, about to change. Just as it had all those years before. Emily was coming home.

Chapter 1

Balancing unevenly on the old wooden swing in her parent's backyard, under the enormous, gnarled oak tree with its twisted and deformed branches reaching out into the night's sky, Luca knew Emily would find him there. The place they'd spent so many hours as children; laughing, talking, and dreaming. How long had it been since they'd seen each other, he considered. 10 years maybe? How quickly the years had passed without her in his life. Like a split second, and an eternity all at once. Their last goodbyes had been in this place. Sitting together on the same swing, talking about how their lives would be, pretending to be older and wiser than their 17 years. Just babies.

"I swear I'll come and visit every summer," Emily had promised. "And I'll call you every week so you can tell me all about your training. You're gonna be the best fighter in the world one day Luca."

With her beautiful, innocent brown eyes, the colour of dark chocolate, he'd believed every word Emily had said that day. He always did. And she'd almost been right.

He remembered how he'd felt the day she told him she'd received the scholarship to attend college in North Carolina. On the other side of the country. A far cry from the broken and battered streets of the housing commission suburb they lived in. He'd been confused and hurt at first. That she would want to leave... to move away from her home, her friends, her family... him. Then he'd been angry. So angry he hadn't spoken to her for almost two weeks. He'd regretted that for a long time after she'd left. If he was being brutally honest, he regretted a lot of things in his life, both before and after that time.

She'd phoned him a few times from college. Short, excited, and enthusiastic calls. She told him she'd found a great apartment in the city; with a girl she'd met in her class. That her schedule left her with no time for a social life, but she loved it anyway. Medicine had always been her passion, even from an early age. Luca smiled as he remembered the time he'd dragged his ass home one afternoon, no older than 13, covered in blood, sweat and dirt after a brawl with some older guys from the block. Five against one: and he'd won, he thought proudly. He always won street fights as a kid. It had been his thing; his calling card in the neighbourhood. At the time he'd wanted to avoid his father, who was sure to give him a good beating for fighting so he'd jumped the back fence into Emily's yard. He found her where she always was; sitting on the swing, book in hand, learning something completely unimportant, if you asked him. She was always reading. Always learning. For the life of him, he could never work out why? Everything he'd ever needed to know was always right in front of him. He learnt from seeing and doing… from feeling and living… not from what some smart dude wrote in a book once.

He walked towards her, dirty and bleeding with a satisfied look on his face as she looked up from her book. Her own face, he noted, went from warm and friendly, to shocked and scared in an instant. Sitting on the old weathered swing now, many years later, he remembered how much fun he used to have trying to shock her, or surprise her, or occasionally even scare her. At the age of 13 years, he liked to consider it his own form of personal entertainment. And if she refused to speak to him for a week or two afterwards, it was always worth it for the look on her face, the fire in her eyes. She'd leapt up and run over to him, talking a million miles an hour about responsibility, and risk-taking behaviour, and all he could think about was how he might have preferred a beating from his father then a lecture from Emily! He was granted a short reprieve as Emily, quick as a flash, raced inside her parents' home and returned with all the equipment of a small medical centre, ready to patch him up.

She actually wasn't too bad at it, except when she pushed the dressing on a little too hard. Probably on purpose, he thought to himself now. But in that moment, he remembered thinking he was probably lucky to have her, even if she was a girl. She'd always been there when he needed her. In fact, he couldn't remember a time in his life when she hadn't been there. Despite her annoying him constantly, and always telling him what to do, at the age of 13 he knew they were going to be friends forever and nothing was ever going to come between them. Luca chuckled to himself, reminiscing about old times. He was never usually sentimental; never one to ponder. "Keep it together man," he muttered under his breath.

It had been a long time since he'd found himself sitting on the swing in the Rodrigues's backyard. He'd tried to keep coming, for old time's sakes, after Emily had left for college. He would jump the fence and sit in the peace and quiet of the yard, with its overgrown, well-loved flower beds exploding with colour and the smell of spring. The vegetable garden in the back corner grew all manner of tasty treats including tomatoes, lettuce and broad beans which he often enjoyed sampling. In the centre of the garden sat the piece de resistance- a little stone birdbath no wider than a dinner plate. Emily's father called it his water feature, which always made them laugh hysterically. Sitting in this place, while ambulance and police sirens blared in the distance, he would try to remember things they'd talked about, life decisions they'd made and promises they'd said they would keep. He especially found himself spending time here after her phone calls, while her voice was fresh in his mind. But as happy as he was to hear from her, to hear her funny and witty stories, it always left him saddened by just how much he missed his best friend; just how much he had relied on her before she'd left him behind.

As time went by, weeks turning into months, Luca began missing Emily's phone calls. He always told himself he'd call her back. He genuinely intended to. But for one reason or another he just never got around to it. Sometimes he was hanging out with friends from the local area. Surfing usually. As past times went, surfing was Luca's all-time favourite. He loved the feeling of paddling onto a wave, doing battle with the power, fury, and fierceness of nature, and coming out the victor… mostly. He could literally surf all day… rain or shine, and never get tired of it. But more often than not, he was at training with his boxing coach John Graham. A local legend in the area, John owned and ran a boxing gym just five minutes from Luca's house. Almost as soon as he started training at Inner City Boxing, it became one of Luca's favourite places. Somewhere to escape the dramas of life in a poor neighbourhood. To dream about success and achievement; to beat away at the stiff hand that life often dealt him. Inner City Boxing Gym had undoubtedly saved Luca's life… in ways even he was yet to realise.

So, when Emily eventually stopped calling, and life kept marching forward, months into years, Luca found purpose and drive in his daily training regime. In pushing himself to his limits, testing his strength & endurance, his will power and courage. Without even realising it, Emily slowly became a distant memory. A warm, friendly, and heart-warming one… but a memory all the same. Now, sitting in this place full of memories, waiting for her to walk back into his life after so much time had passed, Luca tried to recall the last time he'd spoken to his childhood best friend. The shy, unassuming, brown eyed, brown haired girl with glasses and her nose always in a book, who had shaped his childhood like no one else. But he couldn't. It had been too long. A feeling of apprehension began to creep in. What if she'd forgotten about him after all this time?

Emily hoped he would be there. She had imagined a thousand times over what it would be like to see him again after so many years. Would it be the same? Would he be the same? In her sensible, analytical mind, she knew that he wouldn't. That he couldn't. She knew for certain that after so much time, so much water under the bridge, so many new experiences, places and people, she wasn't the same girl who'd left all those years before. That shy and quiet little girl, who'd have happily chosen to melt into the floor rather than stand in front of a room full of people, let alone say anything, was well and truly gone. As were the dorky glasses, purchased when Emily was 14 to help her read, replaced by clear contact lenses, and the short bob of dark brown hair which was all the rage at 12, replaced with a long, naturally wavy style that Emily was very proud of. It had taken her almost the whole 10 years she was away to grow her hair halfway down her back and be damned if she was ever cutting it again! If you asked her friends in North Carolina to describe Emily now, they would say she was a go getter. A warrior for social justice. A kind and generous soul who listened more than she spoke, but who gave her opinion openly and honestly. When she didn't have her head in a book researching the latest and greatest evidence on some new medical procedure, she was working to heal the sick and injured with a passion and drive that many admired. She had certainly changed.

As she pulled her car up to the curb at the front of her parents two-bedroom home, her childhood home, with its dusty windows, overgrown front lawn and paint peeled white fibro walls that looked like they had weathered many storms… Emily wondered who her childhood best friend had become? Would she even recognise the face of the person who had, at one time, been more important to her than anyone else? Emily turned off her car, a 2018 Jeep Wrangler, bought second hand three weeks earlier to make the epic trip across the country, from North Carolina to LA, and closed her eyes. The stress and strain of packing up her entire life, selling almost all of her possessions and saying goodbye to her friends, mixed with spending the last couple of weeks exploring and sightseeing across the US on her drive home, had worn her out. She was tired. More than tired, she was exhausted. Both physically and mentally. The last few years had really taken its toll on her. Between studying and passing her exams, to working 60 to 80 hours per weeks to prove herself in her chosen career, Emily hadn't been left with much time for anything else. She sighed as she recalled the texts and phone messages left on her phone each weekend by friends, begging and pleading with her to go dancing or drinking or to the movies. She'd always intended to go. But most times something had come up. Work, study… life.

It was time for her to take a break, she thought. Recharge and recuperate. To take stock of her life and what she really wanted from it. To finally, after 10 long years away from home, spend some quality time with her family. Her parents weren't getting any younger. She worked every day with people the same age as her parents. People who suffered from chronic disease and illness. She saw firsthand how fragile and futile life could be, and how quickly it could all change. Only a month before, she'd cared for a patient who'd come into the Emergency department feeling unwell, only to have a heart attack and pass away not 10 minutes later. It used to shock her when someone died in front of her. It used to deeply affect her. Seeing the patient deteriorate in front of her eyes, having spoken to them only shortly beforehand. Witnessing their families' grief at losing a loved one. As much as she loved her job, loved helping people, those times really made her pause and reflect on the career she'd chosen all those years before. She often wondered how different her life would have been if she'd just stayed in LA? Sitting in her car, head resting heavily on the back of the seat, eyes closed, Emily wondered if coming home now, after all this time, was the right choice?

"I guess only time will tell," she mused.

The anticipation of returning home after so long had almost made her sick these past few weeks. Sick with excitement at seeing her friends and family after so long. Nervous and uneasy at all the changes she knew had taken place since she'd driven away all those years ago. From the moment she'd completed her medical training, and even before then, she'd thought about coming home. How could she not return to the place she was born? The place she loved more than anywhere. The place where she'd seen so much poverty and illness, crime, and injustice firsthand. The place she saw so much opportunity to use her medical knowledge and skills to make a difference to the people who mattered most to her. Growing up in one of the poorest areas of Los Angeles, in government housing no less, had given Emily a unique perspective on life. A perspective she always made sure was at the front of her mind when she was studying her medical degree.

As a second generation Hispanic, the daughter of Mexican immigrants, Emily knew hardship and struggle. Her parents both worked two jobs when she was little, to put food on the table. The day Emily received her letter, advising that she'd been awarded a full scholarship to attend university and study undergraduate medicine, her parents had cried. Emily often wondered if it was because they were proud of her, or relieved they no longer needed to pay for her big dream.

University had been incredibly challenging. Emily had known it would be hard, but she'd never guessed just how hard. From studying textbooks to lectures and tutorials, to unpaid work experience and practical exams… life had been one rollercoaster after another for years. Weeks and months flew by without notice. She often forgot birthdays and anniversaries. But she kept her head down and worked harder than she'd ever worked before. She knew she owed it to her parents who'd given her all they could spare. Loved her and supported her to follow her dreams, even if it meant working too many hours and sacrificing their own wants and needs. They were always in the front of her mind, through every success and failure.

When she completed her undergraduate studies, she was accepted into medical school and the whirlwind had continued… working nights and weekends to put food on her own table, spending hundreds of hours studying and learning, not sleeping nearly enough. Her hard work had certainly paid off, as she was fortunate enough to obtain residency in one of the best hospitals in the country. Here she'd perfected her craft. Lived and breathed her work. And she'd loved every second of it. The feeling of saving a life, of making a difference. It was something she could never describe to her friends, no matter how much she tried. And now, finally, she was a fully qualified doctor. Dr Emily Rodrigues.

Driving into the town she'd known so well for so long, Emily was surprised at how much had changed, but also how much was still the same. From the new shop fronts in the main street, Cafes and bars with trendy names, to the old rundown basketball court, with its cracked concrete and roughly painted court lines on the corner where the local elementary school stood; still with rusty unkempt chain surrounding the net. She drove past her old high school, with its thick steel security gates and faded brown brick buildings. Trash cans overflowed at the front of the building, covered in graffiti and roughly scrawled expletives. As she drove by, she was reminded of her first day of high school… feeling both excited and terrified at the same time. A feeling she'd felt so many times since embarking on her life after school. Luca had been there with her that day. Standing at the gates about to walk in for the first of many thousands of times, with his piercing blue eyes and short ashy blond hair sticking out in every conceivable direction, looking like he'd just rolled out of bed… as he probably had. She remembered he'd said sarcastically, "How long do you reckon I'll last in this hell hole?" At the time she'd shoved him playfully, rolled her eyes, and laughed it off. In actual fact, he had made it almost three years.

As kids, Emily & Luca had been inseparable… almost from birth. Their mothers had worked together in a local grocery store for years before they were born. Their fathers drank together on Friday nights. It was a tradition. Or so they liked to say. When Luca and Emily were born only two weeks apart, their parents had called it fate. Said they were destined to grow up together. And that they had. They started walking and talking at the same time. They began elementary school together, and then high school. It was only when Luca was expelled at 15 for fighting with a teacher, that he and Emily were separated from one another at school. But never at home. Their houses shared a fence, running the length of their yards. A second-hand gate had been installed into the bottom corner of the yards when the kids were both eight years old after Luca had almost pulled the whole fence down high jumping over it at full pace into Emily's yard.

From the moment the gate went in, the two households had become like one. Two families sharing BBQs and weekend activities; the gate always open. Even now, as she climbed out of her car and stepped onto the sidewalk, she could hear music and voices in the distance… coming from Luca's parents'- Mireya and Carlos Mendes' yard. She knew without a doubt, that both families would be gathered there ready to celebrate her homecoming. And from the sounds echoing around the neighbourhood, both families had already begun celebrating. She took a deep breath and smiled as the butterflies began doing flips and spins in her stomach again. She was really here. Finally, she was home. In a few short minutes she would see all the people she had yearned to see for so many years. But first, there was something she needed to do. Someone she knew she needed to see. She turned towards the side of the house and walked down the dark, narrow path leading to her childhood backyard, to where she had left him all those years before, and where she hoped he would be waiting for her.

He sensed her presence even before she spoke. "Please don't tell me you've been sitting here for the last 10 years waiting for me?"

Chapter 2

Luca felt his heart skip a beat; jump into his throat; race like he'd run up a flight of stairs. The sounds of music, laughter and joyful voices reverberating from across the back fence, suddenly dulled; faded away. He felt like he was overheating. As if all the lights in the world had turned on and were all pointing right in his direction. He took a deep breath and swallowed. He wasn't sure if he could speak… or move at all. But he didn't really care. Nothing mattered in that moment. Nothing but Emily. She was beautiful. Standing there in the light of the porch, her long chocolate brown hair cascading gracefully around her face and down her back. It was much longer than he remembered. In a figure-hugging floor-length navy sun dress with an intricate pattern of red and pink flowers, she looked like she'd just stepped out of a beauty magazine. Perfect. He had no words. He was glad he'd chosen to sit on the swing, as he clung to the ropes like his life depended on it. Tight enough that his knuckles turned white. Realising he probably looked like a complete loser, and remembering that in most circles, he was considered rather good with the ladies, Luca cleared his throat, smiled, and stood up.

Emily hadn't realised she'd been holding her breath until her head began to spin. Taking a couple of quick breaths, she stepped forward onto the wooden deck attached to the back of the house. He was waiting for her. She'd known he would be. Even after all these years, Luca was still predictable. And gorgeous. Undeniably gorgeous. The second she turned the corner she registered how much he'd changed. From the gangly, goofy and overly confident 17-year-old she'd known so long ago, to something markedly different. Sitting in front of her was a strikingly handsome man. Despite sitting, she could see he was taller. His ashy blond hair much longer and tied in a knot at the back of his head. Any comprehension of words left her brain as she stood on the deck feeling like a 13-year-old at her first party; awkward and shy. Get a grip, she thought to herself as Luca stood and smiled. A cheesy grin that made his dimples show. A grin she'd seen a million times before. In that instant she recognised her best friend. He was right there. As if no time had passed at all.

Emily felt her body and mind relax. The anticipation, the fear of not knowing him, of him not knowing her was gone in an instant and she let out a nervous laugh.

"You gonna come over here and give your old friend a hug?" Luca said, in a voice that was both familiar and new, holding out his arms.

Without hesitation, Emily half ran, half skipped the short distance between them and threw herself at him. She felt herself being swung around in circles as she laughed and buried her face into his shoulder. Such strong shoulders, she thought to herself. The guy obviously worked out. He smelt like chocolate and spices. The recognition that he still used the same cologne after all these years surprised her. How hilarious that she still remembered his smell, she thought to herself. Luca put her down and leaned back. He was so relieved. Her face was still the same; her eyes; her smile was all the same as he remembered.

"Hi you," he said smiling, relief obvious on his face.

"Hi back," Emily replied, warmth and familiarity overtaking her.

"Where are your glasses?" He quizzed.

"Contacts… thought I'd better get with the times," she replied with a chuckle.

"Well you're lucky I even recognised you," he joked as she let go of him and turned to survey the backyard of her childhood.

Even in the moonlight, she could see it had fallen apart. The flower gardens were overgrown and taken over with weeds. The grass had grown up so high it was difficult to see the vegetables she hoped were still growing in the back. She really had come home at the right time. She sighed as her initial euphoria subsided. Luca watched her intently. Turning back to him, Emily smiled; a smile he'd never seen before.

Sadness flickered in her eyes as she walked over to the old swing and took a deep breath in… and then out.

"I can't believe they still have this old thing," she noted, as she took a seat on the swing.

"It's definitely seen better days," he said, joining her.

Luca smiled as he thought about all the times they'd sat on that swing. All the problems of the world they had tried to solve.

"So… how's life?" He quipped, then laughed when she gave him an elbow in the ribs.

"What a question," she retorted, "Got a spare 10 years to hear about it?"

He laughed; a laugh she recognised almost as well as her own. Without thinking, Luca threw his arm around her shoulder like he'd done so many times before.

"For you, my dear, I have all the time in the world."

Turning to him she surveyed her old friend. It was amazing to her, that even after so long, they fit right away. Back into their regular scheduled program. Him cracking jokes; her telling stories. It felt good. It felt like home.

"Well then, let me see…" she began.

While the music played loudly next door, and the police sirens blared in the distance, Emily relayed the cliff notes version of the last 10 years of her life while her best friend sat, listening with purpose. She began by telling him all about North Carolina; about her colourful friends and flat mates. She talked about her university, describing the tall buildings and large lecture rooms, that fit up to 500 students at once. She went on to explain how she got into medical school, and after that her residency. Whilst talking, without thinking and completely by habit, Emily took Luca's hand in hers. It was something she'd always done, mostly to make sure he was listening. This time she knew he was listening, but it felt nice all the same.

When the smell of steak and BBQ chicken wafted through the backyard, Emily realised they'd been sitting and talking for over an hour. She'd been so caught up talking to Luca she'd forgotten she still had her whole family to see! Still holding onto his hand, she gave it a quick squeeze and smiled. Sitting with him here on the swing, their swing, she felt like she was 17 again. As if nothing had changed; no time had passed at all. Like she'd never left. "We should probably get to the party," Emily said, begrudgingly. As much as she was dying to see her parents and her friends… something held her here. There was something so familiar about this place; about him. His eyes, the colour of a bright blue sky, were still the same as she remembered. She felt an immense sense of relief. For so long she'd worried that she would return, and they would be strangers. That all the memories she held dearest would be forgotten. As if her childhood was someone else's to remember. But for all the physical changes in Luca, his eyes were still the same. Warm, friendly, and kind. Her best friend.

Walking towards his parents' yard arm in arm, the butterflies that had done so much damage earlier, had finally settled. Emily stopped just before the open gate and looked up at Luca. "I really am so glad you're here," she said, almost in a whisper, squeezing him tight around the waist. Turning to face her, Luca smiled and kissed her on the top of the head, saying, "I am too Em". He knew in that moment; he'd never made a truer statement. He couldn't describe the feeling that held him there right then. If anyone had asked, he would have just shrugged… or laughed. He imagined it felt something like someone who was lost being found. Giving her one last squeeze, Luca led her into the yard.

"Hey everyone, look who I found wandering around in the dark", he called out, as they walked through the gate and towards the party arm in arm. Emily grinned as she took in the scene before her.

The Mendes' backyard had always been somewhere Emily had loved to play. With its spacious and beautifully manicured lawn; its well-kept and sculptured garden; large concrete entertaining area with BBQ set up and seating, it was a complete contrast to the hap hazard, overgrown and hectic yard they had just walked out of. Even after all these years, the yard was still immaculate. Tables and chairs were set up in perfect sequence, end to end along the edge of the BBQ space. Coloured tablecloths were placed strategically to match the chairs, as well as the variety of brightly coloured decorations set up around the yard. Music was playing loudly from within the house, spilling out into the yard, as were the children and young adults dancing to it. The smell of cooking meats and spice wafted from the BBQ and made her mouth water. This was home. This was her family. Loud and colourful. The realisation that the guest of honour had arrived, swept the crowd all at one. At that moment, cheers erupted, and a swarm of people descended on Emily, pushing Luca out of the way like he was a fly being swatted. He didn't mind at all. All he could do was smile at his friend. A stupid smile that he knew probably looked ridiculous. He didn't care.

From the kitchen window, Carmen and Mireya watched their children walk together from the back of the yard. After 30 years of friendship, the ladies were easily able to communicate without words. They looked at each other with eyes that had seen many things. The birth of their children; their younger years; teen years, and now their young adult lives.

"I think we're going to enjoy watching this," Carmen said, as she and her best friend laughed and walked towards the back door, to welcome her daughter home.

The party was well and truly in full swing. The food was being served and the drinks flowed, while Emily said hello and hugged what seemed like every friend and family member she'd ever known. Her head giddy with love and affection, she finally made her way to the closest table and sat down. Taking a deep breath, she looked around her. Loud and excitable children chased each other around the yard. Women stood cradling babies in their arms whilst trying to herd toddlers into chairs to eat their meals. Boys on skateboards practiced tricks behind the BBQ area. Teenagers sat at tables staring at their mobile phones, paying no attention to what was going on around them. Only the smell of the food roused them from their trance. Men stood around the BBQ, discussing the football game playing on the TV inside. So many faces of adults she recognised, but so many children she didn't know. Had everyone had babies while she was away?

She knew Luca had. Two children. When her mother had first called to tell her the news that Luca was going to be a dad, Emily had just finished her undergraduate degree. She was about to embark on medical school. And she hadn't believed her mother. Not at first. In all their years as friends, Emily had never imagined Luca as a parent. Sure, he'd had plenty of girlfriends, especially as a teenager. There always seemed to be a new girl hanging around him, feeding off his every word, at least every other week. Some stuck around for a little while, others only a week or two. He never seemed to worry too much. But they had never, ever talked about having kids… they were still only kids themselves! So, when at the age of 20, Emily found out that Luca was going to be a dad, she was shocked. More shocking was when she discovered that the mother of his child, just happened to be one of their closest friends.

Emily, Luca, Claudia, and Ricky became friends at the age of 14. Emily and Claudia shared a maths class, while Luca and Ricky sat together in English. They were the awesome foursome and did everything together. From weekends at the beach spent surfing and sunbaking; to sitting watching Luca train at his gym; to working weekends together at Claudia's uncle's café; to wandering the streets looking for mischief… the four amigos were inseparable. Claudia and Emily shared a love for storytelling. They would spend hours sitting together in Emily's room, plotting a new twist or turn in an adventure story they were writing together. And when they weren't writing, they would talk about all the adventures they were going to go on when they were grown up.

Travelling the world, visiting the Eiffel tower; the Great Barrier Reef; the Pyramids of Giza.

Luca and Ricky couldn't stand to write, let alone read. They would spend their spare time building skate jumps and ramps in Luca's backyard, then walking the streets finding precarious and dangerous places to test them, while the girls looked on in horror. Many terror filled screams had come from Claudia and Emily, when the boys tried a death-defying trick and got it wrong. That was when Emily's skills for first aid had been most useful. They would all laugh as Emily scolded them for their stupidity, and Luca would tease her about being so uptight. Some of Emily's favourite childhood memories contained Luca and Claudia. But none of them included any sort of romance between the two. For all Emily knew, Luca and Claudia had never looked at each other as more than just friends. Or so she'd thought.

Watching Luca now, loading his plate with chicken and vegetables, then covering it in way too much hot sauce, Emily wondered if his children were here. She looked around, surveying the crowd, looking for anyone young enough to fit the bill. Her gaze settled on a young man, around seven or eight, with baby blue eyes and bright blond hair sticking out in all directions, like he'd just scampered out of a sleep. The resemblance was uncanny. This was Luca's son. A stab of sadness touched Emily's heart. Sadness that she'd missed knowing this little person, who looked so much like his father. That at the same age, she and Luca had already been partners in crime for years. She wondered if this little guy had someone to share secrets with. God, she thought to herself, she didn't even know his name. Talk about friend of the year. Just then, another little guy with ashy blond hair and deep brown eyes popped up from behind the table. He too cut a stark resemblance to Luca.

"Riley, get me some food," the little guy insisted.

"Keep your pants on Joey, you can wait your turn", his big brother retorted.

A shoving match began in the line, as the two boys jostled for plates and position.

"Do I have to come over there and show you guys some manners," Luca growled from the other end of the line.

His tone surprised Emily. She'd never heard him speak like that before. He sounded like his father. She doubted he'd be particularly happy to hear the comparison. Carlos Mendes was a hard man. A proud man. Proud and stoic. He believed in learning lessons the hard way. Old school. Luca and his father had never really seen eye to eye. Emily wondered if that had changed while she'd been away.

She watched the altercation between the two boys with curiosity. How strange that these little men shared so many traits of their father, and yet looked so much like their mother. Crazy times, she thought to herself. Serves me right for staying away for so long, she placated. Luca walked over to the table and sat down next to her. He noticed the odd expression on her face and touched her arm. Emily jumped, not realising he was sitting next to her. She'd been so enthralled in her own thoughts and memories, she'd stopped paying attention to what was happening around her.

"What's up?" he queried. "You look like you're about to cry."

"No, no" she replied, "I was just thinking."

"About what?" he asked, with a mouth full of food.

"Don't talk with your mouth full, it's rude," she quipped.

"Yes Mum," he replied, with a sarcastic grin.

She continued, "I was just thinking about… everything really. It's so strange being back here after so long."

Luca nodded. "I can't imagine" he said, "Must be a real spin out. You planning on staying with your parents for a while?"

He stopped filling his mouth with food to listen intently for her answer. He'd thought about it a few times since he found out she was coming home. Would she be living a two minute walk from his place? Would they be neighbours again, after ten years living on opposite sides of the country?

"Why do you ask? Planning on sneaking in my bedroom window?" she teased, trying not to laugh.

Luca coughed and tried not to choke on his chicken. He swallowed hard and turned to look at her.

"And what if I did?" he asked suggestively. She laughed hard. He hadn't changed a bit.

"Then my Daddy would have to beat your behind, just like he used to, all those years ago!"

Laughter roared from Luca as he resumed his feasting. God, he'd missed her.

She continued, "I'm staying with Mum and Dad until I find a place of my own. I'm actually seeing a realter tomorrow to look at a few local places if you're not doing anything?"

He thought for a minute. "Sure I can come. Hey, you better get in there and get some food", he said, glancing at his kids. "The way these guys eat, there'll be nothing left in under five minutes!"

Sitting across the table, Luca's two boys quietly observed the interaction between their dad and the pretty new lady. They hadn't seen him be silly like this with anyone except their Mum, and that had stopped a few years back, when their parents had split up. They grinned at each other and following their Dads lead, began shovelling food into their mouths as if their lives depended on it.

Hours later, when all the food had been consumed and the children had been put to bed, Luca found Emily in the kitchen helping their mothers wash the dishes. Standing at the door of the kitchen, he watched the three women work together. His mother had always loved Emily like a daughter. Mireya often joked that she'd wished Luca had been a girl, until Emily had come along. Then she got the best of both worlds. A son to love for his rough and tumble, and a pseudo daughter to braid hair and paint nails.

Emily sensed him behind her and turned to smile. He really was incredibly good looking, she thought. Standing there, all tall and handsome. She caught herself looking him up and down, and silently scolded herself. God has it really been that long since I've been on a date that I'm checking out my best friend, she thought. Luca noticed the odd look on her face and wondered what she was thinking. For as long as he could remember, it had frustrated him not knowing what Emily was thinking. It was usually something smart, but he had always wondered just the same. Putting down the dishcloth, Emily said to no one in particular, "I think I'm going to head off to bed."

"Ok sweetie, you must be exhausted… driving so far and entertaining so many people tonight." Carmen said affectionately.

"Yeah I think I could probably sleep for a week," Emily noted, as she gave her Mum and Mireya each a big hug.

Turning to face the doorway, and Luca, Emily held out her arms. Quicker than she expected, he lurched forward and scooped her up into his arms to give her a bear hug. He placed her gently back on the ground and kissed her on the top of the head as he had done earlier in the evening.

"What time can I pick you up tomorrow?" He queried.

"You mean what time can I pick *you* up tomorrow?" She laughed as he looked at her with a semi amused, semi confused look. She'd forgotten he wasn't used to the new, confident Emily.

"I'll meet you on the swing at 11am if that's ok?" she replied.

"It's a date," he joked, as she walked out of the kitchen.

Making her way towards her parent's yard and her childhood home,
Emily grinned happily, as Luca stood wondering what had just happened.

Chapter 3

Waking up in her childhood bedroom was something Emily had yearned for, almost since she'd left for college. As she lay in the steel framed single bed, still covered in the pink and yellow bed cover she'd chosen for her 12th birthday, she was overwhelmed with calm. And happiness. She was home. Her family were all with her. And Luca was still Luca. All that she'd hoped and wished for over the past few months had become a reality. She sighed deeply and rolled over to look at the pile of suitcases that filled the corner of the room. Her worldly possessions. She'd sold or given away all of her furniture to friends in North Carolina. All that was left of the ten years she'd spent away was in these suitcases. Clothes and small items; keepsakes from friends and colleagues. She'd wanted a fresh start. A new beginning. The irony of starting fresh in the one place she had the most memories was not lost on Emily. She considered it poetic. Stretching out so her feet touched the bottom of the bed, she confirmed what she'd been thinking when she first climbed in to sleep the night before; she needed to find a place of her own. If nothing else, then to buy and sleep in a queen-sized bed. She smiled as she remembered all the times she'd laid in her little bed, surrounded by pictures of fairies and unicorns on the walls, dreaming about the world. How young and naïve she'd been.

Her thoughts drifted back to the beginning of the year; to Michael. She'd tried really hard not to let herself think about him since she'd left North Carolina weeks earlier. Since she'd left the life behind that had included him. An Emergency Consultant at the hospital she'd worked, Michael had been one of the deciding factors in Emily's return home to LA. Having met at a work function, introduced by the General Manager of the hospital, Emily and Michael had been inseparable. From the moment they'd met, they'd done everything together. Worked, played, even run a marathon together. Friends and colleagues often remarked they'd never met a more perfect couple. Emily and Michael were sure to get married and live happily ever after. The world-renowned ED physician, whose work in trauma medicine was revered and respected on every continent, and the brilliant Emergency resident whose quick-thinking problem solving, was the toast of the hospital Executive team. Many a crisis was averted by the quick thinking of Dr Emily Rodrigues and the exceptional skill of Dr Michael Matthews. They were the power couple of Carolina General, the largest trauma hospital in the state. Rock stars in the medical field. It was a huge shock to everyone, when Emily reported that she and Michael had gone their separate ways, and she was moving back to her hometown. No one quite knew what to say, and as happens in most hospitals, the rumour mill went into overdrive. Amongst some of the most outrageous rumours included that Michael had run off with a prostitute, Emily had fallen pregnant and refused to keep the baby, and that Emily was in fact a lesbian. None of which had any truth but entertained the masses none the less.

Only Emily and Michael knew the truth. That Michael, despite loving Emily as well as he knew how, felt that she was holding his career back. That he would be more successful single. As much as it had stung, Emily had not been heartbroken. Michael was a brilliant doctor, an exceptionally intelligent man. He was calm in the face of disaster. There was no doubt in her mind that he felt great affection towards her. But in the two years they had dated, they had never really loved. They had never disagreed on anything. Mostly because Michael was a skilled negotiator, but also because Emily disliked conflict. They were cool, calm, and calculated at work and at home. Theirs had become a relationship of status and convenience… not of passion, want and need. Even their engagement had been without excitement. Michael had taken Emily to a jeweller, one of the best in town, and let her choose a ring. He'd given it to her then and there, telling her she could wear it. And that was that. They were engaged. No fanfare; no bended knee. No surprise or elation. He hadn't even spoken to her parents to ask their permission. It was emotionless and efficient. Just like their entire relationship.

Emily closed her eyes and tried to shut out the feelings of guilt and shame overtaking her. She'd been as much to blame for the failed relationship as he had. She'd been so star struck at first. So inspired and impressed at the intellect, the perfection and skill of the man, that she'd fallen for his brain well before she got to know his heart. She'd relished meeting all the high-flying constituents Michael conversed with. Liked the fancy dinners and beautiful outfits she was given to wear… on loan of course. It was so far from anything she'd ever known. So far from the second-hand stores she bought all her clothes as a child and young adult. So far from the school dance hall, the college dorms, the dank, pokey two bedroom apartment she shared with her friend Amy, during their medical school days. Finally, she was drinking expensive champagne and discussing politics with important people. And for a while, it was everything she thought she'd always wanted. Beauty. Status. Respect. But eventually, the sparkle and excitement had worn off. The parties, once so glamorous and exciting, became boring and drawn out for Emily, with the same boring people discussing the same boring topics as if they were on autocue.

For all the status and importance it gave her and Michael, Emily witnessed others come and go as if they meant nothing. Once an important part of the group, colleagues were cast out on a whim based on which suburb they purchased their home, or which brand of car they chose to buy. For Emily, this blatant display of snobbery did not go unnoticed. As hard as she tried to look past it, something inside her could not let it go. The one time she tried to discuss how she was feeling with Michael, he'd remarked matter of factly, "Honey, you're letting it get to you because you were poor. Most middle-class people would be grateful for the opportunity to spend time with these people." It was at that point, that Emily began to see the writing on the wall. She stopped attending the events, faking headaches, and work commitments. Slowly, Emily and Michael drifted apart. 'Like we were ever really together,' Emily thought.

Hearing whistling coming from somewhere in the yard, Emily pulled herself back into the present and smiled. She recognised the noise, like the sound of her own breathing. Luca had arrived early to help her hunt for a house. How funny, she thought, that she had experienced more feelings of joy and happiness in the first five minutes of seeing him last night, then in the whole two years she'd dated Michael. And Luca was only her friend! Looking at her watch, she realised he was very early… almost two hours earlier than the time they'd agreed to. What was he up to? As she pondered, the window next to her bed flew open and Luca's face greeted her.

"Morning sunshine," he said, with a cheesy grin.

"What the hell are you doing?" Emily said, in a stern tone used only for Luca.

Realising that she was still in her pyjamas, consisting of a small tank top and figure-hugging shorts, Emily pulled the pink and yellow cover up to her chin.

"I thought I might see if I could still fit through this window… for old times sakes," he laughed, as he tried to push himself through the small opening in the window.

The wood holding up the wall began to creak and groan under the weight of the full-grown man trying to gracefully enter the room.

"Shit, I think I'm stuck," he commented, as Emily tried all she could not to laugh at the idiot of a man trying to break into her house.

"Just wait till my Daddy catches you stuck in the window," she remarked, attempting to stifle snorts of laughter.

Without warning, Luca's whole body slid through the window and he landed in a mess of arms and legs on the floor next to her bed.

"Smooth, very smooth," was all she managed, before she roared with laughter.

Picking himself up from the floor, he stood tall and pretended to stretch out the imaginary muscle injuries that he hadn't actually received. He took in the room. It was exactly the same as the last time he'd been here… many, many years before. As a teenager, Luca had given Emily hell about the décor of her room, with pink and yellow colour scheme and fairies on the walls. Emily had largely ignored him. She liked her room just how it was… as it had been when she was five years old. She was like that, he thought. Old school; traditional.

"Again, what the hell are you doing?" Emily repeated, as she looked up at the attractive man standing in her bedroom.

Luca replied, "I was thinking we could grab some breakfast before we see the realter? Do a bit of sightseeing around the old neighbourhood. So much has changed since you left."

Emily nodded. "I noticed some of it as I drove in last night. What happened to the old butchers on Logan Street?"

Luca replied, "Old man Sanchez had a stroke a few years back, and his sons decided to sell it up. It's a café now. Something to do with vegan smoothies?"

Things really had changed, Emily thought to herself.

"Ok, breakfast sounds good. Just let me get up and dressed first," Emily remarked. She waited for Luca to move towards the door, so she could get out of bed. Instead, he turned to face her with a cheeky grin.

"I don't mind waiting here," he said, with obvious intent.

"Get the hell out of my room before I hit you over the head with a lamp," Emily said, reaching over to grab her pink frilly lamp off the side table.

"Ok, ok, I get the picture. Can't blame a guy for trying." Luca said sarcastically.

Walking to the door, he opened it fully and called down the hallway, "Morning Mr and Mrs Rodrigues."

Looking back before closing the door, Luca winked at Emily who lay in her childhood bed trying her hardest not to giggle.

Jumping out of bed, Emily quickly threw on the clothes she'd laid out meticulously the night before, tied her hair in a rough ponytail at the back of her neck, grabbed shoes and her bag, and made her way to the backyard where Luca sat swinging on the wooden swing. Calling to her parents that she'd be home later in the afternoon, they made their way down the side of the house and onto the street. Here, parked out the front was Emily's Jeep in all its glory. It had cost her a fortune but was the car she'd always wanted. She'd had a little disposable income from the contract payout she'd received when she left Carolina General, and figured what better way to spend it then on a reliable piece of machinery.

"Nice ride," Luca remarked. "Very upper-class."

The comment, meant in jest, cut a little close to home. Since leaving Michael, Emily had tried her hardest to remove herself from the upper-class life she'd lived. She'd sold or given away her expensive clothes and jewellery. She'd bought herself a run of the mill mobile phone, selling the top of the line model she'd owned in North Carolina. She just wanted to be a regular person again. A girl who grew up in a pink and yellow room surrounded by fairies.

"So… what's first?" she asked, to change the subject.

"Breakfast my dear," Luca announced. "The Mexican place in town is still going strong… and still does the best breakfast burritos on the planet!"

"Done," Emily replied as she pulled the car away from the sidewalk and her stomach growled appropriately. They were going to have such a fun day; she could already feel it.

Driving the streets of her childhood had a cathartic effect on Emily. Every corner she turned, every traffic light she stopped at, every child she drove past riding their bike on the sidewalk, she felt stress and strain exit her body. Driving in her car with the best friend she'd ever had, chatting about how the landscape had changes these past 10 years, Emily found herself smiling a smile she'd almost forgotten she had. The smile of someone who was free to do what she wanted, when she wanted. The smile of someone not weighed down by expectation and duty. As free as a bird.

"Are you even listening to me," Luca said, as Emily tuned back into the conversation.

"Sorry I wandered away for a minute," she replied, glancing over at him as she pulled up at the lights.

Sitting there in the passenger seat, with his white surf shirt and blue denim shorts, Luca was as far from a snob as anyone on the planet. There was no pretence with him. No expectation of how she should look, behave, or think. She loved that he was just himself. No matter what.

"What were you saying?" she asked.

"I asked if the nightclubs are any good in North Carolina?" he said.

"I wouldn't know," she replied. "I never really went to many."

Luca looked at her like she'd gone mad. "I'm sorry what? Are you trying to tell me you were in another state for 10 years, and hardly ever went to a night club?"

Emily smiled an embarrassed smile. How could she explain it? It wasn't that she hadn't wanted to go out partying with her friends every weekend. At first, when she'd turned 21, she'd been too busy studying at university, and then at medical school. And after she became a resident and met Michael, she didn't dare go to a nightclub. He didn't like them. Too trashy, he'd say.

"I guess I just didn't have time with studying and working," was all she managed.

As they pulled into the carpark of their all-time favourite Mexican restaurant, Luca wondered if there was more to the story then she was saying.

Sitting waiting for their food to arrive, the two friends quizzed each other on events of the last 10 years. Luca told Emily about Riley and Joey, and the funny stuff they got up to, now that they were seven and five years old. Emily could see the love Luca had for his kids. Every word he spoke about them was dripping in it. He talked about Ricky, their childhood friend. After finishing school, Ricky had moved away to work. He'd only returned to the local area a couple of years earlier to start his own business. Married with three kids, Ricky was an average, suburban guy from all reports. Despite not catching up all that often, Luca proudly admitted that Ricky had been to every one of his fights. And always cheered the loudest.

"I heard that you fought a couple of weeks ago?" Emily asked, in between bights of her burrito.

"Yeah I fought in a big show in central LA about three weeks ago. It was on a main card for the American Boxing League. A pretty big deal. I've fought in their shows before but never anything that big. There were 20,000 people in the stadium watching. 20,000 Em! At one point, I thought the roof was going to lift off. It was wild!" Luca remarked. "I like fighting at home. It means I can get tickets for all the family. Everyone was there. Mum and Dad, the kids… it was an amazing feeling. I wish you could've been there too."

Emily paused, putting her food down to ask, "Do still love it like you used to?"

She often wondered if his passion had changed. She remembered so many conversations they'd had as kids. Conversations where he would talk about being the best, about beating the best in the world and holding the golden belt above his head. He used to practice what he'd do if he ever won the world title. Emily smiled as she remembered how cool she'd thought he was at the time. And how cool he still was, sitting across from her now.

"Yeah I still love it. Even more than I did back then. When we were kids, it was just a dream. It was made up; a fantasy. Now it's close to being real. That makes me want it even more. Every day I wake up and think about that belt. About holding that belt up in front of my family and friends. It's what drives me more than anything else."

The look in his eyes when he talked about his dream, made her long to have that same passion again. She used to feel that way about medicine. About saving lives. Now she wasn't sure what she believed in, or what she wanted.

  "Come on, it's almost 11am. We'd better get over to the real estate place and grab some brochures," Luca said, not commenting on the unhappy expression on Emily's face.

Chapter 4

As soon as she saw it, she knew she had to have it. It was perfect. And dreadful. Pulling up to the front of the building, with Luca sitting lazily in the passenger seat beside her, Emily wound her window down and took in the façade of the old home. She saw rust and holes. Broken windows and damaged fence palings. It had obviously been vandalised, and maybe even used as a temporary homeless shelter at one point. She couldn't be sure from the road, but she could have sworn she smelt burning wood. The front garden was horribly overgrown, with thick green and black vines weaving a mischievous path up the drainpipes and into the gutters on both sides. The front door was a bright, almost fluorescent orange, and looked like it was off its hinges. The garage door, once a shade of blue, was covered in poorly designed graffiti, with many of the comments and roughly sketched pictures making Emily feel like she should probably blush.

"Moving on," Luca retorted, as he gave the old house a once over.

"Hang on, I want to have a closer look," Emily replied, turning off the engine and opening her car door.

"Why, so you can catch a disease?" Luca snorted with laughter, as he looked over at Emily standing on the footpath.

Seeing the look of utter disdain on her face, and the fact that she was already turning to walk towards the front gate, he realised she was serious.

"You're not serious Em… this place is a dump!" He called, as he climbed out of the car and walked towards her.

"It needs work," Emily replied. "The brochure said it was a fixer-upper."

"That's an understatement," Luca muttered under his breath. "More like a demolition job."

But Emily wasn't listening. She'd already begun picturing the home she'd live in, once she'd re-painted and fixed up a few holes. A lot of holes, she mused. Once she'd cleared out the gardens and replanted the flower beds with her favourite flowers. She could even get a bird bath, like the one her father was so proud of in his own garden. She'd paint the house a light shade of grey, helping it to blend in better with the homes around it. And to make the garden stand out as a feature. It would be beautiful, and it would be hers. All hers.

Luca stood next to her on the footpath, watching her think. It was one of his favourite things to do as a kid. Watching the wheels turn in the head of Emily Rodrigues had always been a sight to behold. Her face would change expression at such a pace, it was often difficult to keep up. The frown lines above her eyes would crease and un-crease a hundred times, as she mulled over something or other. Her lips would curl into a pout and her eyes would narrow as she concentrated. It made him smile to realise her mannerisms hadn't changed, even after all this time. Even before she spoke, he knew she'd made up her mind. And once Emily made up her mind, there was no turning back. This would be her new home.

"Guess I'd better get the toolbox out of the garage," Luca quipped, as Emily glanced up, breaking her train of thought.

She grinned at him; a smile that made his heart skip a beat.

"Guess so!" she laughed, leaning up to kiss him on the cheek. "Let's go see the real estate and get this party started," she said, turning and walking back to the car.

For a split-second, Luca felt like his feet were glued to the concrete. Like his legs had turned into tree trunks; putting down roots right then and there. He shook it off, cursing himself for being a loser, and turned to jump back in the car. Starting the engine and slowly pulling away from the curb, Emily took one final look at the dilapidated building in her rear-view mirror. It would be hers. She knew it. No matter what she had to do, how much she had to pay. There was something about the place that she had to have. It spoke to her heart. More than anything had in a long time.

Half an hour later, as she stood in the real estate office negotiating a sale price, Emily was pleasantly surprised by how accommodating the real estate agent was being. She'd heard such horror stories from friends in North Carolina about agents playing hard ball and squeezing every available drop of cash from prospective buyers. In Emily's case, the agent, Martin, had been a real gentleman. He asked Emily about her renting history and finances, about her motives for buying in the area and seemed genuinely interested in her return to LA after so many years. When the topic of price came up, Martin was very keen to point out that the price was negotiable, and open to all offers. It almost seemed like he was relieved to get rid of the place, Emily reflected as she climbed back into the car with a newly signed deed of sale and the keys to her very own three bedroom home. Her first home.

A deceased estate, Martin advised the building had been vacant for around five years after the elderly owner had died. Luca, always looking for an opportunity to tease Emily, had asked if the lady had died in the building? If maybe it could be haunted? This led to a couple of sharp elbows in the ribs for Luca, but he didn't care. He was having too much fun. Martin reassured Emily, who looked a little panicked, that the elderly lady had in fact died in hospital and would definitely not be haunting the house. Following some online application forms and finance checks, and of course the signing over of a substantial amount of her life savings, Emily found herself signing the paperwork to make it final. She glanced up at Luca as she signed her name on the last piece of paper.

"I'm glad you're here for this," she said quietly.

"Will you both be moving in together?" Martin queried as he copied and stapled the paperwork.

Emily blushed. She smiled and replied politely that no, Luca was her friend and he had a home of his own. Thanking Martin, Emily and Luca made their way out of the building and towards the car.

"We could be flat mates you know," Luca said nonchalantly.

"Yeah sure" Emily retorted, "Did you want the room filled with mould or the one with half a roof?"

Laughing together, they drove towards their parents' homes, neither mentioning it again, but both thinking long and hard about the proposition.

Over the coming weeks, Emily got stuck into project planning, something she was very experienced and competent at. To date, every element of her life had been well planned, almost to the day. She loved the feeling of a good plan coming to fruition. The feeling of accomplishment at achieving a goal. And this goal, the renovation of her first home, was one of her greatest projects to date. She had been through the place with a fine-tooth comb, measuring walls and door jams, roof heights and window lengths. She'd hired a builder, Adam, to come and look at the place with her; to tell her if her grand plans could be achieved. And so far, she'd been pleasantly surprised. He listened to what she thought she wanted, giving his input and technical knowledge, and even coming up with some great ideas of his own. In a short period of time, she'd made some big decisions. She'd agreed to knock out the back wall of the house and extend it out into the large yard space. This would give her more room in the bedroom, located in the back right hand corner of the building, and give her added space in the living area directly opposite the bedroom. She'd also worked out that if she knocked out the kitchen wall, she could create an open plan kitchen that linked directly with the living area, making one large space for eating and entertaining. Finally, she'd worked with Adam to plan a large wooden deck off the back of the house, giving her more entertaining space and linking the currently overgrown garden to the house.

Standing in what had become a construction zone, pondering wall paint colours and light fixtures, Emily felt incredibly pleased with herself. It was all coming together. It'd been three weeks since she'd returned home and purchased her house. With all the noisy, dusty, and destructive work going on there, she'd decided to stay sleeping at her parents' house for the time being. At least until the bedroom walls were put back up.

She was so excited to move in. So excited to paint the walls and add in the flooring so it looked just like she'd imagined it in her head. The gardens were starting to come together too. While workers demolished walls and put in insulation on the inside of the property, Emily and Luca had spent the last couple of weeks pulling out weeds and odd-looking plants from around the house. Both back and front gardens looked much improved, with a clean slate to add in garden beds, plants, and lawn. There was even a big tree in the backyard that Luca joked would look great with a swing hanging from it. He suggested pinching the one from Emily's parents' yard, but that daring plan was quickly shut down with a discerning look. They'd spent the previous day at the local hardware store buying solid wood posts and beams to lay along the fence line, to create flower beds and a vegetable garden. Out the front, rocks and small boulders had been delivered to create a garden feature that would look beautiful and would be low maintenance.

Emily had thoroughly enjoyed the last couple of weeks she'd spent with Luca. Between his boxing training and helping his parents out around their house, he'd spent every other waking minute with her. Drawing plans, cleaning garden beds, wiping down walls and just generally being handy. She really appreciated the time he'd spent with her and all the help he'd given her. It reminded her of their teenage years. He'd even offered to bring his kids around to help out with the manual labour, but Emily thought better of it. Young children and construction sites didn't mix.

'Maybe I'll invite them over to help paint the walls, 'she thought to herself. Once there were walls to paint.

With all the time required at the house, Emily hadn't really found any time to think about work. If she was being honest, she was avoiding thinking about it all together. When she'd put in her resignation at Carolina General, the General Manager had been shocked. He'd offered her pay raises and bonuses to stay, but she'd already made up her mind. All he could really do was wish her well and offer to put in a reference for her at local hospitals in LA. And that he had certainly done. It seemed like every General Manager of every hospital in the area had left a message on her mobile in the last couple of weeks. She hadn't replied to any of them yet. She wasn't sure if she wanted to.

Being here in her hometown with her friends and family, had really caused her to reflect on the career she thought she'd wanted. Did she want to be the best Emergency Consultant in LA? Did she want the stress of working at any and all hours of the day? Of being on call for anything that came her way. Of working so much she didn't get to spend time with the people she loved, like her father had all his life. She just didn't know anymore. In some ways, it was so much easier when she was in North Carolina with Michael. Her decisions, especially around her career, had almost always been made for her. By him. Her plan had been to work where he worked, to follow him around the country wherever that would take them. Now, it was just her. And she wasn't even sure who she was anymore, let alone what she wanted from her career. All she knew was that she didn't have time to think about working. Her house had become her fulltime job.

"Emily are you here," Adam called, walking down the long hallway from the front door into the open living area and soon to be kitchen.

"Hey Adam, I'm in the second bedroom," Emily called out.

Backtracking down the hall, Adam turned into the door on the left and found her washing walls in one of the bedrooms that had been finished a few days earlier. Needing new walls and a refit of the wardrobe, this room had been a simple fix for the work team. The rest of the house, Adam thought, had been a much harder task. But they'd made so much progress in such a short period of time. Usually builds like this took months, if not years. It had been very fortuitous for Emily that the building team had been between jobs when she'd called to offer the work, and they were able to give the job their full attention, as well as a complete team of workers for the build. To date, the whole back of the house had been extended out; large glass doors that opened up onto the newly built deck had been installed; the internal roof sheets had all been replaced throughout the whole house; the kitchen wall had been ripped out and the space gutted, with a new kitchen arriving soon. The plumbing hadn't been as damaged as they'd first thought, so apart from needing some new tiles, the bathroom and toilet was fully functioning. Adam was extremely grateful for that. With up to 10 workers onsite at any one time, a functioning toilet and bathroom were more than essential spaces.

Emily had also hired a crew of painters to give the outside of the house a refresh. Adam had been impressed when he'd pulled up outside the old property earlier that day. To anyone who walked past, the home now resembled every other property on the block. Clean, fresh, and modern. The outside had been painted a light colour of grey with the roof a darker shade of the same colour. White trims surrounded the window frames and a brand-new white mailbox on the newly painted front fence, finished off the look. As renovations went, Adam thought this could possibly be his favourite.

"Just wanted to let you know that the back of the house is all done, and all the walls are ready for painting… except the kitchen," Adam said, as Emily turned to greet him.

As a happily married man, Adam would never admit it, least of all to his wife, but he had enjoyed working with Emily. Not only was she easy on the eye, he appreciated the attention to detail she gave to every element of the house re-build. Most people he worked for, gave him vague requests and disappeared for months, only to return at the end to complain about the work done. Emily was different. She was interested and engaged in making her home exactly as she wanted it. Pity the poor guy who falls for her, he thought to himself one day, after she'd asked him to go over the specifications for the kitchen benches for the 15th time.

Adam could definitely see why Luca hung around the girl so much. Even as a man in his late 50's, Adam could appreciate the vibrance and enthusiasm of Emily. She was such a bright light in an otherwise dull work environment. Even when she occasionally seemed sad and disconnected, she would still brighten the room.

"That's so awesome Adam, thank you so much. My parents will be happy to hear its almost done," Emily replied, "As much as I love them and they love me, I know they'll be happy to see me move to my own place and give them back their peace and quiet." She smiled warmly.

"Well, I think it could be sooner rather than later," Adam advised, "There's no reason you couldn't grab a sleeping bag and camp out here tonight. The walls, doors and windows are all secure. There's nowhere to cook, and no power for light switches… but if you get takeout and use the torch, you should be ok. We won't be back until the end of the week to install the kitchen. You have the place all to yourself!"

Adam watched as pure joy spread across Emily's face at the realisation that she could stay in her home for the very first time.

"Oh Adam, I could just kiss you!" Emily declared, as Luca wandered into the room.

"Hang on there, how come he gets a kiss hey?" Luca joked, as he took in the look on Emily's face. She had clearly received some good news.

"Adam says I can stay in the house tonight! I need to go home and grab some stuff. Luca can you stay here. I'll be back." She spoke so fast, he struggled to register what she was saying, but was able to nod a couple of times before she flew out of the room towards her car, keys in hand.

"And there goes hurricane Emily," Luca remarked laughing, as Adam patted him on the shoulder like he did his own son and made his way out of the house to his truck. Pity the poor guy all right, he chuckled to himself.

Chapter 5

Fighting was Luca's life. It had been his constant companion as long as he could remember. From scrapping in the backyard with his cousins when he could barely walk, to the day he walked into the Inner City Boxing Gym to begin learning a new style of fighting; one that didn't involve cheap shots and fence palings. Fast forward to his current reality, as one of the top 145 pound fighters on the planet. He'd worked hard to get to where he had, sacrificing more than anyone realised. His friends, social life, time with family, and especially time with his two kids. He knew he'd make it up to them one day. To all the people who'd stuck by him from the very beginning. The real ones. It was a constant struggle; a burden he was meant to bare to get where he needed to and achieve his dreams.

When he first started out in the professional scene, he'd worried about so many things. Worried about having enough money to put food on the table. Worried he would disappoint the people he loved. And most of all he worried that he wouldn't be good enough. He'd never shared his fears with anyone, but those thoughts had plagued him for so many years, they'd become his constant companion. Even with all his friends and family, his coach, and even now his fans telling him he was the best… he struggled to believe it. He knew his weaknesses and he worked hard to hide them from the world. He always had. Even his coach John, who knew him better than almost anyone, had no idea of the level of self-doubt that plagued Luca internally. If he did, he would surely be pissed.

Inner City Boxing Gym, located only five minutes from his house, had become like an oasis in a sea of chaos for Luca, from the very beginning. As a 14-year-old, with an attitude for trouble, and a healthy distrust for authority, it had been a rude awakening for Luca when he first walked through the frosted glass doors and began training with his now long-time coach, John Graham. A seasoned trainer, experienced and well-thought of in the Los Angeles local community for his work helping troubled kids get off the street and into boxing, John had seen something in Luca almost from the first moment he laced up his gloves. The kid had skills. And heart. He'd seen it on that first day. When paired up to spar with a boxer three years older than him, much taller, stronger and faster, Luca got stuck into him from the first bell, keeping his chin down and working the guy until he collapsed on the floor of the ring out of breath. It was at that moment that John recognised Luca's talent. And it was the next moment, when Luca jumped on the guys back and tried to choke him out, that he recognised the kid had baggage.

"Dad, Dad… over here!" Luca glanced up as he stepped inside the front doors of the place that had, without question, changed his life.

"Hey boys, what are you doing here?" he remarked in surprise.

He hadn't expected to see his two boys until the weekend, and he definitely hadn't expected to see them at his gym of all places. Despite not having a formal custody arrangement after they separated, Luca and Claudia had worked out a schedule that seemed to work for all of them. The boys lived mostly with their mother. Close to their school and in a good neighbourhood, it made sense that they spent most of their time there. Especially as Luca spent so many hours training every day; morning, and night. Every second weekend, they would spend two days with Luca at his parents' place. He also tried to drop into Claudia's place after training sometimes, to put the boys to bed and read them a story.

Luca loved his time with his sons more than anything else. Even more than boxing. His kids were the greatest love of his life; his motivation and strength. Without them, there was no way he would have had half the success he'd experienced in his career. A fire had been lit in him the day Riley had been born, and then again with Joey. A fire that he couldn't sometimes control, but one that had pushed him to train harder than he'd ever trained; to perform better than he could ever have imagined over the past seven years. His boys had given him purpose. Given him a reason to hope that he could be the best fighter in the world one day. It was this fire that had fuelled the hours and hours of training; the weight cuts; the black eyes and bruises that stayed around for weeks after fights. It was his boys that kept him going, through all the hard times and the good.

When he and Claudia first separated, and he'd moved out of the home they'd lived in together and back in with his parents, Luca had struggled being separated from his boys. He and Claudia had been growing apart for a long time before their split. They both knew it, but neither wanted to give it words until the end. When it happened and they split, he was hurt, but resigned to the fact that they just weren't right for each other. Their relationship had ended on good terms, which he was grateful for. They'd been such good friends for so many years as kids; to separate and hate each other just wouldn't have sat right with Luca. It just wasn't his style. What he hadn't expected, or been ready for, was the grief he'd felt at leaving his children behind. He missed his boys so much his heart had hurt every day. He went through some dark times during those first few months, when he questioned if what he was doing was worth it; if being a fighter was what he wanted from his life. It was his coach John, who'd dragged him out of his funk. John, who held him up and pushed him forward when he couldn't see past his sadness. He would always owe him for that.

"Mum had a date,' Riley advised, with a look of disgust on his face. "She said we could come and watch you at training, so we didn't annoy her."

Despite being a little pissed off that she hadn't called him and asked, Luca didn't actually mind that Claudia had dumped the boys on him. In fact, he was pretty excited to spend some extra time with them. And it wasn't every day that Claudia went on a date. Luca smiled a devious smile as he thought to himself, 'poor bastard doesn't know what he's in for.'

Scooping his boys up into his arms and hugging them so tight they began to protest loudly, Luca said "That's awesome guys, I'm so happy to see you. Let's head in and you can say hi to John and find somewhere to sit and watch."

Walking into the main room of the gym, Luca was always overwhelmed with the sheer height of the ceilings and the vast space available to him for training. All kinds of training happened in this place, not just boxing. There were spaces and equipment like bikes and treadmills for fitness classes; spaces for martial arts training like Muay Thai Boxing and Jiu Jitsu; weights rooms and mats for training of every kind of athlete. It was an incredible place, with an atmosphere that always kept Luca motivated and inspired. Watching other athletes training and working out gave him the constant push to better his own craft, and it was always cool to meet other professional athletes. Only a week earlier, he'd been chatting to a professional football player who stopped into the gym to do some strength training with one of the coaches. They shared training tips and ideas for meal preps. Luca found it pretty cool.

"I see you bought some extra sparring partners," John commented, as Luca and the kids walked into the gym.

Luca grinned, "Apparently Mum has a date!"

Raising his eyebrows at Luca, John looked towards the two little boys standing with their dad. The resemblance always blew him away. The apple didn't fall far from the tree with those two, he thought to himself. It wasn't often John got to see the boys anymore. Since Luca and Claudia had split a few years earlier, she'd stopped bringing them around to spend time at the gym while Luca trained. John missed their little faces around the place. He'd been like a second father to Luca for many years. And when the boys came along, he'd felt a little like a grandfather to them. His own grandkids, living on the other side of the country with his daughter and son in-law, only visited at Christmas and John missed them terribly. It was times like these that he lived for.

"So how are two of my favourite little guys?" John remarked, holding his arms out for the boys to get the hint.

Running and laughing, they jumped up into his arms and gave him a huge bear hug, arms and legs entwined around him, and each other, so that they looked like a giant octopus all wrapped up.

"Ready to watch me torture your Daddy!" John queried, as both boys looked back at their dad and yelled in unison, "Yes sir!"

"Oh hell," Luca muttered. He knew he was in for a good workout.

As Luca did some shadow boxing to warm up, he watched his boys play around in the boxing ring. It still amazed him just how fast they grew. Each time he saw them, only two weeks apart, they were bigger than the last time. Riley, who turned seven earlier in the year, was a tall and lanky kid; very much like Luca at the same age. With crazy blonde hair and blue eyes, Riley exuded a confidence that was well past his age. Joseph, who was five and preferred to be called by his nickname Joey, was shorter than his brother and a little stockier. He too had blond hair like his brother and father. His eyes were his mother's though, dark brown and serious. Luca described Joey as a little bulldog. He was determined, fiercely independent and hated his big brother telling him what to do. Many a scrap and blood nose had occurred when Riley had given his little brother advice he wasn't interested in hearing. Even now, as Riley attempted to show Joey the correct technique for his fighting stance, Joey crash tackled his big brother into the mat and proceeded to pound on him from the top mount position.

"Dad!" Riley called, "Joey's hurting me again."

Joey, who always loved pounding on his big brother when he got a chance, looked over to his dad with an expression of pure joy on his face.

"Get off your brother Jo," Luca insisted, giving his smallest boy a wink. He quietly appreciated the technique Joey displayed in taking down his brother so efficiently.

"Ok you two crazy cats, time to move onto the bags," John called out, as the two boys scrambled to their feet and high tailed it towards the row of boxing bags on the back wall of the gym.

At least if they were hitting bags, they weren't hitting each other, Luca thought to himself. He smiled as they laced up their junior gloves; special editions bought for them by John and kept at the gym especially for their visits.

"You're turn now my friend," John said, as he pointed towards the boxing ring. It was time to work. And work they did.

Two hours later, exhausted and satisfied, Luca lay on the canvas and inhaled long, deep breaths. To anyone not averse to the Inner City Boxing Gym's gruelling training schedule, it might have looked like someone had dropped a bucket of water over Luca, such was the volume of sweat that surrounded him where he lay. It was this training schedule, the hours upon hours of drills, technique classes, and sparring sessions that made the fighters of the Inner City Boxing Gym some of the best in the world. And Luca was no exception. His hand eye coordination and footwork were his biggest weapons. His record spoke for itself. He'd fought 16 times since he made his professional debut at the age of 22. With around three to four fights per year, he was an active fighter who enjoyed the training process, the preparation process and the camp leading up to a fight, almost as much as the fight itself. He trained every day, whether he had a fight booked or not. He was always ready. And at 27, with a strong work ethic and world class team of coaches behind him, he'd fought his way into the top five world rankings for fighters in his weight class.

He was currently contracted to fight for the American Boxing League, in a fight tournament that spanned 15 states in America, inviting international opponents to go head to head with world class American fighters. Luca had fought only a month or so earlier and had won in a decisive fashion. By knockout in the second round. He'd ended up with a black eye and a few bruised ribs for his trouble, but he'd won convincingly. And now, he waited for advice from his management team on his next move. He hoped he would get a title shot soon. He knew he was ready. The four fighters in the top five ahead of him were exceptional athletes, but so was he. He knew, if given the opportunity, he could be the world champion. It had been his dream for as long as he could remember. He wouldn't stop until he had achieved it.

"You stink you know," came the sarcastic undertones of a voice he knew very well.

Standing at the side of the ring, arms resting casually on the ropes, stood his ex-partner and the mother of his two children, Claudia Garcia. Claudia, a receptionist at a local law firm, had never been backwards in coming forwards, and enjoyed telling Luca just what she thought of him, every chance she got. In the 13 years she'd known him, she had never backed down from a conflict with him; never stepped back from her brutally honest assessment of him and his life. In hindsight, that had been one of the major downfalls of their relationship. Both loved to fight, in different ways. And both loved to win. An unachievable goal, when children were involved.

At five foot three inches, with dark brown hair and sultry brown eyes, Claudia was a gorgeous woman by any standard. She was confident and sexy, and she knew it. It was one of the things that had attracted Luca to her when they were teenagers. She knew what she wanted, and she always got it. At the age of 19, she had wanted Luca. It hadn't taken long for him to want her back. Had they not had children, Luca was sure they would still be together, fighting, yelling, and having fantastic make up sex. But once the kids were born, they both realised their relationship wasn't working; it wasn't healthy for children to grow up in a household where yelling was the only form of communication. Luca had loved Claudia, as she had him. But they both knew that their strong personalities were a devastating force; a collision of passion and fierce pride that when mixed, created destruction for all that surrounded them.

"How was your date Claud?" Luca enquired, in a sarcastic tone that had Claudia instantly irritated.

"None of your business actually," she retorted, as she glared at him lying on the ground covered in sweat.

He was still damn sexy, she thought as she stood next to the ring, trying to look insolent.

"Aww come on," he replied, "the least you can do is give me the gossip since you dropped the kids off with no notice and without actually checking if I could have them."

Claudia's eyes narrowed.

"Like you have a life," she retaliated, "You've been here every waking moment for as long as I've known you… it's a no brainer that you were going to be here tonight. And I thought you might like to spend some extra time with your kids, since you haven't been around at all lately."

Her last comment had some bight in it; a sting he knew well, after years living with Claudia. Luca's thoughts shifted to Emily. To the house she'd bought. The place he was spending all his spare time, helping her renovate. He'd been there to help her tear down walls; clean out drains; rip out overgrown gardens and disassemble what felt like every fixed item on the property. Morning and night, he'd stopped around, both before and after training, bringing her snacks and drinks as they got stuck into some project or other. And he'd loved every moment. But now, sitting in the ring looking at a pissed off Claudia, he realised that he'd been so carried away with helping Emily, that he'd been neglecting his kids. Something he swore he would never do. The feeling of guilt that he'd worked so hard to overcome over the past few years suddenly began to eat away at him again. Damned if Claudia didn't know exactly how to make him feel like shit, when he'd just been feeling so good.

Claudia watched him mulling over something in his head. At one point, his lips curled into a sideways smile that instantly gave him away. It was a smile she'd seen hundreds of times before. At that moment, she knew exactly where he'd been these past few weeks. After years watching Luca Mendes smile that particular smile in one particular direction, she was 100% sure she had guessed right.

"So how is Emily then?" she asked, attempting to feign indifference, but quietly interested in his answer.

"She's great actually," Luca replied, being careful with his words. "She's been back for a couple of weeks now. Bought a house about 10 minutes west of her parents' place. It's a dump, but she's got builders fixing it up."

Claudia straightened. "That's nice," she replied, unsure of what to say next. "I'd better get the boys home for dinner then," she said, turning to head towards the back of the gym where the boys were still bashing the boxing bags with their gloves.

"Claud," Luca called, "You should stop in and say hi to her. I know she'd love to see you."

"Yeah maybe," Claudia replied, without turning.

She wasn't sure how she felt about that idea and didn't want Luca to know it. The boys said goodbye to their dad and Claudia walked them out to the waiting car.

The night air was cool and calm, a stark contrast to the thoughts racing through Claudia's head as she pulled out of the parking lot and began the drive home. How could she just drop in and say hi, she thought to herself. With everything that had happened after Emily had left, everything she had done. Christ, she'd stolen Luca from Emily when she was barely out of the state. She had betrayed the best friend she'd ever had, and the girl probably didn't even realise it. Nope, a visit to Emily Rodrigues was definitely out of the question.

Chapter 6

Luca decided to go straight home after training. Claudia's comments about him not being around for his kids really bothered him. More than he wanted to admit. As he jumped into his truck, a second-hand Ford Ranger he'd purchased a with one of his bigger fight prizes a couple of years back, Luca couldn't shake the irritated mood he was in. After all these years, Claudia still knew how to get under his skin, and it gave him the shits. He loved his kids, more then he could ever express. It killed him that he couldn't see them every day. He'd love nothing more than to have them live with him, he thought. It just wasn't practical. With training and travelling; and the fact that he lived in a tiny house with his parents. Over the past couple of weeks, he'd been doing some serious thinking about getting his own place. Seeing what Emily was doing to her home, how good it looked every time he went over there; he was inspired to create something of his own. He'd never done anything like that before.

When he was younger, he'd always lived with his parents. Then when he and Claudia had been together for a few years, they'd moved into a little house her mother owned and gave to her when she turned 20. It was a tiny place with two small bedrooms, a pokey bathroom, and a living area you couldn't fit more than three people in at a time. But at the age of 20, it was all they needed. Even when the boys came along, it fit them all. Just. When he and Claudia split, and she asked him to leave, he never even considered getting his own place. He went home, to his parents' house, with its perfectly mowed lawn and well-loved spaces. His parents were never bothered by him. They loved having their only son at home with them again. At the time he and Claudia split, he was just beginning to get his name out there in the fight game. People were starting to pay attention, but he was still being paid almost nothing. Even if he'd wanted to, he couldn't have afforded to move out on his own. Now though, now he was in a good place financially. He had a little money in the bank. He had a decent car; nice clothes courtesy of some local sponsorship deals. He was where he should be. A home was the next item on the list.

He thought of Emily's house again as he drove along the quiet streets of his hometown. It was really coming along nicely and was going to be amazing when it was all finished. Her vision for what she wanted was so clear, so specific, even Luca could see it in his mind every time she talked about it. Her attention to detail was something to behold. He'd forgotten how good she was at planning. She'd always planned his life for him, when they were younger. They would sit for hours talking about their futures. He would have the big ideas; she would have the detailed plan to go with it. They were the perfect pair in that respect. Big, bright ideas mixed with cool, calm planning and execution. Add in the fire and passion of Claudia and the easy go lucky Ricky and there was nothing the group of friends couldn't do together. Except they hadn't been together. For a really long time.

'I should do something about that,' Luca thought to himself, as he pulled up out the front of Emily's place.

"God damn it," he cursed under his breath. He'd intended to drive home to his parents' place, but without even realising, found himself out the front of Emily's house. He had to admit, even in the dark of the evening, it looked great. The painters had finished the outside façade and roof. To look at it now, you wouldn't even know it was any different to any other home in the street. He noticed Adam's truck in the driveway as he made his way out of his own truck and up towards the front porch. Adam's a good guy, Luca thought as he walked in the gate and along the path towards the front door. Thoughtful and competent, he'd kept the project on track from the beginning.

'I should buy the guy a beer sometime,' Luca thought, as he opened the front door.

He heard Emily talking to Adam from the second bedroom.

"Oh Adam, I could just kiss you!" she declared, as Luca wandered into the room.

"Hang on there, how come he gets a kiss hey?" Luca joked, as he took in the look on Emily's face. She had clearly received some good news.

"Adam says I can stay in the house tonight! I need to go home and grab some stuff. Luca can you stay here. I'll be back."

She spoke so fast; he almost couldn't register what she was saying. He nodded a couple of times before she flew from the room, grabbing a torch, her bag and keys and heading out the front door towards her car like her life depended on it.

"And there goes hurricane Emily," Luca remarked, laughing, as Adam patted him on the shoulder and made his way out of the house to his truck.

Well, Luca thought to himself, 'what the hell am I supposed to do now? I should have bloody gone home,' he scolded himself, as he picked up another torch and wandered into the living area.

The power was off as the kitchen still hadn't been installed. He could see though, the back walls and glass folding doors had been finished. Even in the dark they looked amazing. The light from the full moon flooded onto the wooden deck outside, casting shadows down onto the bare yard. It'd taken them almost the full three weeks to clear the weeds and shrubs from the space. They would start planting out the gardens soon. Unlocking the sliding glass doors and pushing them all the way open, Luca stepped out onto the deck. The thick smell of wood stain filled the air as a light breeze hit his face. He walked to the edge of the deck and sat down on the wooden steps, surveying the space around him. It really was a great yard. Plenty of room for parties, and for kids.

He imagined his two boys running around kicking a football or throwing a frisbee. They could probably even fit in a pool. Hot summers would be brilliant with a pool. Looking over at the big old oak tree at the side of the yard, he pictured a wooden swing just like the one in Emily's parents' yard, swinging in the breeze. He'd mentioned it to her once before, but she hadn't seemed keen. He would talk her around. Every kid needed a swing to play on. He imagined strings of fairy lights running the length of the branches, creating beautiful, eclectic shapes in the space, and bringing new life to the old tree. He would enjoy sitting out here at night, drinking a cold beer or two. They could put a grill on the deck and add some speakers into the living area so music would flow outside. He imagined dancing with Emily; the lights from the tree casting a soft glow on her beautiful face.

He caught himself smiling and snapped back to reality. What the hell was he thinking? Kids, pools, lazy beers on the deck…dancing? He'd pretty much moved himself and his kids into the space… the space that was owned and occupied by his best friend! He'd gone mad!

"Bloody Claudia," he muttered.

This was her fault. Coming around to his gym, dredging up stuff that he hadn't thought about for years. He must be tired, he thought. And irritated. That was all.

'Nothing to see here,' he thought, as a loud bang echoed through the house from the front porch.

"Luca, help!" Emily yelled.

As quick as a cheetah, Luca was up and racing down the hallway. He threw open the front door, ready and willing to fight off whatever was attacking her. He ground to a halt as he found her standing on the porch, flashlight on the ground in front of her; sleeping bags hung from each arm; pillows under each arm; a box of random stuff balanced precariously in her arms, and a small suitcase rolling beside her. She looked ridiculous. And like she was about to cry.

"Can I help you with some of that," he smiled, teasing.

"Oh for god's sake just take this damn box… its heavy," she retorted.

Launching the box in his direction, Emily felt instantly relieved. She'd thought carrying everything from her car by herself was a good idea at first. Efficient even. She'd quickly discovered this not to be the case, as she struggled up the stairs and onto the porch. Once she dropped the torch and couldn't see where she was going, she'd decided she needed some help after all.

"I thought you were being attacked," Luca said, as he picked up the torch and directed her through the dark house.

"Lucky you're here then," she replied sarcastically.

"What is all this shit?" he asked, sifting through the box of random junk as he put it down on the floor in the living area.

Tealight candles, a small container of what looked like coffee, plastic cups, mosquito repellent… the girl looked like she was going camping… without the tent.

"I'm staying here tonight," she replied, grinning from ear to ear. "Adam said the house is at lock up and there's no reason I can't stay here until they put the kitchen in on Friday."

He could feel the excitement radiating from her; could hear it in her voice. This really meant a lot.

"Nice," he replied, as he surveyed all the random items she was piling into the corner of the living area.

"Why so much stuff though?" he queried.

Emily looked hopefully in his direction.

"I thought maybe you could stay too?" she said. "I couldn't think of anyone I'd rather spend the first night in my new home with then you. And I figured, since we'll be putting in the flower gardens early tomorrow, it would be more convenient for you to stay here tonight?"

That was what she'd told herself anyway, as she was driving back from her parents' place with a car full of supplies. The truth was somewhere closer to not wanting to sleep in an old house, by herself, when there was no power, but she wasn't about to tell Luca that. He'd have a field day making ghost noises and banging around in the dark. No, she decided in the car on the way over that she would play to his ego a little. If it happened to be true, all the better.

"How can I say no to that?" Luca said with a grin.

With the sleeping bags set up in the living room, Luca and Emily began putting out the tealight candles. Battery operated; the little lights created a cosy atmosphere in the empty space. With the kitchen to the front of the room, next to the hallway, and the glass folding doors leading out onto the deck to the back of the room, the space looked enormous with no furniture in it.

"This is going to be such a cool room," Luca said, thoughtfully.

"I'm so excited to go furniture shopping in a couple of weeks," Emily replied, as she put the last of the candles above her sleeping bag and pillow. "You'll have to come with me to pick out a couch, and a coffee table, and a rug. I think a light on a stand would look awesome in that corner too… and…" she drifted off as Luca stepped in front of her and put his hands on her shoulders.

"Hold up tiger," he joked, as she looked up at him. "You need some paint on these walls and proper flooring before you start placing furniture."

She laughed, realising she was getting ahead of herself.

"You're right. I need to chill. I'm just so excited! I've never done anything like this. Never owned a house of my own. I can't believe it's all happening!" Shaking her head, she turned to look out the folding doors onto the porch.

"I was thinking about your idea for the swing in the tree earlier. I think maybe you're right about putting one up."

She turned back to look at him, expecting to see happiness on his face and was confused by the look that greeted her. Like he'd just eaten something bitter.

"Are you ok?" she said.

"What? Yeah sorry, I'm all good. A swing hey? Good thinking," he replied quickly, turning to face his sleeping bag, busying himself searching for something to do so he would stop thinking about his little moment on the deck earlier.

She would die if she knew what he'd been thinking!

"I didn't have time to grab dinner, but I bought some biscuits and cheese if you're hungry?" Emily said, as Luca's stomach growled on cue, reminding him that he hadn't eaten any dinner after training.

"Sounds good to me", he replied, as she sat herself down on her sleeping bag.

"Dinner by candlelight," she joked, as he sat down across from her and she offered him the box of biscuits.

"How romantic," he said, chuckling at the scene they found themselves in.

Emily remarked, "Who'd of thought we'd end up sitting here eating cheese by candlelight hey?"

Tell me about it, Luca thought to himself.

"I really appreciate everything you've done for me lately Luca," Emily said quietly. "I know how much of your time I've taken up. There must be so many other things you have to do that you aren't, because of me. I just want you to know, it really means the world to me having you back in my life. I promise I'll repay the favour one day." And just like that, the crap mood Luca had wallowed in earlier in the evening, evaporated.

Snuggled up next to each other in their sleeping bags, the two friends reminisced on old times spent together as kids; laughing well into the early hours when the batteries in the tealight candles began to go flat. From the time Luca had attempted to break into the old man's house next door to steal some beers and had been caught red handed; to the time they'd snuck out and spent the night in an old abandoned house up the road, telling ghost stories and scaring the hell out of each other. They talked about school, with Luca filling Emily in on where everyone had ended up in the years following graduation. A lot had moved away, to college or for work. Many had stayed in town and tried their hand at finding work. Luca talked about turning professional as a boxer, and about each of his fights. Emily especially loved listening to him describe each of his bouts. She wasn't a fan of violence; detested it actually. Too many hours spent stitching up drunk teenagers in the emergency department on a Friday night, had given her an aversion to fighting. But with Luca, it was different. The way he described his fights was like she was listening to someone describing an art form; like a beautiful dance… that just so happened to end with one of them flat on the canvas. She was very glad that in almost all cases, it had been Luca's opponents on the ground at the end of his fights.

 "I'm really looking forward to coming to your next fight," Emily commented, as Luca finished telling her about his most recent fight. "I can't believe I've never actually seen you fight for real."

She'd seen him fight plenty of times when they were kids; at school in the playground; at school in the classroom; in the streets near their homes. But she'd never had the chance to see him fight professionally… in an actual boxing ring.

		"Do you ever get scared?" she asked him, glancing over to where he was laying with his hands resting on his chest, face pointing up to the roof, eyes closed.

He replied without hesitation. "Every time."

She waited silently, willing him to go on.

"Leading up to the fight its ok," he continued, "I'm concentrating on my diet, my cardio, my weight cutting. Even the day before the fight, when I go in for my official weigh in and to do all the press meetings and stuff. I'm still ok; still just thinking about the preparation and planning. It's not until the night of the fight; a couple of hours before it. When you arrive at the venue, you're shipped off to your room to get ready. They have all the gear they want you to wear, all set out in your room. Your gloves, shorts and walk out shirt. You get your hands wrapped up. That's when it kicks in for me. Sitting across from John, watching him wrap my hands up perfectly. I start to think… about where I've been; where I want to be; how much I want to win; what it all means. It's then that the nerves kick in." He looked over at his best friend, laying quietly next to him, listening intently, "It's then that I get scared. Scared that I might get hurt; that I might disappoint everyone; disappoint myself. At that moment, I feel like I could jump up and run for my life. As far away from there as my legs would take me." Luca closed his eyes.

 "So why do you do it then?" she asked quietly.

He thought for a minute. "The same reason you walk into the emergency department to go to work every day," he said, matter of factly. "You must get scared every now and again. I see the stories on the news. Doctors and nurses being attacked by drug addicts and criminals. Being injured by violent patients. Why do you do it?"

Emily thought about what he was asking her. About why she was a doctor. She decided it was far too late into the night to bring up her own demons; put words to her own greatest fears.

"It's my passion," was all she replied, as she closed her eyes and began to drift off to sleep.

"It's the same for me," he said quietly, realising she hadn't heard him.

Luca watched her sleeping peacefully next to him, in the sleeping bag on the hard wood floor. Next to them lay the empty biscuit packet, and tealight candle with a flat battery. She certainly wasn't a princess, he thought to himself smiling. She was one of a kind. He reflected on what he'd told her tonight. He'd never actually told anyone that stuff. Ever. If he was being honest, he rarely liked to think about any of it himself, let alone talk about it. But he had tonight. He had with her. She had a way of making him talk, making him *want* to talk, without her really saying anything. He'd always felt safe with her… even when they were kids. He knew she'd never tell a soul anything he'd said. She was his oldest friend, his very best friend. As he lay there looking up at the roof, slowly falling into sleep, he wondered if their friendship was all he needed now. If maybe, he should dare to ask for more?

Chapter 7

As the birds began to stir in the trees outside, Luca opened his eyes and glanced at Emily lying peacefully next to him. Trying not to wake her, he sat up and stretched silently. At around 4am, when he'd woken up cold and sore, he'd decided that sleeping on the floor was not as easy as he'd remembered when he was younger. He confirmed this now, as he rubbed his shoulders and neck. Not that he was saying he was old. Sometimes when he looked at his kids, he felt old though, he thought. They just grew up so damn quick. Birds started squawking as Emily began to stir. Laying back down on his sleeping bag, Luca looked over to her as she opened her eyes. She had beautiful eyes, he admitted to himself.

"Morning you," she said, smiling a warm, friendly smile.

"Heya, how'd you sleep?" he asked.

"I slept great," she replied. "How about you?"

Luca thought about telling her that he felt like he'd been hit by a truck. That he had more sore muscles then when he fought and may have lost a couple of toes overnight from the cold but thought better of it.

"Great. So, what's the plan today boss?" he asked smiling.

Emily laughed and replied, "Hard work my friend, very hard work."

Standing up and stretching her back, which she had to admit was a little sore after sleeping on the floor, Emily walked to the glass sliding doors at the back of the house and looked out onto her yard.

"I was thinking we could start putting together the garden beds and maybe go buy some plants if we get time?"

Luca groaned and replied, "We just got rid of the damn plants… why are we putting in more?"

Emily turned to face him and said. "Because this time it will be the plants I want, not the random jungle that was there before."

"Ok, but if we're building gardens today, I'm gonna need some breakfast," Luca said, as he walked over to stand next to her at the door. "It will look amazing Em. The whole place is looking incredible. You should be really proud of yourself and what you've done here."

Emily smiled and said, "I'm proud of what *we* are doing here… it's just as much my work as yours. So… what were you thinking for breakfast?"

Luca pondered this as he turned towards her, "You know me babe… burritos for the win."

Sitting at the restaurant, inhaling breakfast burritos like his life depended on it, Luca commented in between bites, "I saw Claudia last night." Emily glanced up, surprised.

"She dropped the boys at training while she went on a date with some random guy."

As soon as he'd said it, he silently scolded himself. He wasn't sure why he'd brought it up at all.

"Really?" Emily said.

She hadn't thought he really spoke to Claudia anymore; at least he'd never talked about it. Reflecting now, she realised how silly that was. They had children together, of course they would speak. Probably every day for all she knew.

"Did she mention coming to see me at all?" she asked in a tone that she thought sounded casual enough.

"No, not really," he replied, cursing himself again for even mentioning it.

"That's a pity," Emily said, "it would be nice to see her again."

Luca decided to prod a little, "When *was* the last time you spoke to her Em?"

Emily thought about it, "Probably a couple of months after I left?" she responded. "We spoke on the phone each weekend for a few months but after a while we both got busy and started missing each other's calls."

Just like you and I, Emily thought to herself. For a fleeting second the thought of Claudia and Luca sitting together, laughing at the phone when she called and they hadn't answered, crept into her mind. As quickly as it arrived, she shook it off. These were her friends, her best friends. They were just as busy as she had been all those years ago. There was no ulterior motive.

"Do you see her often?" Emily prodded a little herself.

Luca, realising he had created the awkward atmosphere they currently sat in, decided it was time to bight the bullet and get a few things off his chest. Things he'd been meaning to say to her since the day she rolled back into town.

He put down his burrito and said, "Em, look at me. Firstly, I want you to know there was never anything going on between Claudia and I when we were all younger. I need you to know that ok?"

Emily nodded and looked down at the table, feeling terrible for her earlier suspicious thoughts.

"We do see each a lot. Every second weekend when I get the kids for a couple of days and they come stay with me. And I drop around every now and again to see the boys and put them to bed. I tell a killer bedtime story you know?"

Emily smiled. Of course he did.

"And I try to get to their school stuff… awards days and meetings with the teachers. You know, all that stuff our parents used to do when we were younger. I don't see them as much as I'd like to, but I do try my best." He paused, "Sometimes I wish my best was better with them; but that's just life I guess."

Emily glanced up to see the sad expression on Luca's face. She felt terrible for even asking him this stuff. It was his personal business, not hers. He didn't owe her an explanation of anything he did.

 "You don't have to explain your personal life to me Luca," she said quietly, as she finished off her breakfast.

Luca responded without missing a beat, "Yeah I do Em. I want to explain it all to you. I don't want us to have any secrets between us. We never have, and I don't want to start now. You mean too much to me to keep secrets."

Emily smiled a weak smile. Leaving the restaurant, she sat in Luca's car thinking about the secrets she needed to tell him. She just wasn't sure if she was quite ready to tell them yet. Soon, she thought to herself as they headed back home to start gardening; soon.

One of the greatest joys of Emily's life was working with her hands. Whether it was saving someone's life by sewing up a wound; putting in a chest drain or central line; or tending to her very own garden beds; she found using her hands to be therapeutic. Relaxing. Calming and creative. She found great joy in her gardens. When she'd lived in North Carolina with her university flatmate, she'd bought a few small planter pots for her windowsill and had planted an assortment of herbs and flowers. She loved tending to them; watching something grow and flourish at her hands. It reminded her of her childhood. Of hours spent in her parents' garden planting and picking with her father. Back then, the gardens were bright and colourful, with semi organised rows of vegetables and flowers spanning the length of the garden beds. Many years later, those rows had turned into chaos. Overgrown and filled with weeds, it now reminded Emily of another garden she had transformed in recent years. Michael, her ex, had never been interested in gardening. He never liked to get his hands dirty outside of work.

 'We have people we can pay to do those sorts of things,' he would say, when Emily began tinkering around in the garden at the front of their home. Emily would smile and tell him she didn't mind doing it herself;

that she actually enjoyed gardening. He would look at her with disdain and slink off to sit in his airconditioned study reading.

Standing in her yard now, dressed in old shorts and a t-shirt, sneakers and a baseball cap, Emily was in her element. She couldn't contain the smile on her face as she helped Luca move wooden sleepers into place to form up the sides of her garden beds. She could see the vision clearly in her head. The left-hand side of the yard would be where she planted her flower garden. An assortment of blue, yellow, and white flowers of all varieties. It would look like a thousand bouquets of flowers had been placed there and grown alongside each other. There would be neat rows; amazing bursts of colour. It was going to look incredible. To the back of the yard, she would build a vegetable garden just like in her parents' yard. She would grow tomatoes, carrots and put in a few berry vines. It would be full of life and hopefully produce enough food for her to share. To the right of the yard was the big oak tree. It was huge, and gorgeous. It created a nice shaded area over to the side of the yard that Emily could use as a seating area. She thought again about Luca's idea to put in a wooden swing like the one in her parents' yard. A nice idea, she mused, but a lot of work. Looking up at the tree, she figured she would need a huge ladder and lots of rope to tie the swing up to the stronger of the branches. It would take a team of people to achieve that one. She decided to put it on the 'to do later' pile, when the house was finished, and she had time to work out the logistics of such a huge venture.

Luca watched her work and think. As he worked, he found himself smiling and enjoying every minute. It was starting to really come together. The sleepers that formed up the frame of the garden beds had been laid, and the dirt that had been removed when they went through flattening and evening up the ground around the previous gardens was sitting there waiting to be put back in the newly shaped garden beds. Grabbing a shovel, Luca began moving dirt. It was a basic task but gave him great satisfaction. He'd always liked working with his hands. He enjoyed taking a blank canvas and making it look amazing. This was no different. As he worked, he began whistling out of habit. It was something he'd done since he was a kid, to keep his mind on the task. For Emily, hearing Luca whistling brought back so many childhood memories. From playing around in the dirt pile in her backyard as little kids; to riding bikes up and down the streets together; to laying on the manicured grass in his parents' backyard staring at clouds in the sky and thinking about the world. Nostalgia caught hold of Emily as she picked up another shovel and started moving dirt into the flower beds. Side by side they worked, through the day and into the afternoon. Occasionally, one would stop and grab a water bottle to share. Luca would stop whistling every now and again to comment on their progress. They worked together in sync; so well that they had the job completed in half the time they'd expected. Standing back and surveying the yard, Emily was ecstatic. All the garden beds were completed and full of rich, dark dirt. The vegetables had been planted and wooden trellis dug into the centre of the garden for the vines to grow up. The only thing left to do, was to plant the flowers and lay some grass in the centre of the yard.

Overwhelmed with joy and excitement, Emily walked over to Luca and catching him off guard, jumped up on his back wrapping her arms and legs around him.

"Oy, what's the go!" Luca remarked as he stumbled, surprised and off balance.

In an attempt to stay upright, he wobbled to the right. He realised too late that he was going to fall and take Emily with him. Quick thinking had him drop to his hands and knees, with Emily sliding off his back and landing on the empty flower bed in front of him with a thud. Concern and worry covered his face as he looked up to see if she was ok. Laying there in the freshly turned dirt, now completely covered from head to toe, Emily burst into laughter. A belly laugh that she hadn't heard from her own mouth in a long time. Luca relaxed as he realised she was ok. He stood and turned to face the opposite direction, flopping down on the garden bed next to her, covering himself in dirt. He began to laugh along as they lay there together, staring up at the cloudy afternoon sky, as they had done so many times before.

"I'm so glad you came home Em," Luca admitted, as their laughter subsided. "I didn't realise how much I missed you, until the last few weeks."

Looking over at Emily lying next to him, covered in dirt and mess, he couldn't remember ever seeing anyone more beautiful. Leaning over, he brushed dirt from her face as he looked into her eyes, glistening in the sunshine. Eyes that he'd looked into a thousand times, but somehow also never before. At that moment he wondered what it might feel like to kiss her; right there in the flower garden. What she would taste like.

Emily, taken by the intimate gesture and feeling both confused and embarrassed at the same time, gave him a friendly shove, and stood up, dusting off dirt from her back, legs, and hair.

"Sorry," she said in a sheepish voice, "I got a bit carried away. I didn't hurt you, did I?"

Luca, still with a foggy head, stood up and began dusting himself off.

"No, you didn't hurt me," he smiled, "I thought I'd hurt you for a second," he said.

Emily grinned. "I'm pretty tough for a girl you know."

She turned to pick up the shovels and started walking towards the deck at the back of the house.

"Don't I know it," Luca muttered, softly enough so that Emily didn't hear him.

What the hell was going on, he thought to himself. He was behaving like a total moron; like a hormonal teenager who'd never had a girlfriend. This was Emily, his best friend. She'd only just come back into his life. He couldn't do anything to jeopardise that. He couldn't lose her again. They'd just spent way too much time together, he thought to himself. He needed some space from her. Yep, that was the answer… a little space and perspective to clear his head. Walking up to the house, rehearsing what he was going to say to ensure a swift exit from the building, Luca caught a glimpse of her through her bedroom door. She stood with her back to him, changing out of her shorts and top and into the dress she'd been wearing earlier in the day. Having had no time to install the new door handles she'd bought the week before, the door stood slightly ajar. All thoughts of space and perspective left Luca's head as he realised in that moment, just how attracted he was to her. He wanted her badly. More than he'd wanted anything in a long time.

As Emily stood in her bedroom, changing out of the old dirt covered clothes she'd been wearing in the garden, she worried she had misread his signals. Surely, she'd been confused. For a second she'd thought he was going to kiss her. But that was crazy! Of course, he wasn't going to kiss her. He was her best friend. God, she thought to herself, I know it's been a while since I got any, but this is ridiculous! Apprehension flooded her mind as she contemplated the disaster it would have caused if he'd actually kissed her. No, she was just being crazy. And probably needed to get out and meet some new people if she was considering kissing her childhood best friend! Dressed and clean, Emily turned and walked back out into the living area. She found Luca sitting on one of the sleeping bags, waiting for her.

"So, what are your plans for this afternoon?" she asked casually, deciding not to bring up what she thought had almost happened. She didn't want to look like a complete idiot.

"Umm, I told my Mum I'd help her with some chores around the house. Other than that, I'll probably head to training?" Luca replied simply.

Emily breathed a sigh of relief. He was being normal; she had dreamt the whole thing up. Thank god was all she could think. Thank god.

Trying his hardest to sound normal, Luca sat wondering how on earth he was going to get the current R rated thoughts out of his head. Emily laying in the dirt; Emily half naked getting changed; Emily laying on the sleeping bag next to him the night before, looking so beautiful. He took a deep breath. His throat was dry as chips. He needed to get out of here before he did something they might both regret. Well he probably wouldn't regret it but… What the hell was he thinking? Standing up and grabbing his car keys from the floor, Luca said as casually as he could muster,

"Well I'd better get moving then; Mum's probably waiting for me now. You know what she's like when I'm late."

He'd almost made it to the hallway before she'd even had a chance to reply.

"Ok…" she said, "you don't want to keep her waiting then. I guess I'll catch you tomorrow maybe?"

He turned and looked at her standing there… looking as gorgeous as ever. Damn it, he was going to hell.

"Yeah I'll see what I've got happening. Maybe we could go grab the plants from the nursery. Or something…"

His train of thought was interrupted as the afternoon sun shone in the glass sliding doors, surrounding her with warm white light. She looked like a bloody angel. Christ almighty, he was screwed. He needed to think… to work out what the hell was going on in his head.

"Ok well I'll text you later then," he said.

And with that, Luca was out the front door and gone.

As soon as the front door closed Emily let out a deep breath and flopped down on the sleeping bag. What on earth had gotten into her? What was she thinking, wanting to kiss her best friend? The one and only person she could rely on. She must be seriously mentally unstable to think that she could just kiss her oldest and dearest friend, like it was nothing. She knew it wouldn't be nothing. She knew it would mean something. It had to. As she looked around her house, all she could see was Luca. The walls they'd painted together; the gardens they'd just finished building. She needed to get out of the house… get some fresh air. That would surely clear her mind and get her back to normal thinking. Picking up her bag and keys, she locked up the glass doors and walked to the front of the house. An outing by herself was just what she needed. And she knew exactly where she would go.

Chapter 8

Emily loved the beach. Feeling the sun warming her back; watching the afternoon shadows lengthen as she walked along the cool, soft, white sand. She felt so blessed to live 10 minutes from one of the most beautiful beaches on earth. As a child, she'd spent most of her summers at the beach. Sunbaking, swimming, or playing some form of sport. Beach volleyball was her favourite. It was one of the only sports she could give Luca a run for his money, she mused. Luca. What the hell was going on with her? As she walked along the shoreline, the waves lapping at her feet, she thought back to the last few weeks with him. All the time they'd spent together. All the things they'd done together. Not once had she thought something was going on between them. In her whole life, she'd never considered anything would happen between them. Even as a teenager, Emily saw Luca as her best friend. More like a brother than anything else.

'Nothing *is* going on between us,' she thought, scolding herself.

Nothing *will* happen between us. How could it? They'd been friends since they were kids. They knew everything about each other. Almost everything, Emily thought, as her mind wandered to North Carolina. To Michael.

She knew she needed to tell Luca about him. About life with him. Being engaged to him. She just hadn't worked out how to say it yet. How to explain it in a way that didn't make her look silly. Because she had been silly; falling for a guy who couldn't see past his success and status to show her love. She knew Luca wouldn't understand it. He was such a loving and passionate person. How could he possibly understand her relationship with Michael? Its dysfunctional functionality. Its calm in a storm of career beginning self-doubt. She needed to think long and hard before she had that conversation with her best friend.

Walking along the sand alone, thinking about her life and the choices she'd made so far… Emily felt that familiar self-doubt threaten to creep in. What was going on with her? She was crazy to think that something could happen between her and Luca. It just wasn't realistic; it wasn't at all practical. And it wasn't what she wanted. She was almost sure of that. As she left the sand and headed towards her car in the parking lot, she was 100% sure it was all in her mind, and that would be where it stayed.

No matter what he did, Luca couldn't get Emily out of his mind, and it was driving him insane. Every time he closed his eyes, he could see her, half dressed. Her skin shining in the light of the afternoon sun. Her hair glistening and flowing free down her tanned and toned back. Christ almighty, he thought exasperated. He needed to get laid. Standing at the grill in his parents yard, about to cook them all dinner, Luca ran the afternoons events through his mind again. He'd figured going over it all a few times would help him get over it. Whatever 'it' was. It hadn't worked so far. Not driving home; not washing his dad's car; training at the gym, and definitely not now. Emily. Why Emily? Of all the girls in the world he could think about… in that way. Why did it have to be her? She was his friend. She trusted him. He was sure she would be shocked if she knew what he was thinking about her.

"Yo, yo, yo," came the call from the side of the house.

Turning towards the sound, Luca was pleasantly surprised to see one of his oldest friends, Ricky walk around the corner towards him.

"What the hell," he replied jovially, as he put down the tongs and walked over to his friend.

They embraced warmly as Luca said, "What brings you to this side of the world my friend?"

Ricky smiling, replied, "Just in the neighbourhood my man. Thought I'd drop by and see what's new with you. It's been too long man."

And it had. Far too long between drinks for Ricky and Luca. The friends, who'd spent so much time together as teenagers, could almost be taken for strangers they'd had spent so little time together over the previous couple of years.

"Take a seat buddy," Luca said as he walked back over to the grill, flipping the meat before it burnt. "How are Rachael and the kids?" he asked.

In Luca's opinion, Ricky and Rachael were the perfect couple. They had loved each other at first site, or that's what they told everyone. Even after having three kids, they still loved each other more than anyone Luca had ever seen. They were inseparable.

"She's great man, still working as a teacher at the kindy and loving it. She just loves kids so much." Ricky replied. "The little ones are great too. The twins turn three in a couple of weeks and Lilly is nine months old. They grow up so quick man," he commented.

"Yeah don't I know it," Luca agreed. "My two are seven and five now… old enough to give me plenty of attitude." he said with a big grin on his face.

"How's it going with you and Claudia?" Ricky asked. "Last I spoke to you; she wasn't really happy with you seeing the kids too often."

Luca considered what his friend had just said. Had it really been that long since he'd spoken to Ricky? He and Claudia had sorted all that stuff out almost a year earlier. Luca instantly felt guilty.

"Yeah man it's all good now. I get them every second weekend and go around to see them at her place a couple of nights a week. Or I was… been pretty busy lately." He said.

Ricky replied, "That's awesome Luc, I'm really happy for you. We should get the kids together for a play soon hey. Maybe head down to the beach for the day or something."

Luca nodded, agreeing. "Absolutely, I know they'd love that. I've got them this weekend if you're not busy?" he said.

Ricky thought about it. "I'd have to check with Rachael, but I don't think we've got anything on so that sounds great. The surfs meant to be good then too so we can catch some waves. I can't remember the last time I went for a surf."

Luca thought about it too. The last time he'd been surfing was the day he found out that Emily was coming home. That was a couple of months ago now. He was definitely due to for a day in the waves.

"So, how's training? Any word on your next fight?" Ricky asked, as Luca piled the cooked food onto a tray to take inside to his parents.

"Training's good man. Still with the same team, still working with John. Still working hard every day. I'm hoping to get some news about my next fight soon. It's got to be someone in the top five. Or at least I hope it is. The other guys above me have all had fights booked in the next few months, so I'm really hopeful it's my turn next," Luca remarked.

Ricky said honestly, "I'm sure it will be man. You've definitely deserved it. I was at your last fight and you were heads above the other dude. You looked so good in there man."

Luca smiled. He often had people telling him how good he was. Mostly he took it with a grain of salt. But with Ricky, he believed every word. Other than Emily, Ricky was the best mate he'd ever had. The most loyal, trustworthy friend. He could always trust Ricky to give it to him straight. To be kind but fair in his assessment of Luca and his life.

Even when Ricky had moved away, Luca used to talk to him regularly on the phone. Ricky had been by Luca's side through all his hardest battles. As soon as Emily had left for college at 17, Luca had relied on Ricky to give him good doses of the truth. No matter what. And up until Ricky had moved away a few months later, they'd been connected at the hip. Surfing together, partying together… Ricky had even tried to train with Luca once or twice. He quickly decided it wasn't for him though.

"Want a beer Rick?" Luca asked, as he carried the food into the house.

"Thought you'd never ask," Ricky replied, resting his feet on the chair next to him and grinning.

Luca returned from the house with two cold beers and sat down at the table nearest the grill. Both men sat quietly sipping their beers.

After a while, Luca broke the comfortable silence.

"Emily's back," he said simply.

Ricky looked at him with a curious expression.

"Really?" he replied. "Little Emily Rodrigues is back in town hey?" He grinned as Luca laughed.

"I can tell you now man, she's not so little anymore," Luca said.

"Have you seen her then?" Ricky asked.

He would never admit it to Luca, but he had always secretly hoped Emily would return home one day. Luca had never quite been the same after Emily had left town.

Luca responded, "Yeah, I've seen her a bit since she got back. She bought a house about 10 minutes away and she's been renovating it. We spent all day today fixing up the backyard. Putting in new garden beds and filling them. It's looking pretty awesome. She's got some great ideas for the place."

He stopped short of telling Ricky about the plans he'd thought up himself for the place. He thought it might sound a little strange.

Ricky sat listening to Luca talk about Emily's house. Yep, he thought to himself, the guys still mad about her. He always found it hilarious, even when they were teenagers, that Luca was so oblivious to how crazy he was about Emily. Ricky had certainly seen it, plain as day. He always suspected that Claudia had seen it to. As teenagers, the four of them had been such good friends. But Ricky had seen the dynamic shift between them all as they'd gotten older. Emily and Luca had always been close. So close that they'd never really seen what was between them. It was just how they were. Like an old married couple from when they were little until she'd left for college. Almost as soon as she'd left, Claudia had changed. From being Emily's offsider, to setting her eyes on Luca. Ricky had seen it firsthand. And he hadn't liked it. They'd talked about it once. Ricky asking Claudia what she was doing with Luca. Claudia had responded with something like 'back off, its none of your business. Emily isn't here anymore. I'm doing nothing wrong.' But Ricky had always felt uneasy about Luca and Claudia. He knew that Luca and Emily were made for each other… meant to be together. It was just the way it was.

Now she was back in his life. Ricky decided it was time to poke the old bear.

"How's it been seeing her again? Spending time with her again?"

Luca wasn't sure how to answer him. He'd always been truthful with Ricky. He just wasn't sure if he was ready to tell him what he thought about Emily. If it was even sane. He thought probably not, so decided to keep it close to his chest for now.

"It's good man. She's still the same old Emily. Still crazy organised; still knows exactly what she wants; still…" he wasn't sure how to finish his sentence.

He looked up to find Ricky with a huge grin on his face.

"What's so funny?" Luca remarked.

"Come on dude," Ricky replied, laughing. "We aren't 17 anymore…"

Luca was confused. "What do you mean?" he said.

Ricky continued, "Dude, you've been in love with that girl for as long as I've known you. We both know it. Christ, everyone that knew you both could see it. You're 27 years old now man. You're not kids anymore. What the hell are you doing about it?"

Luca was a little stunned. He wasn't at all sure how to respond to his friend. What did he mean… in love with Emily? He was clearly wrong.

Maybe a little delusional. Emily was his friend. Yeah, he'd pictured her in some interesting new ways recently, but she was still Emily. His friend. Luca took a big chug of his beer and cleared his throat.

"You're wrong Rick. You know Emily's my friend. You're talking crazy if you think anything else."

Ricky retorted, "Are you trying to convince me… or yourself?"

Luca took another long sip of his beer. He wasn't sure how they ended up having this conversation, but he didn't think he liked it.

"Look mate, I know you're all loved up now that you're married and everything. But not all of us get a fairy-tale ending." Luca said, trying to divert attention.

"Tell me this then," Ricky continued pushing, "Who do you think about when you first wake up in the morning?"

"What has that got to do with anything?" Luca replied quickly.

"Just answer me man," Ricky returned.

Luca was starting to get really irritated.

"So, its Emily… so what?" he said.

Rick continued, "And who do you think about before you go to bed each night?"

Luca definitely had the shits now as he replied, "You know who."

Ricky smiled as he saw how annoyed his friend was getting with him. He was almost there.

"And since she's been back, how many days have you gone without seeing her?"

Luca had had enough. "That has nothing to do with anything Rick. She's just moved back. I'm helping her get moved in and with her house. It doesn't mean anything."

He finished off his beer and slammed it down on the table.

Ricky smiled and said matter of factly, "So let me tell *you* something Luc. When I met Rachael, I loved her from the minute I set eyes on her. I think about her every morning when I wake up, and every night before I go to bed. Since we met, *we've* never spent a day apart."

Luca was starting to see where he was going.

"You tell me… what *does* it mean? I married the girl I couldn't live without. What are you going to do to keep the girl in your life that you can't live without?" He paused, "Whether you want to admit it or not, I think that you know you love her. You've always known you love her. You're just too damn stubborn to say it."

Luca closed his eyes. The truth he'd been struggling to admit to himself since Emily had returned home all those weeks ago, hit him in the face like a well-timed hook shot. He knew Ricky was right. He did love Emily. He'd always loved Emily. What the hell *was* he going to do?

Luca opened his eyes and looked at his friend. His honest and trustworthy friend. And he decided to come clean.

"I can't stop thinking about her man," Luca began, as Ricky settled back, ready to enjoy the show. "She's in my head. Always in my damn head. Every day I wake up and think, 'I wonder what Emily is doing today' or 'maybe Emily might call me this morning.' Even when I'm at training, I'm listening out for my phone… just in case she calls me. I can't concentrate. I can't focus… unless it's on her. I'm completely screwed Rick."

Luca slumped over in his chair and placed his head in his hands. He looked like he was about to cry. The poor guy, Ricky thought to himself. He was a goner. Ricky couldn't help but smile. Luca looked up at his friend.

"Don't you dare laugh at me man… this is torture. Actual torture. I see her every damn day. I almost kissed her today and she looked at me like I was mad. Maybe I am mad. What the hell do I do?"

Ricky stopped to take in this new piece of information. "What do you mean you almost kissed her today?" he asked.

Luca relayed the story of the garden beds, of the two ending up in the dirt. Ricky laughed and leant across the table to punch his best mate in the arm.

"Buddy, you have no idea how much I am looking forward to seeing this play out… maybe more than I've ever looked forward to anything. Except maybe my wedding day." He laughed again. "What are you going to do about it then? How are you going to show her how you feel?"

Luca paused. "I don't know if I can Rick. I don't think she looks at me like that. I really don't. And if I push it, and she doesn't… what if I push her away? I couldn't handle losing her again. I only just got her back."

Ricky considered his friends comments. After falling for, and marrying the greatest love of his life, Ricky understood Luca's fear of losing Emily. He knew himself that he would be nothing without his wife, his partner and soul mate. He wanted so badly to give his friend the right answer. To help him solve this problem that was obviously troubling him.

"Look Luc, I can't give you the answer you want. As much as I want to. You're just gonna have to figure it out as you go man. You'll know when the time is right. You guys are meant to be together, that I know for a fact. And you do too. I've never met two people more perfect for each other. You just have to trust that the universe has a plan for you both. It sure did for me and Rach."

Luca stood up and embraced his friend. "I appreciate you so much man. Thanks for listening to me ramble. I was in such a crap mood earlier thinking about it all… now I feel so much better. We should catch up more often man. I miss you!"

Ricky nodded. "I know man, it's been too long. It's mostly my fault for being so damn busy with work and the kids. I've been meaning to come around for months, but life just gets in the way sometimes."

Luca considered his friend, "Lets lock in this weekend then. Saturday at the beach, near the pier. You bring the kids and Rachael. I'll bring my boys. And I'll ask Emily to come along too. She'll be so happy to see you."

Luca did feel so much better after talking to Ricky. His head felt clearer and his decision was made… he needed to work out how to make Emily see what she meant to him; what he had to offer. How he would do that… he had no clue yet.

"Now how about another beer my friend?" Luca asked, as he and Ricky walked into his parents' house to watch the football.

Chapter 9

Saturday arrived as Luca drove his car towards the beach and what he hoped would be a fun day out with good friends. He hadn't seen Emily for a few days; since they'd fixed up her garden. After his conversation with Ricky, he'd decided to take a few days to get his head clear. He'd spent some time training and seeing his kids. Both well overdue. John had been somewhat surprised when he showed up at training more than two days in a row. Having known Luca for many years, John had seen the strong work ethic Luca displayed. When he had a specific goal to reach. Outside of that, when his goal had been reached and he hadn't yet set another… Luca could wander a little. And lately, he had wandered far. John knew a fight agreement was on the cards. As soon as the news came through it would shake Luca back into action. Until then, he just took whatever time he got from him… whenever he chose to show up.

Claudia had also been surprised to see Luca. Having heard almost nothing from him for weeks, she was a little put off when he showed up to read the boys a bedtime story, four nights in a row. Curiosity got the better of her on the 4th night when after finishing The Cat in the Hat for the second time, Luca kissed his boy's goodnight and walked out into the living area of her small two bedroom home. Sitting on the pale grey couch, pretending to watch some trashy show (when she had in fact, been listening to him read to her kids), Claudia looked up as he walked in.

"Sound asleep," he said smiling, taking a seat on the floor.

It was a simple gesture, but one that pinched at her heart as she recalled all the times he had sat in that exact spot on the floor with their kids. With her. But that was a long time ago, she reminded herself. She had moved on.

"So, what's with you then?" she asked, trying to sound cranky but only mustering mild disapproval.

"What do you mean," he replied, readying for the usual barrage of negativity.

"Why are you here Luca? What gives?" She sat up straighter and continued, "We don't see you for weeks and weeks… then out of the blue you show up every night like you still friggin live here. I want to know what's going on?"

Luca took a deep breath and tried to push what he really wanted to say back down somewhere dark. He wouldn't argue with her today.

Laying on his back on the floor and placing his hands up under his head, Luca said calmly, "Nothing's up Claud. I've been really busy lately and I realised I haven't seen the boys as much as I wanted to. I had a few spare nights, so I thought I'd swing by. If it's a drama I can always call and check with you before I come around?"

Claudia sat looking at him suspiciously. He was never this reasonable. Something was definitely going on. Changing tact, she smiled and relaxed back on the couch.

"Sorry, I didn't mean to snap. I've just had a busy couple of weeks too. What with work and the kids school stuff." She began to prod. "What exactly have you been up to?"

Luca recognised the tone. His ex was fishing, and he didn't feel much like being caught.

"Just training mostly," he replied casually. "I'm hoping I get some big news soon… maybe a title shot."

This wasn't what Claudia had wanted to hear. She'd been hoping he would say something about Emily. Give her some indication of what her old friend was up to. Since Claudia had spoken to Luca at the gym the week before, she'd thought a lot about Emily. She'd even gone hunting for her old photo albums; long packed away in a box in the closet, and spent hours reminiscing on their teenage adventures. She would never admit it to anyone, but she missed her friend. Luca lay quietly on the floor, enjoying the knowledge that the silence would be driving Claudia crazy. And that it was. Unable to pretend she was watching the crap television show any longer, Claudia reached over and switched off the TV.

"Hey, I was watching that," Luca said sarcastically.

"You're an idiot," Claudia retorted, realising he had baited her.

She sat forward on the couch and looked directly at him. "Will you just tell me how she is?" she said.

Luca smirked. Got ya, he thought to himself.

Always happy to irritate her, Luca feigned confusion as he said, "How's who?"

Claudia snapped. "For Christ's sake Luca, stop being a complete loser and just tell me what I want to know. Or get the hell out of my house."

Realising that steam may soon come out her ears, and not wanting to wake the kids, Luca reluctantly obliged.

"Emily is good. She's great actually." He said genuinely. "She's fixing up her house. Re-doing the gardens, painting walls. She'd got a new kitchen going in… tomorrow, I think. It sounded great when she was describing it. She's got some guy coming to replace the floors in a couple of weeks. She wants polished floorboards all through the house."

Claudia listened intently to every word and recognised a familiar feeling as it came over her. One she'd felt for many years standing by her friends' side, and for many years after. Jealousy. New kitchen; polished floorboards. She could barely afford a coat of paint on her place, and Emily was building a whole new house. A mansion by the sounds of it.

'So, nothing has changed then,' Claudia thought to herself.

Emily was still perfect. Still getting everything she ever wanted without giving it a second thought. Beautiful; smart; kind. Claudia felt the old knot begin to turn in her stomach.

Growing up, Emily Rodrigues had been everything that Claudia had wanted to be, but never was. Claudia had spent her early childhood growing up in one of the poorest neighbourhoods in LA. The daughter of a drug addicted father who left her mum when he found out she was pregnant; Claudia had never met her dad. Didn't even know his last name. It was one of the reasons she got so angry at Luca when he was absent for more than a few days. She didn't want her kids to know the feeling of being forgotten; unwanted.

Claudia met Emily in high school. At first, she'd sat next to her to copy her class work. Emily was really smart, and everyone knew it. Claudia… not so much. But after a while, the two had become friends. And when Claudia met Emily's good-looking best friend Luca, she'd decided this was a group she wanted to be a part of. Even if Emily was a massive prude. She wasn't like Claudia's other friends. Friends she hung out with on her block. Emily didn't drink or smoke. She didn't sleep around at 14. Claudia found it odd. She'd never met anyone like Emily before… or since. At first, Claudia had felt sorry for Emily. With strict parents who expected her to be successful, Claudia had wondered how Emily lived without going crazy! Without parties, alcohol, and drugs. It was a foreign world to Claudia... and she assumed for a long time that Emily was missing out because of it. After a while though, Claudia began to realise that it was Emily who really had it all… parents who loved her and supported her; opportunities to get out of the hell hole they lived in; a childhood friend who always had her back… no matter what. Claudia began to quietly resent her friend for her sunny disposition, her goal setting and planning; her big picture ideas. Claudia never told anyone how she felt. She knew it would leave her back where she had begun… alone in the world.

Feeling a headache coming on, Claudia told Luca he needed to leave. She said she had an early morning shift the next day, but they both knew that was a lie.

As he stood and made his way to the door he said, "You really should go see her Claud. She wants to see you."

Claudia nodded indifferently. That wasn't going to happen if she had anything to do with it. She wouldn't chase Miss Perfect down. For a while after he left, Claudia stayed sitting on the couch, deep in thought. Thinking about her life. Mistakes she'd made. Friends she'd lost. Choices she'd made. Emily had never seen the hardship she had, Claudia thought to herself. Had never gone without love in her life. Without the support of the people that were meant to mean the most. Claudia had.

'At least I've got one up on her,' Claudia mused. 'At least I got Luca first… even if it was only for a while. I had him before her.'

Smirking to herself, Claudia checked her boys were still sleeping peacefully, their little faces a daily reminder of the life she and Luca had tried to build together; the life she'd told herself she wanted for so many years, when in fact all she'd really wanted was Emily's life. Turning off the kitchen light, Claudia went to bed alone.

Pulling up to the beach near the pier a couple of days later, Luca surveyed the foreshore in front of him. He really was lucky to live in such a beautiful part of the world, he thought to himself. Jumping out of his car and grabbing his towel and surfboard, he made his way down onto the beach. They'd agreed to meet near the pier that morning. He, Ricky, Rachael, and their kids. And Emily. He'd called her the night before and asked her to come. Emily had been surprised but pleased to hear from him. She'd thought maybe she'd done something to upset him as she hadn't seen or heard from him for days. Walking along the beach, Luca watched a family building a sandcastle together. The two little kids were making a mess of it, as the parents laughed and rebuilt the fallen sections. It made him think of his kids… of all the beach days he'd missed lately. Claudia, after her tantrum a few nights before, had agreed to drop the boys off at the beach a little later that morning. Luca was looking forward to being with them… maybe teaching them to surf.

Hearing his name, he glanced along the beach to where Ricky and Rachael sat with their babies. Even at the age of three, Ricky's twins were still tiny little people, Luca thought. Not like his long, lanky lads.

He smiled and waved as he picked up to a jog and made his way over to them. Putting down his board next to Ricky's, Luca shook his friends' hand and leant down to kiss Rachael.

"Hey trouble," she said playfully.

"In the flesh," Luca replied with a laugh.

Plonking himself down on the sand next to his friends, he was suddenly swamped by little people. The twins had seen their chance and taken it. Laughing and lifting them up in the air, one in each hand, Luca pretended to use them as weights. Giggles exploded from the children's mouths as they were lifted up and down.

Walking towards the group, Emily smiled at the site of Luca playing around with the little ones. These must be Ricky's children, she thought. Luca had told her all about Rachael and the kids a few weeks earlier, when Emily had asked about their old friend. Now she saw firsthand the joy on Ricky's face as he sat next to his wife, arm in arm, watching his children laugh and play. It warmed Emily's heart.

"Hi everyone," she called out, as she walked towards the group.

Putting the kids down on the sand, Luca turned to watch her walk towards them. She looked incredible, he thought to himself. Dressed in a short pale blue sun dress, her tanned skin radiating in the warm sun. Ricky smirked at his friend as Rachael looked at them both, confused.

"Emily Rodrigues… come here and give me a hug!" Ricky stood and walked over to his old friend.

Picking her up, he swung her around in circles until her head spun.

"Ricky put me down," she laughed, as she tried to get her bearings. "How are you," she continued, once she could tell which way was up.

"I'm great… you look amazing!" he said in a friendly tone. "Emily I'd like you to meet my wife Rachael," Ricky said, as he led her over to where his wife sat with their baby.

"Nice to meet you," Rachael said, as she and Emily shook hands and smiled at each other.

She had a kind face, Rachael thought as she looked at her husband's childhood friend. They would definitely be friends, she decided. Any friend of Ricky's was a friend of hers. Sitting herself down next to Luca, Emily squeezed his knee.

"Hey, you," she said, trying to be extra friendly.

She still wasn't sure if he was angry at her or not, since she hadn't really spoken to him in days. Feeling his pulse quicken at her touch, Luca decided he needed to keep moving.

"Wanna come check out the water," he said, as he stood and faced her.

"Sure," she said a little perplexed, but glad he was speaking to her normally.

"We'll stay here with the kids," Ricky said to Luca with a smile, as the two friends exchanged a quick look that neither of the ladies noticed.

Walking towards the water Luca asked, "So… how have you been? Anything exciting going on with you?"

Emily, feeling the tension between them replied quickly, "Luca are we ok? Please tell me if I've done something to upset you?"

Luca looked at his friend, with her concerned face and felt terrible. He hated worrying her.

He smiled as warmly as he could and replied, "Of course we're good Em… never better."

Emily smiled; a look of relief clear on her face. Everything was ok.

"Dad, Dad" the two boys called, as they ran as fast as they could down to the water's edge.

Catching them in each arm, Luca swung them around as Ricky had done to Emily, although this time they called out "faster, faster!" After sending himself dizzy, Luca stopped and caught his breath. He put the boys down and said, "where's your Mum?"

He had quietly hoped that Claudia would make an appearance. It would have been nice to have the friends back together again.

"She didn't want to get out of the car. She said to tell you to drop us home before dinner, and we aren't allowed to get burnt."

Disappointment registered on Luca's face as Emily watched him converse with his kids. Obviously, Claudia was still someone he liked to spend time with, Emily thought as she said hello to the boys.

"You're the lady from the party, aren't you?" Joey asked Emily.

Emily smiled. He was such a sweet kid.

"Yep that's me," she replied.

"My mum said you used to be friends when you were little," he said matter of factly.

"We sure were," Emily continued, "We used to get into lots of trouble with your Dad."

She laughed as both boys looked at their father with wide eyes.

"But Dad said he was really good when he was little," Riley chimed in.

Looking at Luca, Emily raised her eyebrows, trying not to laugh.

"I said I was *pretty good* boys. Why don't you both go jump in for a swim."

Not needing an invitation, both boys threw off their shirts, turned and ran into the water.

"Pretty good hey?" Emily said sarcastically, as she leant over to grab the kids shirts from the sand.

"I may have forgotten to tell them exactly *what* I was pretty good at... getting in trouble." Luca said smiling.

"That sounds more like it," Emily quipped, as they both turned to watch the boys tackle each other in the waves.

Rachael and Ricky sat together on the sand, with their babies playing around them.

"What's the deal with these two," Rachael asked, as she watched Emily and Luca talk at the water's edge.

"Oh my dear," Ricky said brightly, putting his arm around his wife, "We don't possibly have enough hours in the day for that epic story."

Smiling, he glanced at his wife who was looking at him curiously.

"Give me the cliff notes version then," she replied, genuinely interested.

"Ok let me see… best friends since birth… spent every waking moment together as kids… and teenagers… she left for college 10 years ago and is now a doctor… he stayed here and built a professional boxing career, but you know that bit… then he had two kids with her other best friend while she was off becoming a doctor… she moved home a few weeks ago… he's finally realised he loves her… even though we've all known it for years… and she has no idea how he feels about her. That should just about do it." Ricky finished dramatically.

Rachael let out a long, overexaggerated breath. "Wow," she said. "That was a story alright."

Ricky smiled and said, "They'll work it out eventually… she's too smart not to. And he's so stubborn he won't let her get away again."

Ricky and Rachael looked at each other and smiled. As one of the three year old's began eating sand, and Rachael realised the baby needed to be changed, she felt incredibly grateful her life was as simple as nappy changes and sandcastles. It was going to be fun hearing about the Luca and Emily show though, she thought to herself.

After Luca and Ricky had swum, surfed, and spent awhile showing Luca's two boys the basics of surfing, they made their way back to Rachael and Emily who had been happily talking and playing with the babies. Taking a seat next to his wife, Ricky remembered something he wanted to talk to his friend about.

"Luca, I have to go to this club tonight for a work thing. It's a new one just opening in town. You should come check it out with me."

Luca considered Ricky's offer. It had been a while since he'd been out on the town. He'd heard about the new club opening from some of the boys at the gym and had wanted to check it out.

Turning to Emily and Rachael, Luca said "How about all four of us go and make a night of it?"

Rachael looked from her small children to Luca and laughed, "Yeah right Luc. I'll just leave the kids in the car, will I?"

Feeling a bit foolish, Luca said, "Sorry. I forgot how hard it is to find a babysitter at short notice."

Rachael replied, "It's fine. You three go. I'll come to the next event… with plenty of notice."

Luca smiled. He looked at Emily, covered in sand from the twins climbing all over her.

"How about it Em? Wanna go out on the town tonight?"

Emily thought about the offer. She wasn't a huge fan of nightclubs. But deciding she needed to be braver, and live a little, agreed to go along. She also wanted to spend some more time with Luca. Despite what he'd said earlier, she still wasn't 100% convinced they were ok.

Later, as she drove home to shower and finish off some chores around the house, she wondered how on earth she'd gotten herself into this; and what the hell was she going to wear.

Chapter 10

The base reverberated off the walls making Emily's heart beat faster as she entered the building. It'd been a long time since she'd stepped foot in a nightclub. She wasn't entirely sure that was a bad thing. Walking down the long corridor leading to the main room with its red walls and Spanish inspired artwork, Emily wondered if she should turn around and run back out. What the hell am I doing here, she thought as she turned the corner and found herself in an enormous room filled with hundreds of people. Strobe lights flashed in all directions, illuminating sections of the crowd happily dancing away to the beat. The music pumped loudly from the large speakers scattered across the front of the room near the DJ booth.

Emily looked up to find a high ceiling covered in artwork. Colours were splashed hap hazardously in every direction. Small lights filled up the blank spaces, like stars illuminating the night sky. The packed dance floor in the centre of the room was huge; probably bigger than her entire house. Emily felt like a small fish in a big fishpond. How was she meant to find anyone in this place? Earlier in the day, she'd agreed to meet Luca and Ricky in the club at 9pm. She regretted that now, as she wondered if she would spend the whole night wandering around looking for them. Dressed in a tight black and red patterned dress, that didn't leave much to the imagination, Emily felt a little exposed. In actual fact, she looked stunning. With her hair out and flowing down her back, she looked like a Spanish dancer ready to go on stage. More than a few sets of eyes followed her as she walked around the outside of the dance floor. Looking around at the other women dressed in significantly less than her, Emily relaxed a little.

'It's going to be ok,' she repeated in her head.

Still searching in the semi darkness, she stopped and squinted at a group of men standing near a wall at the side of the dance floor. She was pretty sure it was Luca. Climbing a small set of steps, she found herself on a raised platform section, where chairs and tables were set up and couches lined the walls. As she walked towards the men in the group, she spotted Ricky and waved. Ricky waved her over, nudging Luca in the ribs. He turned and glanced up, spotting Emily walking towards him. His head spun a little. She looked gorgeous. Wolf whistles filled the air around him as the guys he'd been talking to; guys he worked out with at the gym, spotted Emily too. Blushing bright red, Emily quietly wished the floor would open up and swallow her.

Pull yourself together', she thought as she reached the group.

"Hi, you," she called out to Luca as she smiled the biggest smile she could muster.

He felt his feet shuffle forward as he reached her and held out his arms for a hug. Obliging, Emily gave him a squeeze. She smelt so good, he thought as he held onto her.

Stepping back, Emily looked up at Luca and yelled, "It's really loud in here hey!"

Hardly able to hear her, Luca moved in closer as she repeated what she'd said. Nodding in agreement and pointing up, Luca took her hand and began leading her towards the back corner of the room; the opposite direction to where she'd entered. Curiously she followed, being led up a long flight of stairs and emerging onto the roof of the building, to find a courtyard set up with tables and chairs.

It was a gorgeous night outside. Emily was surprised by the beautiful space she found herself in. It was calm and quiet. A distinct contrast to the loud chaos that ensued below them. She much preferred this space.

"Wow," she commented, as Luca led her over to a couch seat set up along the side of the space.

"I know right," Luca replied as he looked around.

He loved it up here. Arriving early, he'd discovered the spot and knew Emily would love it too.

"You look amazing," Luca commented, as he took a seat on the couch.

Emily looked at her feet, embarrassed.

"Not really," she replied. "I couldn't find anything to wear so I just grabbed this from the bottom of my suitcase. I bought it a couple of years ago for an event, but never ended up wearing it."

"Why not?" Luca quizzed.

Emily paused. "Guess it just didn't match the scene I was going to."

In actual fact, Michael had told her she looked cheap in the dress. A dress that she had loved the minute she'd seen it. It had reminded her of Spanish dancers she'd watched on TV as a kid, and of dancing in the streets with her family as a teenager.

"Well it certainly matches this scene Em. You're the most beautiful woman in the club tonight." Luca said genuinely.

Emily was taken aback by the comment. Luca often paid her compliments, so much so that in most situations she took it with a grain of salt. He was her best friend… he was supposed to say nice things to her. But somehow, it felt different this time. His tone was so… genuine. Tender even. She felt like maybe it meant something more. Something she couldn't quite grasp. Looking at Luca, Emily felt butterflies flutter lightly in her belly.

"Emily, you look amazing!" Ricky called, as he made his way up the stairs and across the roof towards them.

Standing to greet him, Emily was embraced in a warm, friendly hug.

"I have to tell you before I forget, Rachael she said to say hi and she had a great day today. She wants to take you for coffee and lunch soon."

Emily smiled and nodded. Since she'd returned to LA, she hadn't really had a chance to make any new friends. Rachael was definitely someone she wanted to hang out with again. It had been nice to talk girl talk for once.

"This club is pretty amazing hey," Ricky continued. "Rach and I used to go out all the time to clubs like this before we had the kids."

Emily commented, "I'll have to babysit for you one night, so you can bring her here for a night out."

Ricky's eyes lit up. "I won't say no to that!" He laughed and gave her a squeeze. "So, what's the plan people?" He asked to no one in particular.

Luca looked at Emily and said, "Did you want to go for a dance downstairs?"

Emily thought about it for a minute. "Could we maybe stay here for a bit? I much prefer hearing the voices of the people I'm talking to."

Luca smiled and nodded. He had hoped she would say that. Ricky pulled up a chair as the three friends sat together and chatted about their day and all the fun they'd had with the kids.

"I'm going to grab a drink," Ricky said, after they'd been talking for a while. "Do you want anything?"

Luca replied, "I'd love a beer thanks," and Emily responded, "A vodka for me please."

Ricky nodded. "Coming right up," he said, as he turned and walked back down the stairs.

"I missed Ricky," Emily commented after he'd left.

She smiled, thinking about all the adventures they'd had when they were younger.

"Yeah he's a great guy. I feel bad I don't see him more often," Luca responded.

Emily thought aloud, "You know, when the house is finished, we should invite him and Rachael around for dinner."

Luca smiled. He was starting to like it when she spoke as if her place was their place.

"Em, there's something I wanted to…"

Luca was abruptly cut off as loud laughter and commotion came from the stair well. Half a dozen of Luca's mates appeared on the roof top followed closely by a group of young women.

"Luca my man, we were wondering where you went with your beautiful lady," one of the men said, setting his eyes on Emily.

She didn't like the look of the guy. He seemed a little too sure of himself, and a little too drunk. Luca stood and turned to Emily, gesturing for her to stand close to him.

"Ben, I'd like to introduce you to Emily. She and I were friends when we were kids. She's just moved back to town from North Carolina."

Ben made a bee line for Emily and without hesitation, gave her a crushing hug that made her feel a little sick. He smelt of alcohol and cigars. About as tall as Luca, the guy obviously worked out. Seeing the disturbed look on Emily's face as she stepped back from Ben's embrace, Luca moved to stand directly in front of his drunk mate.

"What are you guys doing up here? Isn't the dance floor going off down there?" Luca said, to divert his friend's attention.

"Nah man," Ben answered, turning to the other guys. "We were thinking of bouncing. Heading over to the clubs on the other side of town. Looks like they've got some sort of Latin dance night on here tonight and it's not our thing."

Luca let out a quiet breath. He was relieved to hear they were all leaving. When he and Ricky had arrived and run into these guys, Luca had known he would struggle to have a good time. They were nice guys, trained hard at the gym almost every day, but had an attitude that didn't really gel well with Luca. He wasn't a fan of people who were massive fans of themselves… and spent time telling everyone who would listen just how great they were.

"Well don't let us stop you from partying boys. Have a great night. I'll catch you at the gym next week."

The men, not needing an excuse to leave, shook hands with Luca and retreated down the stairs towards the music and the exit.

"Oh, thank god," Emily sighed as they left.

Luca laughed and turned to her. "Not a big fan then?" he asked.

"Hell no," Emily replied, as they settled back down on the couch, sitting much closer this time.

"That guy seemed like a massive creep," she said, making Luca grin.

Ricky smiled as he appeared at the top of the stairs with three drinks. There sat two of the most important people in his life… for more than half his life. And from what he hoped he was seeing; they might just finally be getting their acts together.

After an hour or so, they finished their drinks and hoping the coast was clear, the three friends descended the stairs back into the club. The atmosphere was electric. Latin beats pumped through the speakers as everyone on the dance floor moved to the sultry music.

Looking at his watch, Ricky yelled, "I have to go guys. Rach is expecting me home soon and I'll be in big trouble if I'm too late."

Shaking hands with Luca and giving Emily a big hug, Ricky moved off towards the exit and waved as he turned the corner and disappeared.

"Guess it's just you and me," Luca called, as he led Emily towards the dance floor.

Finding an empty spot on the packed dance floor proved to be a challenge, but finally the two settled on a space towards the back corner, the furthest away from the large speakers that pumped out the music. Picking up the beat, both began moving to the Latin tunes. Emily loved to dance. It was one of her favourite things. She had spent the last couple of days putting the first coat of paint on some of the walls in her house and had broken up the monotony of the task with music and the odd dance move. She grinned at Luca as she watched him move. He was a good dancer. Always had been. Fighting had given him good foot work. She remembered all the times he'd told her about boxers taking dance classes to improve their movement in the ring. As she watched him, she wondered if he'd done the same. He certainly had a swagger about him that was incredibly attractive. As she danced away, the music swirling around her, the butterflies returned.

Luca was paying close attention to Emily as she moved to the music. Truthfully, he couldn't take his eyes off her. As she moved her hair fell beautifully around her face; her dress twisted and turned to the music; her eyes glinting in the shifting lights of the dance floor. He'd decided earlier, as they sat upstairs, that he needed to tell her how he was feeling. How he'd been feeling over the past couple of days.

'If he even knew what that meant,' he thought to himself.

Ricky had been right a few days earlier, when he'd said life was too short.

Luca thought, 'I've already wasted 10 years of my life without her by my side.'

He didn't want to keep wasting time.

The music slowed a little and Luca took the opportunity to move closer to Emily. Taking her hand in his and placing his other hand on her waist, he began moving her around the dancefloor. Couples came together around them, dancing arm in arm. Emily's butterflies went crazy as she stood up close to Luca.

'Get a grip,' she muttered to herself as she moved around the floor with him.

Her head felt foggy, like she couldn't think straight. With her hand in his and her body up against him, she felt like she couldn't breathe. What on earth was wrong with her, she thought. She glanced up and looked directly into his eyes. Eyes the colour of the sky. Eyes she knew as well as her own. Her breathe caught in her throat as she felt her heart beat faster and faster. She forgot they were in a busy club. She forgot they were surrounded by hundreds of other people. All she could see was Luca. Shifting her hand from his shoulder to his chest, she noticed his heart beating fast… almost as fast as hers. At that moment, all she could think about was how much she wanted to kiss him.

Completely taken by the moment, Luca drew her close to him as they swayed together to the music. God he wanted to kiss her, he thought to himself as she looked up and directly into his eyes. He looked deeply into hers as he leaned in towards her. Out of the corner of his eye, Luca saw a movement. Without thinking, he grabbed Emily and swept her out of the way as two large men crashed to the floor, right where she'd been standing. Arms and legs flew as the two men laid into each other, with a fury Luca recognised from his many years in a boxing ring. This was a fight. A drunken brawl. Luca moved to stand in front of Emily to keep her out of harm's way as several large security guards arrived on the scene to restrain and escort the two heavily intoxicated, and now badly bloodied men to the exit. Turning, Luca saw the shocked look on Emily's face and realised any romantic moment between them had passed.

"Let's get out of here," he called to her, as he took her hand and began leading her towards the exit.

Arriving outside the club, Luca was still struggling to hear properly. Leading Emily along the street he headed towards his car in the parking lot next to the club.

"I feel like I'll never hear properly again," Emily said, a little too loud.

Luca laughed and threw his arm around her shoulder in a friendly gesture as they sighted the car.

"What a night hey," he said casually, smiling his cheeky smile.

She laughed as she thought how close she'd come to potentially embarrassing herself by trying to kiss him.

Opening the passenger side of the car, Luca helped Emily climb into her seat.

"And they say chivalry is dead," she said flippantly.

Without thinking, Luca took her hand and kissed it pretentiously, as he'd seen men do in old movies.

"I am at your command my lady," he said, in an attempt at a British accent.

Emily laughed. "Nice try buddy," she replied, as she punched him on the arm with her free hand.

Pretending he'd been wounded, Luca stumbled back clutching his chest.

Emily rolled her eyes at the drama of the whole thing and said in a matter of fact way, "Are we going home tonight, or will you be performing Shakespeare's sonnets next?"

Looking both mildly confused and amused, Luca muttered "I don't even know what the hell that is."

He made his way around the front of the car, opened his door, and took his place next to her.

"What's a sonnet anyway?" he asked, as he started the car and began moving towards the exit.

"It's a type of poem," she replied, with a hint of amusement in her voice.

She'd known he wouldn't have any clue what the hell she was talking about… he'd never bothered to pay attention in English when they'd learnt about Shakespeare, or any kind of poetry for that matter. She was pretty sure he'd been suspended for fighting the week they learnt about Shakespeare.

"William Shakespeare was a famous poet who wrote 154 poems… called sonnets. They're very famous." Emily explained, as Luca drove along the highway towards their suburb.

"Not in my street they're not," Luca retorted.

Emily smiled and began quoting, "Shall I compare thee to a summer's day? Thou art more lovely and more temperate. Rough winds do shake the darling buds of May, And summers lease hath all too short a date."

Stopping at a red light, Luca glanced over to Emily and commented "What the hell does that even mean?"

Emily laughed and replied, "It's a love poem. It's really beautiful when you read the whole thing."

Luca snorted and said, "I think I'll give it a miss thanks."

Emily smiled, "We'll see… I'll have you quoting Shakespeare before I'm done with you."

As Luca rolled his eyes dramatically and scoffed at the suggestion, Emily looked out the car window at the lights and signs scattered along the side of the highway, her mind still dancing to Latin beats.

Chapter 11

Pulling into his driveway, Luca killed the engine and looked over at Emily. She'd fallen asleep as they'd driven home and was now tucked up in an awkward position, seemingly sleeping peacefully. As he'd driven along, he'd thought about taking her home to her place but figured she would be more comfortable at his place. In an actual bed. He knew she'd been sleeping in the sleeping bag on the floor of her place for over a week now. The kitchen was being installed and she planned to spend the next week painting walls and preparing the floors for the wooden floorboards that were being laid in two to three weeks' time. Then all that was left was to buy some furniture and Emily's masterpiece was complete. The house looked amazing, he thought to himself. Each time Luca visited he'd been surprised at the changes she'd made. He wondered how much had changed in the days since he'd been there.

He knew the gardens were all in and, according to Emily, looked great. She told him she'd bought a table and chairs earlier that day, for the back deck. He imagined he would now find her most mornings sitting out there in the sun drinking her coffee. Tonight she could sleep in a real bed, he thought to himself as he stepped out of the car and walked around to the passenger side. Opening the door slowly and carefully so she didn't fall out of the car all together, Luca took Emily's arms and placed them around his neck. He scooped her up into his arms as she began to stir.

"Where are we?" she mumbled, as she partially opened her eyes and looked at him groggily.

"We're home Em. Go back to sleep… I got you."

Snuggling into his neck, she did as she was told. Kicking closed the passenger door and hitting the lock button on the keys he was balancing precariously in his left hand, Luca walked towards his front door.

The sensor light flicked on as he pushed his house key into the lock and turned it, all the time holding her in his arms. He opened the front door and stepped inside. The house was silent; his parents surely retiring to bed hours earlier. Quietly shutting the door with his foot, Luca silently walked down the hallway and turned into his room. It was a mess. Clothes and shoes thrown around the room, as if a whirlwind had passed through.

'Lucky she's asleep,' Luca thought to himself.

Emily would not be pleased if she saw the state of his room. He smiled as he recalled all the times she had given him a stern talking to about being tidy.

'A tidy room is a sign of a tidy mind,' she would say, as she stood in his door frame waiting for him to get ready for school.

He would grin and make some smart comment about his mind being a rat's nest for random thoughts or something along those lines. By the time he was ready for school, she'd usually done a pretty good job of tidying it for him, which he never minded. Standing here now, with her nestled in his arms, he figured he'd probably better do a clean-up before the morning. Placing her down gently on the bed, he covered her up with his blanket and got to work picking up pieces of clothing. He even found a pair of shoes he'd thought lost for at least a couple of weeks.

Tidy enough for his standards, Luca pulled out the foam mattress that lived under his bed. Used to sleeping on it when his boys were staying over, Luca grabbed the spare pillow and blanket from his cupboard, switched off the bedroom light and settled down to sleep. But he couldn't sleep. He couldn't stop thinking about the woman lying in his bed. He could hear her breathing. He could smell her perfume on his skin, from carrying her inside. He could still feel her skin on his as she'd snuggled into his neck to sleep. He sat up and looked at Emily, sleeping peacefully. He really had to tell her how he was feeling. He almost had tonight. If it wasn't for the brawling idiots on the dancefloor, he would have kissed her. Sitting there looking at her, he decided tomorrow would be the day. He would finally tell her how he felt.

Early morning light pierced the room as Emily rolled onto her back and opened her eyes. Disorientated and sleepy, she felt panic take over as she struggled to register where on earth she was. She sat up quickly and looked around her. Glancing down, she saw Luca sleeping on the mattress on the floor and realised where she was. She was in his room. His childhood bedroom. She knew this place like her own. Feeling a profound sense of relief, she looked around. The place was a damn mess. Frowning, she figured she probably needed to give him another talking to about cleanliness. Next to her, Luca began to stir. Drawing her knees up to her chest and resting her chin on them, she watched him roll around on the mattress. She hadn't realised she'd been so tired last night. She hadn't even meant to rest her head down in the car, let alone fall asleep.

'How sweet of him to bring her back here,' she thought.

He could have just driven her home and dumped her on her sleeping bag. But he hadn't. He'd taken care of her. She'd always been able to trust him to look after her. From the time she'd run away from home, after her parents wouldn't let her start boxing classes alongside him, and ended up spending the night at his place, to when she got ridiculously drunk at a 16th birthday party and he'd had to carry her home, stopping every few metres to let her vomit in the gutter. Luca had always watched over her and made sure she was safe. Even last night, when she'd almost been flattened by drunk guys trying to kill each other, he'd been there to pull her to safety. He really was her guardian angel, she thought as he opened his eyes and looked up at her.

"Morning," he muttered, as he stretched his body out the length of the mattress. "How did you sleep?"

Completely pre-occupied by the fact that he was laying on the floor in an old pair of grey track pants and with no shirt on, looking incredibly sexy, Emily looked at him blankly.

"What?" she asked, distracted.

"I said how did you sleep?" he repeated, wondering about her tone.

"I slept great," she replied in a friendlier tone. "Thank you for bringing me back here. It was nice to sleep on a mattress for once. My neck and back definitely thank you. I can't believe I was that tired! I don't even remember falling asleep… or getting here." She pointed to the bed.

"How did I get here?" she asked him.

"I carried you," he replied simply, closing his eyes, and stretching out on the mattress again.

In her mind she played the scene out… or at least what she thought the scene might look like. Him picking her up out of the car; carrying her to the door and down the hall in his arms. She felt herself blush. Glancing down at Luca, she hoped he hadn't noticed. Luckily, he'd rolled over and was reaching for a shirt from a pile of clothes in the corner of the room.

"Do we need to have a talk about this room," Emily said, with a disapproving tone.

Luca smiled under his shirt as he pulled it on over his head.

"I figured we would have to at some point," he replied, amused. "What's the plan today Ma'am?"

Emily sat back and thought. What day was it again? She thought it was probably Sunday since they'd gone out the night before, but she couldn't be sure. Ever since she'd moved back to LA, she'd mostly lost track of days. Not working had helped. With no routine to set her week by, it had started to seem like one day and one week floated into the next. She didn't really like the feeling of time passing quickly, and it seemed to have sped up recently.

"I really need to get some painting done today," she said. "With the guys arriving in the next couple of weeks to put in the flooring, I've got to have all the walls done 100%."

Luca replied, "OK, so we have some breakfast and then we head over and get it done." He smiled at Emily and she returned the gesture.

"You really are pretty amazing you know," Emily said genuinely.

Luca stood and held out his hand as his stomach made a growling sound.

"Let's go eat ourselves stupid," he said, as he led her out of the room.

Following Luca down the hall into the kitchen to grab some food, Emily was confronted with the faces of two women she knew very well.

"Morning you two," Carmen and Mireya commented, glancing at each other with raised eyebrows as their two children arrived in the room.

Still dressed in the clothes she'd worn out the night before, hair messy and eye makeup a little smudged, Emily looked somewhat dishevelled. Which was very unlike her. Luca on the other hand looked very relaxed in old track pants and a creased-up shirt.

Realising what it must look like to the ladies drinking coffee in the kitchen, Emily, talking way too quickly stated, "We went out dancing last night and I fell asleep in the car on the way home and Luca let me stay in his bed… and he slept on the floor… and it's not what it looks like."

Realising she sounded unhinged, she stood at the door of the room praying for the floor to swallow her whole.

"Honey, what you do or don't do in Luca's bedroom has nothing to do with either of us." Carmen said, trying not to smirk.

Mireya glanced at her son who leaned lazily against the kitchen counter with an amused look on his face.

"I'm glad to see you're looking after your friend," she said, giving him a playful wink when he smiled at her.

"We were just heading out into the garden to plant some new flower beds if you'd both like to join us?" Mireya said.

Luca turned to take the pan out of the cupboard.

"I think we might cook up some breakfast if that's ok?" he replied.

"Absolutely, there's bacon and eggs in the fridge… help yourselves."

Stopping to give Emily a kiss on the forehead. Mireya and Carmen both headed out of the kitchen and into the garden. Luca could hear the two women giggling to themselves as they went.

"Looks like we gave them a good show," Luca mused, as he grabbed the bacon and eggs from the fridge.

"How embarrassing," Emily replied, as she planted herself on one of the kitchen chairs and put her head in her hands.

"I hope they don't think we… you know," she said, with a pained expression on her face.

Luca laughed, "Em, you are such a prude… who cares what they think we did. And anyway… what's so wrong with me hey? You know some women find me very attractive." Luca said, feigning insult.

Emily rolled her eyes and smiled. She'd always been embarrassed talking to her parents about sex. It was a topic that had very rarely come up in her house, and she was happy to keep it that way. Seeing that she was obviously uncomfortable, Luca changed the topic.

"So how much painting have we actually got to do?" he asked, setting up the pan and turning it onto high.

Emily thought about her house. Calculating room by room, she worked out that they had 10 walls and the hallway to paint. She had completed one of the spare rooms and the bathroom the day earlier and so had the main bedroom, other spare room, and main walls in the living area to finish off. She'd done the laundry and kitchen when the new benches and cabinets had gone in, so those spaces were done too. Watching Luca standing at the cooktop sizzling the bacon, Emily couldn't wait to cook in her new kitchen. It was so beautiful, with its clean white walls and fake white and grey marble looking bench tops. She had considered buying the real deal, but after reviewing the quotes, figured she would need to sell her car to afford it and decided to go with the fake stuff. Michael would have been disgusted. In actual fact, it looked just as amazing as she'd seen in the kitchen place… and had cost a quarter of the price.

"What are you pondering over there lady," Luca said, breaking her train of thought.

Looking up she replied, "I'm just thinking about how much I'm looking forward to cooking in my new kitchen," Emily said.

Luca smiled. "I bet you are… we should have a huge cook up once you get all the appliances in. Have you thought much about a housewarming party?"

She hadn't given it any thought at all but considered the idea as she sat there. She hadn't been all that enthusiastic for parties since she and Michael had split. She thought it might be nice though, to get all her family together to show them the finished house project.

"Sounds like a good idea to me," she said, as Luca handed her a cooked plate of food. "This smells so good… you've definitely still got the expert cooking skill."

Emily took a bite and let out a noise that backed up her statement. It was delicious. Luca had always been a better cook than her. Even as kids, he'd kicked her butt in the kitchen. She didn't mind really… it was nice having someone to cook for her every now and again. Since she'd been staying at her half-finished house, her diet had consisted of foods that didn't require cooking. For her, this meal was worth a million bucks. Tucking in, she shovelled food into her mouth like she hadn't eaten for a week. Luca watched on in amusement.

"Classy," he commented, in between his own bites.

Pretending to give him a pissed off look, Emily polished off the plate and sat back in her chair. Holding her full stomach she sighed and closed her eyes. This was what it meant to be home, she thought to herself.

Finishing his own plate and seeing the satisfied look on Emily's face, Luca stood and took her plate over to the sink. Setting them down and turning on the water, he began washing the dishes.

"Hang on a minute," Emily said, appearing next to him. "You cooked… I clean."

Using her hip to shove him out of the way, she took over the filling of the sink.

"I guess I'll dry then." Luca said, picked up the tea towel.

Standing side by side, the two worked perfectly in tandem, polishing off the dishes and putting them away. Luca was reminded of their childhood… standing side by side at the sink. Emily washing, him drying as their parents watched television together or played cards. It made him smile. He was also reminded of another event that had often occurred when they had washed the dishes together. As if by ESP, Emily also remembered… right as Luca drew back the curled tea towel and whipped her clean on the back of the legs.

"Ouch, you asshole!" Emily yelped, as she turned and launched at him laughing, trying to wrestle the tea towel from his hands.

Much faster than her, Luca stepped back and whipped again, getting her on the knee.

"Jesus…stop! That hurts more then I remember," Emily said, trying to grab a hold of his wrists, still laughing.

With wet hands covered in bubbles, she couldn't get a good grip and tripped, hurdling towards the ground. Thinking fast, Luca dropped the towel and grabbed her around the waist. Sweeping her off her feet and around so that he was holding her inches from the ground, stopping her from hitting the floor. At that same moment, his father Carlos entered the room. Looking at the two entangled in a rather intimate looking position, Carlos rolled his eyes, turned, and walked back out of the room without a word. Emily burst into laughter. More out of embarrassment then actual amusement.

"Are you ok?" Luca asked, as he tried to muffle his own laughter at the situation they found themselves in.

Standing her up, but holding onto her still, he pretended to check her over for injuries.

"I'm fine," she said in between giggles.

It was ridiculous… and hilarious.

"You are seriously an idiot," she said amused, punching him lightly on the chest.

"Hang on," he retorted, "I'm not the idiot who nearly knocked herself out on the floor just now. Then I never would have heard the end of it… in 20 years' time, you'll still be saying, remember that time you got me with the tea towel, and I broke my nose!" he said, trying to sound like her.

They both cracked up laughing as it struck Emily just how comfortable she felt with him. She'd never felt that with Michael. Never in a million years would they have stood in their kitchen like this. With arms around each other laughing. Never would they have messed around like this… had fun like this. Sensing the change in her, Luca looked at her face and saw flickers of sadness.

"What's up Em?" He said gently.

Emily smiled and said, "Nothing at all. I'm just happy to be here mucking around with you like we used to when we were kids."

Luca looked into her eyes and knew she was lying. There was definitely something she was keeping from him, but he didn't push her.

"Em… I want to talk to you about something …" he began, as he finally mustered up the courage to tell her how he was feeling.

"EMILY COME QUICKLY… Oh my god!"

Screams erupted from the backyard as Emily and Luca stood together inside. Hearing the panic in Mireya's voice, Emily turned and raced to the back door and out into the yard. There she witnessed a scene that stopped her in her tracks. Her mother, Carmen, was crumpled on the ground… not moving at all. Standing near her, shocked and pale, Mireya waved Emily over.

"Quick Em, she just collapsed. Help her quickly."

Running to her mother, Emily crouched down over her, looking for signs of life. She was sickened to see her mother like this… pale and unresponsive.

Luca, following directly behind her said quickly, "Em, what is it… what's wrong with her?"

Emily was confused. This wasn't happening… this was her mother. Looking down at the lady that had raised her; cared for her; given her life, Emily felt frozen with fear. Time stopped. She couldn't concentrate on anything except the look on her mother's face. She looked like she was dying.

"EMILY," Luca yelled in her face, bringing her back to reality. "Do something," he implored, with panic in his voice.

Emily snapped into action. She rolled her mother onto her back and began checking for signs of life.

"Tell me exactly what happened," she said to Mireya, as she felt for a pulse and listened at her mother's mouth for any breath sounds that might be escaping.

There was nothing.

"We were talking… just talking and planting flowers," Mireya said in between sobs, tears flowing unchecked down her cheeks.

"We were laughing… she stopped suddenly… she clutched her chest. She just collapsed in front of me. What's wrong with her Emily?"

Recognising the symptoms of a possible heart attack, Emily looked into Luca's eyes and said assertively, "Ring 911…NOW."

Moving around to her mother's side, Emily began a task that she'd done a thousand times before on a thousand different people. She began delivering CPR. One thousand, two thousand, three thousand… she counted in her head as she pressed hard on her mother's chest. The adrenaline began coursing through her system as she pumped away. She'd felt it so many times in her medical career. The rush; the surge; a result of her body attempting to give her superhuman strength to combat the fatigue that came with this level of physical activity. Resuscitating a person whose heart had stopped was not an easy task. Emily knew it. As she pumped, statistics swam around her head like fish in a barrel… 10% survival rate for out of hospital cardiac arrest… every minute without oxygen to the brain increases the chances of brain damage… doing something is better than doing nothing. She had recited these same statistics during seminars and training sessions for the past 10 years, never thinking they would hold any real relevance to her life outside of the hospital setting. She had been wrong.

Around Emily, chaos ensued as she systematically and methodically worked. She blocked it all out, singularly focussed on the task at hand. Saving a life. Hearing the commotion, Carlos walked to the back door. Quickly taking in the scene confronting him, he raced next door through the open back gate, as fast as his aged legs would take him to alert Jose, Emily's father. Having only returned from his night shift a few hours earlier, Jose appeared confused and disorientated as he made his way with his old friend to the adjoining backyard. He quickly came to his senses when he saw the scene unfolding. His wife was blue… his daughter pushing furiously on her chest with a force that was sure to break some of her ribs, if it hadn't already. He gasped, his legs threatening to give out on him. He was held steady by his oldest and dearest friend. Together they stood, watching the distressing movements. Sirens called in the distance; a sound they had all heard thousands of times before, but now recognised as having an urgent purpose. Emily worked furiously. Up and down; up and down. Counting in her head to block out the feelings of hopelessness and despair now threatening to overtake her. Wake up, wake up, wake up, she repeated as she pumped. For Christ's sake, just open your eyes. Tears began falling down her face and onto her mother's chest as she continued to push hard.

Somewhere in the distance she could hear voices she recognised. Voices encouraging her to keep going... to not stop now. Luca was there; she could feel it. She knew he wouldn't leave her side. With a second surge of energy, Emily refocussed her efforts and kept pushing. It felt like an hour had passed since she'd started CPR. Where the hell was the ambulance? As if from her mind to their ears, the ambulance officers walked quickly through the house and out into the yard. Directing them over to Emily, Luca moved out of the way to give them room. He didn't want to leave Emily. He wouldn't leave her alone. He watched her continue to press on her mother's chest; calm and concise; almost robotic in her actions. He could tell she'd done this before. He wondered what was going through her head as she pushed away.

Emily conversed briefly with the ambulance officers who had begun opening bags, inserting drips, and sticking cables onto Carmen's lifeless body. Around the side of the house another officer walked with purpose, pushing a stretcher. Like a well-oiled machine, the three officers worked together with Emily to move Carmen onto the stretcher without missing a single chest compression. Emily climbed up onto the stretcher, on top of her mother and continued to push on her chest as the stretcher was wheeled quickly back down the side of the house and out to the waiting ambulance. Luca stood still; not sure what to do.

"Go Luca… go with Emily," Mireya called, as Luca leapt into action and chased the group towards the waiting ambulance.

An eerie quiet returned to the yard as the sirens moved off into the distance. Sitting on the edge of the flower garden, surrounded by newly planted flowers, Mireya wept for her best friend.

Arriving at the local hospital, Carmen was pushed into the resuscitation bay and Emily was forced to climb down from the stretcher. She no longer had any say in what was happening to her mother. No power in this place. She was a visitor, like all the other family members who stepped foot in this emergency department each year. Her qualifications meant nothing; her years of experience of no value to the medical staff who now worked furiously on her mother. She felt helpless. And hopeless. She knew the score. The realisation that her mother might never take another breath hit her hard as shock began to set in. Beside her, Luca saw her sway. As he had done less than an hour before, he caught her before she hit the floor. Scooping her up into his arms, he was ushered out of the room and into a side room. The plaque on the door read 'Family room' and Luca felt the truth in the statement at that moment. This was his family.

He sat down with Emily, holding her tight. The woman he cared about more than anything on the earth, sobbed uncontrollably in his arms. Her mother, who cared for him his whole life like he was her own son; who held his hand to cross the road when he was little; helped ice his injuries after his fights as an adult, was in the room next to them fighting for her life. He knew his only choice was to be strong for them all. For Emily more than anyone. Sitting on the couch at the back of the room, Luca cradled her in his lap as she cried. They sat this way for an hour before the door opened and a doctor entered the room.

"Miss Rodrigues, my name is Dr Khan. I am the Director of Emergency here at Los Angeles General."

Emily stood as the doctor introduced himself. She recognised the spiel he was giving. In her head she began reciting it, as if she were saying it herself.

"Your mother came to us in a critical condition. She is a very unwell lady. We were able to stabilise her, and she has been rushed upstairs for emergency cardiac surgery. We can't say how long it will take. As soon as we know anything, we will let you know."

Emily nodded despondently, as the doctor left the room. Her mother was in surgery. She was still alive. Collapsing back onto the couch, Emily buried her head in her hands. This wasn't happening. This couldn't be happening. Her mother was fit and healthy. She walked five miles every day; rain, hail, or shine. She ate healthy food that she picked from her home-grown vegetable garden. It just didn't make any sense. Exhaustion overcame Emily as the weight of everything she had done, everything she had been through over the last few hours overwhelmed her. She had no tears left to cry now. No words left to say. Laying her head down on Luca's lap and lifting her feet onto the couch, the muscles in her arms and upper body burning and aching from saving her mother's life. Unable to keep her eyes open or her head upright, Emily resigned herself to sleep. A fitful, broken sleep filled with panicked screams and vision of her lifeless mother.

Four hours later, as Luca's sat watching her toss and turn in her sleep, Dr Khan returned.

"Emily, time to wake up. The doctor's here." Luca whispered in her ear as she stirred.

Emily opened her eyes to find not only Dr Khan in the room, but Carlos and Mireya Mendes, and her father sitting across from them. Emily held her breath as the doctor began speaking to Jose.

"Mr Rodrigues… I have some news. The cardiac surgical team were able to re-start your wife's heart. They found a 90% blockage in one of her arteries and needed to do what is called a coronary artery bypass graft. This is where they take an artery from her leg and stitch it into her heart to bypass the blockage. The surgery was a success, and your wife is currently in the Intensive Care Unit on life support. We are hopeful she will wake up over the next couple of days but are unable to say if her brain was affected by her heart stopping for so long."

Looking to Emily he continued, "The surgical team wanted me to tell you that without your exceptional CPR skills, the chances of your mother surviving would have been 0."

Unable to speak, Emily nodded as the realisation that her mother might survive, filled a small pocket of her broken heart.

"Can we see her?" Jose asked quietly.

Emily looked at her father. She had never seen him look this way. Dejected; dishevelled; broken.

"We can only allow visits from immediate family, and only one visitor at a time. Come with me Mr Rodrigues and I'll take you up to the ICU," the doctor stated.

Jose nodded and followed Dr Khan out of the room.

Carlos and Mireya sat back down on the chairs across from Emily and Luca. The four sat in silence for a few moments; the only sound in the room was the clock on the wall ticking the seconds away.

"We should probably head home love… we won't be allowed in today," Carlos said to his wife, breaking the silence.

"Luca what are you going to do?" he asked his son.

Luca looked at his father. He didn't need to say anything. His dad understood.

"Ok, well we might see you back at home later then," Carlos said as he and Mireya stood and walked over to Emily.

Standing tentatively, Emily gave them both a hug. Luca shook his father's hand as Carlos clasped a hand onto his sons' shoulder and looked him in the eyes.

"Look after her son," he said quietly as Luca nodded.

Turning to the door, his parents left the room.

"Can I get you anything? Something to eat or drink?" Luca asked, as Emily sat, resting her head on the back of the couch.

Emily shook her head. She couldn't eat or drink. She'd probably be sick. Her head hurt. Almost as bad as her arms. She'd never felt like this. Even after performing CPR on patients in her own emergency department, she'd never felt as physically drained as she did in that moment. She just wanted to sleep some more. Thinking about laying down on Luca and trying to get a few more hours in, Emily looked up as the door opened and her father re-entered the room. She could see the toll the last few hours had physically taken on him. His eyes we surrounded by dark circles, his skin red and blotchy from crying. He stood hunched over. He looked at least 10 years older than he had the day before, Emily thought.

"They're ready for you Em… we can only have five minutes at the moment," he said, gesturing to the doctor waiting at the door.

Standing up, Emily said to her father, "What will you do now?"

Jose replied, "I'm going to head home. The doctors said there's nothing more I can do here today. Carlos and Mireya drove two cars over and left one for me to drive back."

Seeing the exhaustion on her father's face and knowing he'd barely had any sleep since he'd arrived home from work earlier that day, Emily shook her head.

"No Dad, I'm not letting you drive home in your state. You'll have an accident."

Tears began to well in Emily's eyes again.

Luca, seeing her distress said quietly, "Don't worry Em… I'll drive your dad home and come back for you."

Nodding in agreement, unable to speak for fear of falling apart again, Emily turned and gave Luca a tight hug. He held her for a split second before she pushed away and turned to her father. Repeating the gesture, she hugged her father, then walked out of the room following the doctor. Luca and Jose stood looking at each other for a moment, before Luca walked over to the older man. Placing his arm around his shoulders, he led him out of the room and to the waiting car.

Walking into the ICU, Emily was surrounded by familiarity. She had spent many hours in and out of Intensive Care units during her career. One of her first rotations in medical school had been in a ten bed ICU in North Carolina. Emily had immediately found the environment appealing. Everything was structured and organised. Despite the many tubes and lines hooked to the patient, all were labelled, and colour coded accordingly. For a student with a touch of obsessive compulsiveness, this was the place for Emily. She had thought for a long time that the ICU would be where she would find her home and hone her craft. It very easily could have been. It wasn't until she spent six months as a resident in a busy Emergency Department; the favourite student of a flamboyant Trauma Consultant, that Emily realised her place was in fact firmly secured in the Emergency Department. A place she could create calm amongst chaos. Where she could take broken pieces and put them back together, if only for a couple of hours. Emergency medicine was her greatest joy. And she was good at it. Damn good at it. A feeling of uneasiness crept into Emily's mind as she was reminded that she hadn't worked in almost three months. She decided she couldn't think of that now though; there were more important things to consider.

The young doctor at the desk looked up and smiled as Emily walked past.

"Emily… Emily Rodrigues?"

Recognised her name, she looked up. The young man looked sort of familiar. Too exhausted to really think, Emily just stared at him blankly.

He continued, "It's Ryan. Ryan Johnson? From Medical school?"

Recognition dawned on Emily. She knew this man. He had studied medicine with her in North Carolina.

"Ryan… how are you?" Emily said without emotion.

Picking up on it immediately, Ryan replied politely, "I'm good thanks. I wondered if Carmen Rodrigues in bed four was a relative of yours… I remember you talking at school about living in this area of LA."

Hearing her mother's name, Emily's heart began to hurt. "Yes, she's my mother," she replied quietly.

Ryan walked around the outside of the reception desk and put his arm on her shoulder in a familiar and friendly gesture.

"Don't worry. I'm here all night and I'm going to take really good care of your Mum, Emily. Let me take you to her and introduce her nurse."

Walking over to an area with a curtain pulled, Emily couldn't mask her shock, when Ryan pulled back the curtain. Lying in the bed was her mother. Except she didn't look like her mother. Not the way she had ever seen her. On a breathing ventilator, and with tubes and drips coming from every limb, Carmen Rodrigues looked like a ghost. Over her chest was a large white pad that covered the scar where the surgeons had cracked open her chest to repair her heart. The only signs of life came from the multitude of monitors that beeped regularly, telling everyone that Carmen was still with them. Seeing her mother like this made Emily want to run away. As far away as her legs would take her. Instead, she took a deep breath and walked to the side of the bed that held the woman who had been her rock for her entire life.

Taking her hand gently, Emily kissed it lightly. A machine in the corner beeped faster as the nurse at the end of the bed looked up and smiled.

"She can tell it's you," she said kindly, "you should talk to her."

Emily looked at her mother and wondered how on earth she could possibly know it was her. Just in case, Emily began talking to her softly.

Telling her how much she loved her, how much she needed her in her life, needed her to get better and wake up. She talked small talk, to fill the quiet that threatened to overwhelm her. Mostly about Luca. About the night club they'd been to the previous night; the roof top balcony and the dancing. She smiled a little as she recounted the story of the drunk guys almost crashing down on them. She talked about how he had sat with her the entire day while she waited on news about her mum. Recognising it may be one of the last times she might ever speak to her again, Emily told her unconscious mother about Michael. She'd never mentioned him to her parents before; despite dating him for almost two years. She'd always meant to tell them. But if she was being honest, she was embarrassed to talk about him. About their relationship. Seeing her parents so in love with each other, she felt like a fraud saying that she had loved Michael. Because she hadn't, not really. Emily talked on, as her mother lay unconscious in the bed next to her and the machines let off the occasional beep. It wasn't until a nurse came up to Emily and told her a young man was waiting outside to drive her home that Emily realised she had been talking to her mother for much longer that her five minutes. She figured Dr Ryan Johnson had something to do with that. She just wished her mother had talked back.

Walking to the car, Luca held her hand tightly. The radio remained off and they didn't speak as he drove carefully back to his home. Walking up the stairs and into the house in silence, Luca wanted desperately to say something; anything, to make her feel better. But he had nothing. There was nothing to say. Entering his room, Emily took off her shoes and jacket and climbed immediately into the bed she would now sleep in two nights in a row. Looking at the mattress on the floor and then to Luca, Emily shifted to the far side of the bed, making enough room for him to lay next to her. Luca removed his own jacket and shoes and climbed into bed. As Luca lay holding Emily, the light of the early afternoon sun casting shadows around the room, all thoughts of romance were long gone. The sudden and painful realisation of the futility of life had made sure of that.

Chapter 13

Emily slept deeply. Without dreaming. Without moving a muscle. When she woke the next day, it was lunchtime. She had slept for almost 24 hours. Her body was exhausted. Her arms and chest felt like they'd lifted 1000 heavy weights and her heart weighed heavily in her chest. She lay in Luca's bed, thinking about her mother. About the pale, lifeless body that in no way resembled her mother in the hospital bed the day before. She pulled the covers over her head and tried to go back to sleep. To ignore the sadness in her head and in her heart. But she couldn't. She just couldn't. Sitting up slowly, she realised Luca wasn't there with her. She remembered falling asleep next to him the afternoon before. Of feeling warm and secure in his arms. She wished he was there with her now. She stood up and tried to stretch, but her arms hurt too much.

It was then that she saw the glass of water and pain killers sitting on the side table next to his bed. The guy's a damn mind reader, Emily thought to herself. In actual fact, Luca had been watching her sleep earlier that morning. He'd seen the grimace on her face when she moved in the bed and realised she was in pain. Emily stood, swallowed the tablets, threw the bed cover over the bed untidily and opened the bedroom door. The house was silent. Walking down the hallway and into the kitchen she saw the note on the table and walked over to read it.

"Em, Dad is next door hanging out with your Dad. I have some errands to run… will be back this afternoon. The hospital rang… no change with your Mum. Luca."

Emily sighed heavily and turned to the fridge. She was hungry… and sad. Food usually fixed both. She grabbed some ingredients and began making herself a sandwich, when she heard a car door close. She hoped it was Luca returning. Grabbing her food, she walked to the hallway as the front door opened.

Emily was confronted with the largest bunch of flowers she had ever seen walking through the door. Behind them stood Luca with a warm smile on his face.

"Morning you… or is it afternoon?" he said, as he walked into the kitchen, stopping to kiss her on the top of the head, and putting the flowers on the table.

"Are those for my Mum?" Emily asked, between bites of food.

"They sure are. I thought we could take them up to the hospital this afternoon if you're feeling up to it?"

Smiling a little at her friend, Emily nodded.

"I'd like that," she replied.

"Good," he replied. "But first we need to take you back to your place to get you some other clothes. You've been wearing the same dress since the night club the other night. People are starting to talk."

Emily looked down. She hadn't even noticed what she was wearing. It felt nice to hear him joking.

She smiled and said, "Imagine what the neighbours might think."

Luca laughed and turned to the kitchen window in time to see his father walking back from next door. Carlos walked into the house and made a beeline for the kitchen.

"Emily, you're up," he said with a smile. "I've just been to see your Dad. He spoke to the hospital just before and they say your Mum is off the breathing ventilator and is breathing on her own so he's very relieved. They have her on some strong pain medications after such a big operation, but they say signs look good that she might wake up in the next day or two."

Relief overwhelmed Emily as she took a seat on a kitchen stool. Her mum was breathing on her own. Emily knew that this was good. That she was starting to head in a good direction.

"I'm going to take Emily over to see her Mum in a while Dad," Luca said to his father. "Is there anything you need us to do or get while we're out?"

Carlos surveyed his son. He would never admit it, but he was incredibly proud of the man Luca had become. He had certainly proved his character over the past 24 hours. Being a support for Emily during this tough time. Luca and Carlos had always had a difficult relationship. Carlos was old school. He didn't believe in any of the mushy stuff and made sure he raised Luca to be tough. Real tough. At any cost. He wanted to tell his son he was proud of him. Proud of how he was stepping up to care for his friend. He hesitated.

"No thanks, I'm fine. Your mother should be home from work soon and she's bringing me home a few things," Carlos said.

"No probs," Luca replied, turning to Emily. "Wanna head off then?" he asked her.

She nodded in agreement and retreated down the hall to collect her jacket and shoes. They walked outside, Luca carrying the enormous bunch of flowers, and climbed into his car. For a moment, she thought she could smell a familiar scent of fresh paint but figured she was just going a bit crazy after everything that had happened over the previous few days. Luca turned on his car and reversed out of the driveway and onto the street, heading towards her home.

Arriving at her place, Emily was surprised how quiet the street was. She had been so used to seeing Adam and his workmen's trucks in her driveway and in her street, it was strange seeing the street so empty. Parking behind her car in the driveway, Luca turned off the engine and climbed out his door. Emily began sifting through her bag for her front door key and started to panic a little when she couldn't find it. It was the only house key she had. How on earth were they meant to get inside without it.

Stepping out of the car, Emily called out to Luca who was already on the front step, "Luca I can't find my key. We can't get in."

Smiling, Luca turned and unlocked the front door. Confused, Emily walked up the driveway towards the front steps.

"How do you have my key?" she asked, perplexed. "I left it in my handbag when we went out the other night and I haven't been home since."

Smiling his cheeky smile, Luca stood aside and ushered Emily into her house. Walking in, Emily was taken by the strong smell of fresh paint. Again confused, she walked down the hall and into the living area. The house shouldn't smell that badly of paint, she thought to herself. She hadn't done any painting in a couple of days. Looking around, she was shocked to realise that all the walls were coated with paint. Completely covered… finished. The bedrooms, the living area had all been completed. She looked at Luca, still grinning like a cat who swallowed a canary.

"What the hell is going on?" was all she could manage to get out.

Seeing the confused, and somewhat distressed look on Emily's face, Luca explained quickly, "I remembered you said yesterday morning that you wanted to get the painting done, and I thought I'd try and smash it out for you. I figured you'd have more important things to think about then painting. Adam and his boys came over and helped yesterday afternoon and this morning, so we got it done pretty quick. Looks good doesn't it."

Luca turned around in a circle, surveying his handy work with pride. Emily on the other hand stood dead still, staring at him, still a little fuzzy.

"You mean to tell me you painted my whole house while I slept?" she asked incredulously.

"Yep," he replied lightly, obviously pleased with himself.

Emily didn't know what to say. She was genuinely lost for words. The gesture touched her heart like nothing else. She looked around the room at the finished paint job and loved it instantly. Not only had he bought her mother flowers; sat with her throughout the previous harrowing day without a word of complaint; supported her and comforted her throughout the night… but he'd painted her whole damn house for her… in 24 hours! Emily began to cry. Joyful tears that took Luca by surprise.

 "Are you ok Em?" he said tentatively, hoping that he hadn't sent her over the edge into complete madness.

Emily felt a weight lift off her shoulders. She'd been worrying so much about finishing the house. Even without realising it, it had played on her mind these past few days. How was she going to fit it all in? Paint the walls before the flooring, be there for her mother when she would need her to be there. Luca had just taken a weight off her without even realising it. He was so kind, and thoughtful. So selfless and giving. He had displayed all those qualities in the previous 24 hours when she had needed him the most. He had been there for her. Without thinking Emily walked over to Luca standing in the middle of the empty living area, looking at her with a concerned look, and put her arms around his neck. Reaching up on the tips of her toes, she kissed him lightly on the cheek.

Leaning back but keeping her arms where they were on his shoulders, she said genuincly, "You know, I think you are possibly the most wonderful human being on this planet."

And she meant it. She smiled and her tired face lit up. Looking into her eyes, Luca felt butterflies flip flop in his stomach and he instantly felt conflicted. He wasn't sure what to do next; if it was even an appropriate time to do what he'd been thinking about doing over and over for weeks. God… he just wanted to kiss her. Thoughts rolled around and around in his head as he looked down at her standing there with her arms around him, smiling sweetly. Her mother was sick. Really sick. Luca didn't want Emily to think he was trying to take advantage of her at a time when she was vulnerable. He didn't want her to think he was trying to push her into something, when her mind was in another place. Christ, he didn't even know if she had any feelings for him anyway.

He felt so conflicted. He didn't want to make the wrong decision. He couldn't bear the thought that he might hurt her.

'Oh screw it,' he said to himself, as he stopped thinking.

Putting one hand around her waist, he drew her closer. Wiping away her tears, he rested his forehead on hers.

"You mean the world to me Em," he said quietly. "I'd do anything for you."

Emily felt her own butterflies take hold as she looked up into his familiar face. A face she had looked at a million times, and for the first time in that moment.

"I know," she replied simply.

She touched his cheek and smiled, "You mean the most to me too."

Luca took her hand and kissed it lightly without taking his eyes off hers. She looked so beautiful standing there, her eyes sparkling and damp. Looking into his eyes she saw a look that was new to her. A look of longing… of wanting. Luca saw her face change too, saw the realisation in her eyes as she stood in front of him, knowing what he would surely do next. Surrounded by the smell of fresh paint and the sounds of birds in the trees outside, Luca did something he had been wanting to do for a long time. He kissed her.

Softly at first. As if she would break at any second. Warmth surrounded him as he tightened his grip on her waist. She tastes like strawberries and cream, he thought to himself. Recognition flooded in as he realised she still used the same lip gloss as she had as a teenager. Feeling like the room was spinning, Emily tightened her grip around Luca's neck. She could feel his pulse beating in his chest… strong and fast. Reacting to her movements, Luca kissed her again with an intensity that took him by surprise. He was used to taking his time… taking things slowly. But with Emily, he couldn't restrain himself. Or maybe he didn't want to.

Years of wanting… of yearning, was welling up inside of him. He was rapidly losing control and he didn't care in the slightest. He just wanted her. All of her. She felt the air escape her lungs as desire coursed through her body. This was what it felt like to be wanted, she thought. Slowly, she moved her hands to rest on his chest. She felt his heart beat faster and faster as their kiss deepened. Luca ran his hand up her spine to rest at the back of her neck. He entwined his fingers in her soft, long hair. She felt him groan as she ran her own hands down the front of his shirt, resting on the top of his belt buckle. Passion surged through her body, setting her skin on fire. Every touch made her crazy for more; every movement making her head spin. All she wanted was him.

Breathless and barely able to control the urge to throw her down on the wooden floor and have his way with her, Luca, using every ounce of willpower he possessed, instead pulled away, keeping his eyes firmly and longingly locked onto hers. His was a look she had never seen from him before, but one she knew she wanted more of.

"I've wanted to do that for a long time," he said in a rough voice. "Since the day you came home, I've wanted you so badly. God, I want you so badly now Em."

Feeling giddy and a little overwhelmed at the feelings coursing through her; with him looking at her with such intensity, Emily struggled to find any words to say. She'd never felt like this before. Wanted… needed so urgently.

"I… I…" was all Emily could manage as she struggled to find the words to tell him she felt the same way.

Giving up on words, she kissed him again. Hard and fast. She wanted him to want her more. The feeling of wanting… of being wanted like this made her feel incredible. Invincible.

She heard her phone ringing in the background but ignored it. It could wait, whatever it was. Luca moved his lips down her neck, nibbling on her collar bone and making her tremble all over.

"You should probably get that," he said begrudgingly. "It could be the hospital."

Realising what he was saying, Emily stepped back unsteadily, almost tripping over her handbag on the floor at her feet. Luca steadied her and smiled. She looked so sexy when she was flustered. He'd enjoy making her look like that again. Reaching down, he picked up her handbag and removed the mobile phone from it. Pressing call accept, he handed the phone to her and watched her carefully as she answered.

"Hello, this is Emily Rodrigues," in a tone that hadn't quite recovered from the previous activity. "Yes, thank you we will be right over."

She hung up the phone and looked at Luca. Her facial expression had changed dramatically. Where three seconds ago she had been all passion and lust, now her face resembled someone who had received bad news.

"What's wrong? Is it your Mum?" Luca asked urgently, all thoughts of what he had been planning to do to her on the floor, gone out of his mind.

"That was the hospital. They said I need to get down there. They couldn't give any information on the phone, but they said it was important."

Without a second thought, Luca grabbed Emily's hand and led her out of the house. Slamming the door shut behind her, they climbed into his car and he pulled out of the driveway. It wasn't until they were almost at the hospital, that Emily realised she was still wearing the clothes she'd worn out to the nightclub days earlier. Her trip to get changed had certainly taken an interesting turn.

Chapter 14

Thanks to Luca's knowledge of local backstreets and a few potential speeding infringements, the two friends arrived at the hospital in record speed. They walked with purpose into the hospital, jumping into the closest lift. As the elevator music jingled brightly away, and the lift rose excruciatingly slowly towards their floor, Luca put his arms around Emily and held her tight. She was shaking.

"It's gonna be ok Em," he said quietly, not sure if he was trying to reassure her, or himself.

As the lift reached the 14th floor and the doors opened, Luca and Emily stepped out into the ICU. Luca had never been in an ICU before and he found it uncomfortable. It was a quiet and eerie space. The only noise in the room coming from beeping monitors behind each of the curtains. The place smelt like shower cleaner. Walking towards the reception desk, Emily recognised the doctor she'd spoken to the previous afternoon.

"Emily, hello again," he said cheerily, as she tried to muster a smile. "I'm glad you could make it in. Is this your partner?" he asked, referring to Luca.

"Hi Ryan, thanks for calling. This is my best friend Luca. Luca, Ryan, and I went to medical school together. He's been looking after Mum."

The two men shook hands as Emily looked over to the space she knew her mother was in. The curtains were pulled shut.

"How is she?" Emily asked, not sure if she was ready for the answer.

"Come and see for yourself," Ryan said with a smile.

He walked to the bed space and pulled the curtains back. Emily's eyes widened as she took in the scene before her. Feeling a mixture of confusion and disorientation, she stared at her mother. What on earth had happened?

Laying in front of them, Carmen opened her eyes and smiled. A faint and pain filled gesture, but a smile all the same. Where previously a ghostly figure occupied the bed, today Carmen had returned to the colour that Emily was used to seeing; life now in the face of the mother she loved more than anything. Emily broke down and began sobbing, not understanding how it was possible that her mother could look so much better after being so close to death only 24 hours earlier. Luca glanced at Emily nervously. Concerned that she might collapse again, he took a tentative step in her direction. Pure elation coursed through Emily as she tried to compose herself. Never had she felt so relieved; so happy. The stress and tension of the past couple of days began to evaporate as she wiped away her tears and walked to the side of the bed to gently take her mother's hand.

"You scared the shit out of me," she said, not caring who heard.

This was her mother. With pink cheeks. Warm hands. Her mother was going to be ok. She just knew it. Luca, seeing the mixture of relief and joy on Emily's face, let himself relax a little. He walked to the opposite side of the bed and took Carmen's other hand. Realising that he was no longer needed, Ryan mumbled something about doing rounds and abruptly left the space, pulling the curtains around the three of them. Unable to speak more than a whisper, Carmen instead just lay looking at them both.

She knew she had almost died. From the huge cut reaching from the top of her sternum to the bottom, to the ribs she knew were broken, she *felt* like she had almost died. And it frightened her. The doctors and nurses had been wonderful since she'd woken earlier in the day. They'd spoken to her calmly and quietly; told her all that had happened and all that she had been through. Carmen found it difficult to believe what had occurred. She had felt perfectly fine; perfectly healthy. It was only when she moved a fraction and the pain returned like she was being hit by a freight train, she realised that maybe she hadn't been as healthy as she'd thought. The pain took her breath away and made her want to scream. But she wouldn't, not in front of her daughter. She looked at Emily now. Eyes red and filled with tears. She owed her daughter everything. The doctors had told Carmen what her daughter had done for her. What it had meant. She had saved her life.

"Mum, we thought we'd lost you," Emily said quietly. "Seeing you lying there on the grass, not moving… I… I love you so much," she said, tears pouring down her cheeks.

Carmen carefully and ever so slowly lifted her swollen hand. Placing it on her daughter's cheek, she began wiping away her tears.

"I don't ever want to imagine my life without you Mum. All I could think about was all the things I haven't told you… all the things I wanted to talk to you about," Emily remarked.

Carmen smiled and whispered, "My darling, we have all the time in the world."

Emily smiled back at her mother and lifted her head to glance over at Luca. The two shared a look of relief.

Turning her head to look up at Luca, Carmen squeezed his hand and whispered, "Have you been looking after my girl these past few days?"

Luca smiled and nodded. "Yes Ma'am," was all he managed, before the curtains opened and Emily's father, Jose stood in front of them grinning.

"Emily, Luca… I'm so glad you came down," he said jubilantly.

Emily was surprised to see her father so enthusiastic. She couldn't remember another time he had looked so happy. For as long as she could remember, her father had looked serious; sometimes just tired, but always serious. This man standing before them was not the same father she had kissed goodbye a few nights earlier when she'd visited for dinner. Emily smiled at her dad as he walked over to stand beside her. He leant over and gave her a squeeze. Emily moved a little to let her father shift along the bed side, so he was standing directly next to Carmen. Taking her hand in his, he leant over the railing and kissed it gently, murmuring something in her ear. Carmen smiled. Luca and Emily, almost at the same time, began retreating to the end of the bed, not wanting to interrupt the moment.

It was then that Jose looked up at the two, and said to Emily with a perplexed look on his face, "Honey… are you wearing the same clothes you had on two days ago?"

Letting out a loud laugh, Emily covered her mouth quickly. This didn't really feel like the place for laughter, she thought to herself.

"Yes I am… and it's a long story," she said looking at her mother.

Carmen, intrigued, gave her daughter a warm smile and winked.

"We should probably go." Emily said, taking Luca's hand in hers without thinking.

Luca nodded, surprised at the comfort he felt with her hand in his. Emily said goodbye to both her parents and promised to visit her mother again later. As they walked away, Carmen and Jose smiled together.

Emily sat in the passenger seat of Luca's car in silence. She had no words left to describe how she felt. No tears left to cry… they had all been used over the past few days. Instead she sat, looking at her best friend while he drove. Sensing her look, Luca glanced over.

"Are you ok?" he asked, worried.

"Yep," was all she could reply, smiling.

He continued to drive along as she watched him intently. Emily wondered how she would ever make it up to him. How she could ever describe to him how grateful she was for his unwavering support over the last couple of days. She didn't think there were even words for that kind of gratitude.

"Did you want me to drive you home to your place, or did you want to stay at mine again?" Luca asked, trying his best to sound casual.

She should probably go home, she thought to herself. She should go back to her freshly painted house, have a shower, get changed for the first time in three days and curl up in her sleeping bag. But something was stopping her. Something held her where she was.

"Can we go to the beach?" she asked instead.

"The beach…now?" Luca replied, looking outside into the soon to be dark surroundings.

They had been at the hospital for quite a while, and it was getting late.

"Yeah," she continued, "I really feel like walking on the beach."

Luca glanced over at her again. She looked exhausted. Physically spent. He would take her wherever she asked him to. Taking a left at the lights, Luca headed towards the beach and pier where they had spent time with their good friends only a few days earlier.

Walking along the sand the two didn't speak a word for a long time. With the setting sun throwing a beautiful backdrop to the ocean, and the waves crashing gently at their feet, Emily felt herself relax. With every gust of cool breeze hitting her face, she felt the built-up tension and stress leaving her body, floating off into the distance. The past few days had been the worst of her life. She had almost lost one of the most important people in her life. Regret filled her mind as she thought about all the years she had missed with the people who were most important to her. Her parents. Luca. Sensing a change in her demeanour, Luca stepped closer and took her hand in his. Emily looked up at him and smiled, continuing to walk along the soft, white sand.

"You must be so relieved," he said after a while, squeezing her hand softly.

"You have no idea," she replied. "I don't even know if I can describe how I'm feeling right now," she continued. "It's like I've been 1000 times around a rollercoaster track, and I'm finally stopped at the finish."

Smiling, Luca replied, "You hate roller coasters Em."

Laughing lightly, Emily nodded in agreement. She really did hate roller coasters.

Arriving at a flat section of sand, Emily let go of Luca's hand and sat down. Following suit, Luca joined her.

Sitting together, looking out at the darkening sky, the sun almost completely past the horizon line, Emily said, as much to herself as to Luca, "Do you remember when we used to come down here when we were kids? When our parents would bring us to the beach in summer and we'd spend the whole day building sandcastles and running up and down the sand?"

Luca nodded in agreement, smiling at the memories flooding in.

 "Sure do. Some of the best memories of my whole life," he said.

Emily replied, "Mine too. Do you ever wish you could go back in time and re-live it all? The fun; the freedom?"

Luca thought about her question as he looked at the sad expression on her face.

"You know Em, I don't think I would," he said, as he thought about all the things he had done so far in his life, all he had worked hard to accomplish.

Emily looked up at him, "I wish I could say the same."

Luca said softly, "Em… what's going on with you? And don't tell me nothing. I know that's crap. I've known you long enough to know when somethings bothering you. I see you thinking in that brain of yours all the time. I see you looking sad. Even before everything with your Mum. What is it you're not telling me?"

Emily stared at the darkened ocean, not wanting to look at him for fear of crying again. He knew her so well, she thought. She'd tried to stay positive, even before her mother had fallen ill. She'd tried to keep her feelings bottled deep down, and she'd been doing ok. She'd kept busy with the house… making it perfect. But now, with everything that had happened with her mother, Emily didn't feel she had the energy to keep on hiding how she was feeling. Letting out a deep sigh, Emily began to talk honestly to her best friend. More honestly then she'd even been with herself lately. Months of pent up worry and anxiety came flowing out in a storm of words. She talked about North Carolina; about her work as a doctor. She told him how she'd been feeling lost for a long time; questioning her choice of career and pathway. She described how passionate she had felt when she first began, how rewarding it had been to make a difference; a real difference. She told him she was frightened she had lost that feeling. That all her years of hard work and sacrifice all felt like they were for nothing. That she feared she had missed out on too much in the pursuit of her singular dream. At one point, Luca put his arm around her waist and drew her closer while she talked. Leaning in, she rested her head on his shoulder and kept talking. About her feelings of regret at not being home for so many years… her feelings of time moving too fast, and not living in the moment.

Luca sat quietly and listened to her words; her fears. He struggled to understand how someone so sure of themselves could be so unsure of their life. He thought about his own fears for his career; of not feeling good enough, not working hard enough. He thought he could understand some of where she was coming from. He knew he didn't have the words to make her feel better. He had never been good with words… but he desperately wanted to make her feel ok. Hearing the person he cared for so much talk about feeling so alone made him want to wrap her up and run away with her. Away from everything that was bothering her, everything that had hurt her in the past. When she finished talking, they sat quietly for a while, listening to the waves crashing on the shoreline, the distant sound of cars driving along the beach roads. Emily felt a little better. She always felt better after she'd spoken to Luca. Even as kids, when she was struggling with a problem, she would always go to him. Sometimes he would give her advice, sometimes he would just listen. Either way, it made her feel better.

"Luc, can I ask you something," she said into the darkness.

"Anything," he responded almost immediately.

Standing, Emily walked a short way from him and turned. The lights from the pier gave off just enough light to see the silhouette of him sitting on the sand. She wasn't sure if she should ask this; if she was brave enough right now to hear the answer. But she was on a roll… why not get it all out into the open. Plucking up a lifetime's worth of courage she jumped in headfirst.

"What's going on with us?" she asked quietly.

Sitting on the sand trying not to smile, Luca recognised how hard it would have been for Emily to ask him that. Frankness was never one of her strong points. Standing and walking over to her, Luca swept her up and spun her around. Laughing, Emily held onto him tightly, feeling his body warmth against hers. He smelt so good.

Placing her down gently in front of him, Luca took her face in his hands and looking into her eyes, said simply, "Everything Em, everything."

Standing in the dark, Luca kissed her as the waves crashed gently at their feet, washing away any traces of old footprints in the sand and any sense of hesitation they'd felt for each other.

Later that night, while she lay alone in her sleeping bag, showered, and finally dressed in clean clothes, Emily couldn't wipe the smile off her face. Even in the dark she was grinning from ear to ear. She wanted to pinch herself; to scream from the rooftops. Luca. Her Luca. She couldn't quite believe what was happening. Her friend, her childhood best friend was now… something more. What exactly was he though, she thought to herself? Her boyfriend? Sounded a little teenager, she decided. Lover? Not quite an accurate description, she contemplated. Yet. Thinking back to the afternoon, standing in the same spot she now lay, she pictured his hands on her body, his mouth on hers. Shivers ran up her spine as she recalled his eyes looking at her with so much passion. So much need. She knew he would be an amazing lover. When and if they got to that point, she mused. Emily wasn't silly. She understood what it would mean if they slept together. How much it would change them; change everything forever. She thought back to her time in North Carolina. To Michael. He had been a skilled lover without a doubt, a calm, calculated operator who knew the right things to say and the right places to touch. But she had never felt any passion towards him, she thought. Even in the beginning. She had never felt the feelings of longing, of wanting that she felt now for Luca.

Thinking about Michael again made Emily stop smiling. He always did have a way of ruining a moment, she thought sarcastically. She knew she had to talk to Luca about Michael. She couldn't keep it from him any longer. It would look like she was hiding something. Was she hiding something? She knew she should just be able to talk to Luca about Michael. To explain what had happened and why it had happened. Just as he had done for her, when he'd explained his relationship with Claudia so openly and honestly. But Emily knew it wasn't that easy. Luca wouldn't really understand. She wondered how he would take her story; her description of her loveless, convenient relationship. Her engagement. She didn't want him to think she was weak, or greedy to agree to marry someone like Michael. Concluding that she would leave her decision to tell him to another time, Emily closed her eyes and drifted off to sleep; Luca's blue eyes in the forefront of her mind as she slept.

Chapter 15

Days later, Emily found herself back at the hospital with her mother. She was alone this time. Luca had needed to go to training. They had been inseparable the past few days. Spending most of their time cleaning and preparing for the laying of the floors at her house. It was almost finished. Her excitement at the conclusion of her house project was increasing by the minute. Earlier that day they'd been planning what furniture she could put into which spaces in the house. Emily had to admit; Luca had good taste. They'd decided to go shopping for furniture in the next day or two and Emily couldn't wait. To buy all her own things, things that were special to her; meant something to her. She hadn't done that in a long time. Michael had chosen most of the furniture in their place in North Carolina. Sleek and sophisticated pieces, worth way too much money. Emily would stare in disbelief whenever he would have something delivered that cost in the thousands. She would always estimate how many people she could help with that same amount of money. She never mentioned that to Michael though. He wouldn't have been happy. When they'd separated, she'd sold or given away most of her furniture. She hadn't wanted any of it anymore; hadn't wanted any memory of that time in her life to linger. And now here she was, ready to start fresh and find things that made her smile. Like Luca.

For days now, she'd struggled to keep her hands to herself when he was around. It still felt so strange to admit that, she thought. She smiled as she recalled that he also seemed to suffer from the same problem. From making out while wiping down the shower screens in her finished bathroom, to making out while cleaning out the kitchen cabinets that had finally been installed. Then there was the time they were caught making out in the kitchen in his parents' home. By his mother no less. Emily blushed now as she recalled how incredibly embarrassed she'd felt. How Luca had given his mother a cheeky smile, proceeded to pick Emily up over his shoulder and march her into his room. How they'd spent the afternoon there… in his bed… getting to know each other better. The irony of this hadn't escaped her. That the person she knew better than anyone in her whole life, was just getting to know her. In a few ways. They hadn't slept together… yet. She wanted to take it slowly, she kept reminding herself. One day at a time; one new experience together at a time. She wasn't someone who struggled with self-control. But she had to admit, the last few days had been difficult. Watching him work on her home; shirtless and sweaty, with ripped muscles on full display. It certainly had been a struggle, she thought to herself smiling... one that she was more than happy to suffer.

As Emily entered the ICU, she found Carmen awake and sitting up slightly. She had been trying each day to sit up a little more than the previous few days. Still in a lot of pain, her daily improvement was noticeable to all around her. She was able to speak louder than a whisper now, without the pain taking her breath away. She restricted this though, as talking also had the effect of tiring her out. She had slept very well the night before after Jose had visited and she had talked to him a little too much. She didn't care though. She'd wanted to tell him how much she loved him. How she was sorry she hadn't said it a million times more. That she would spend every day for the rest of her life saying it as often as she could. Almost dying had given her an interesting sense of perspective. One that she wanted to share with her daughter. Looking at Emily, with her flushed cheeks and bright eyes, looking much more like the happy, relaxed person she had raised, Carmen sensed there was something that Emily might also have to share.

"Hello, my darling girl," Carmen said, as Emily took a seat on the stool next to her bed. "If I didn't know better, I'd say you'd won a lottery prize with that smile."

Emily blushed. Her mother really did know her well.

"How are you feeling Mum?" Emily said, as she leant over and kissed her mother on the forehead.

"Healthy as a horse," Carmen joked. "Don't change the topic… what's got you so happy then?"

Emily laughed lightly. It was so good to have her mother back. The old Carmen, who joked and gossiped, who prodded her for information more than she liked.

"I'm telling you, lying in this hospital bed gives you plenty of time to think. And I've run out of things to think about… so hurry up and give me some gossip to enjoy before I go crazy!"

Carmen loved playfully teasing her daughter. She'd recognised the seriousness of Emily's personality from an early age and made sure to remind her daughter whenever she could that it was important not to take life too seriously. She'd worried when Emily had first returned home from North Carolina that she'd forgotten this lesson after so many years away. She had seen the worried looks and sad eyes that had held her daughter's attention. This young lady sitting in front of her today though, was quite different.

"I might have some news," Emily said cryptically.

"Well… don't keep an old lady waiting," Carmen quipped.

"Mum, seriously… please don't call yourself old. You are not old!" Emily responded.

Realising that her daughter was stalling, and not wanting to pry into her personal business if she wasn't ready to share, Carmen smiled and took her daughters hand.

"I know honey, I'm just joking. I know I scared you these past few days and I'm sorry for that," she said sincerely.

Emily squeezed her mother's hand. She really was so lucky to have such an amazing Mum. Patient and kind, Carmen had never pushed or pried into her life. She had always given Emily space and time to think, which Emily had always appreciated. Feeling it was the right time, Emily took a deep breath and began filling her mother in on the last few weeks. From the moment she and Luca had built her gardens and she'd realised something might be going on between them; to the fun they'd had at the nightclub; to the love and support Luca had showed her while her mother had been unconscious. Carmen sat quietly listening to her daughter talk. An animated story that made Carmen smile. She had always held a special place for Luca in her heart. He was a sweet kid. And he'd always cared for Emily. Even as children, he had protected her and watched out for her. And, Carmen thought, now he loved her. She would bet her house on it.

Emily finished talking and instantly felt relieved. It was nice to talk girl talk for once. As much as she enjoyed Luca's company, sometimes she really missed female company. In North Carolina she had relied on a couple of good girlfriends to gossip with, and before that it was Claudia. Emily wondered what Claudia would say if she knew that she and Luca were… whatever they were. She was pretty sure she wouldn't be pleased. Carmen sat in silence for a minute after Emily stopped talking, pondering what she might say.

"I'm so happy for you Em. You know I love Luca like he was my own, and the two of you have been so close for so many years. I can't think of anyone I'd rather see my girl fall in love with."

Emily blushed again.

"Mum we aren't in love… that's going a bit overboard. We're just getting to know each other again… seeing if we even like each other that way." Emily replied.

Carmen smiled. Poor girl can't even see it, she thought to herself.

'You've been in love with him since you were 10 years old,' she wanted to say, but held back.

The last thing she wanted to do was stress Emily out and have her overthink everything.

"Well, whatever you are… I'm happy for you." Carmen said. "Em, I don't tell you what to do often, but will you allow me to give you some advice now, as someone whose been married for many years?"

Emily nodded curiously.

"If I could go back and tell myself anything, especially about relationships, it would be this. Take things day by day. Hour by hour sometimes. See each experience as a lesson to learn. See each roadblock as an opportunity to grow. Appreciate the small things. So often we get caught in the need for grand gestures. Notice the things that matter. A smile, a look. Each and every little thing adds up over time and makes a lifetime of memories. I am so lucky to have a lifetime of little moments with your father. And now I have a second chance to make even more."

Taking a deep breath, Carmen closed her eyes and thought about her husband and how lucky she was to love such a kind and gentle man. She prayed her daughter would one day know the love and joy she had experienced in her lifetime.

Hours later, Emily drove home from the hospital smiling. She'd spent the evening talking to her mother about lots of things. About Luca mostly. But other things too. Like her work in North Carolina. Her life away from home. And about Michael. Carmen had brought him up and Emily had been taken aback. She'd never spoken to her mother about Michael. No one in her family knew of his existence. Then Emily remembered the first night her mother had been in hospital in a coma. She'd talked to her mother about Michael, not really believing that she could hear her.

Carmen smiled, "I heard every word you said to me baby," she said. "And I want to know more about the man that kept you from us."

Emily thought, just how accurate her mother's comment had been. When Emily had finished her training and was looking for residency, she had actually been planning to move back to LA, to take up a program in the hospital her mother currently lay in. She'd been offered a number of programs all around the country. Such was her work ethic and graduation results; she almost had the pick of every hospital in the country. It was right before she finished medical school that she'd been invited to a fundraising event for Carolina General Hospital and had decided to go along to check out the competition. Whilst chatting to a couple of friends from medical school, Emily had been introduced to Dr Michael Matthews. Tall and handsome, Michael exuded sophistication. His tone was one of superiority and importance. When he spoke, everyone in the room listened. Emily was immediately taken by his confidence; his assertiveness. The two spent the rest of the evening together, talking about new technological advances in medicine. Later that night, as they lay naked next to each other in his bed, with Michael describing the exceptional work they could do together in the medical field, and Emily picturing her career as an Emergency Consultant in the best hospital in the country; any ideas of moving home faded long into the background.

Arriving at home now, Emily locked up her car and walked towards her front door. As she reached the steps leading up to the door, she noticed an odd shaped object resting against the side of the house. Stepping onto the front stoop as the sensor light switched on and flooded the space with bright white light, she recognised the object as a beautiful bunch of red roses. Emily glanced out towards the road, hoping to locate the gift giver. Instead, the road was empty and quiet. The only noise, a slow bubbling of water coming from the small water fountain in her front garden.

'Interesting,' Emily thought, as she unlocked her front door and collecting her flowers, walked into the house.

Taking off her shoes and leaving them at the front entry, Emily made her way down the hall and into the kitchen. She loved her kitchen. It really had become the heart of her home since the walls had been removed and the space opened up to link with the living area. She imagined all the furniture she would fill the space with over the coming weeks and smiled happily. Placing her bag on the bench, Emily looked at her beautiful flowers, noticing a small card attached to the paper covering the stems.

Reaching in carefully, so as not to cut herself on the thorns, Emily opened the card and smiled as she read the roughly scrawled note, "Beautiful flowers for a beautiful lady. L."

Smelling the amazing aroma coming from the flowers, Emily walked to the kitchen cupboard and pulled a plastic jug from the shelf.

'Note to self, buy glass vase,' she thought, as she filled the jug with water and placed the flowers onto the benchtop.

'Appreciate the small things,' Emily thought, as her mother's words re-entered her mind.

Looking at her flowers, Emily vowed to do exactly that.

At 8am the next morning, Emily was woken by a loud knock on her front door. Stretching out on the floor in her now well used sleeping bag, Emily wondered who could be visiting so early in the morning. She had made plans with Luca to go furniture shopping that morning, but not until 10am. Standing and throwing an old t-shirt over her pyjama top, Emily made her way to the door. She could hear male voices laughing as she opened the door hesitantly. Standing there, toolbelts at the ready, she found Adam, her builder, and his workers.

"What are you guys doing here?" Emily asked, confusion obvious on her face at the sight of them.

Laughing, Adam replied, "We had a job cancel this morning, so we thought we'd come and start on your floors."

Confusion was replaced with sheer elation as Emily opened the door wide and threw her arms around Adam.

"Come on now, my wife will give me hell," he said embarrassed.

"Oh my god, thank you so much," Emily replied, as she let go of her builder and moved out of the way to let the workers into the house.

The flooring was the last step in her house puzzle, and she'd been hoping it would be finished before she bought her furniture.

"Luca and I are going furniture shopping today," she said excitedly, as Adam put down the tools he was carrying and looked at Emily's empty sleeping bag.

"Don't tell me you're still sleeping on that thing," he said incredulously.

"Sure am," she replied matter of factly. "I love sleeping in my house," Emily said.

"Well hopefully we can knock this all out today and be out of your hair," Adam said smiling. "I bought a couple of extra guys along with me today. We should be done with the place by this afternoon."

Emily felt like she was going to burst, so was the excitement flowing through her at the thought that her home would be complete by night fall.

"Let me just pack up and I'll get out of your way," she said, as the men began setting up wood saws and walking packs of floating floorboards through the living area.

"Take your time Em, we're the ones taking over your house on your day off!"

Emily smiled, not wanting to correct Adam that every day was her day off now that she wasn't working. He worked so hard; she didn't think he'd understand. Packing up her sleeping bag and suitcase, Emily quickly dressed for the day in one of the spare rooms and wheeled her gear to her car. It would be easier to keep it all at her parents' place while the floors went down.

"Adam, I'm heading out for the day. Give me a call if you need anything ok?" Emily called down the hall.

"No worries love, have a great day." Adam replied, as the electric wood saw fired up and the guys began cutting lengths of timber to lay on her floors.

Jumping into her car, Emily pulled out of her driveway and headed down the road towards her parents' place. Driving along the quiet streets of her hometown, Emily thought about all the fun she and Luca would have choosing all manner of furniture from the largest furniture warehouse in LA. It was around a 40-minute drive from her place, but after they had looked on the website, they'd decided on the place because of its industrial style, and reasonable price. Arriving at her parents' place, Emily made a beeline for the side of the house, heading towards her parent's backyard. After everything that had happened over the past week, she felt like spending some thinking time on the swing.

Turning the corner into the yard, Emily was surprised to find she wasn't the only person using the swing on that warm, summer morning. Her father sat rocking gently, lost deep in thought. Careful not to startle him, Emily shuffled her feet on the gravel and Jose turned towards her.

"Em, what are you doing here so early?" he said, surprised to see her standing there.

"Hey Dad," Emily replied, "I'm sorry if I scared you. The builders had some spare time this morning, so they arrived early to put down my floors. I thought I'd come over and see how you're doing."

"Well I guess you'd better join me here then," Jose replied, patting the space next to him on the swing.

Sitting down next to her dad, Emily smiled at him as he pretended to go for a big swing and scare her.

"Dad I'm pretty sure that joke hasn't worked on me since I was about five," Emily said smiling.

Chuckling to himself, Jose put his arm around his daughters' shoulders and said jovially, "Can't blame an old man for trying."

Emily looked at her father, "You're just as bad as Mum," she said. "When did all this talk start about being old?"

Jose squeezed his daughters' shoulder and replied, "You know better than anyone Em, we aren't getting any younger. This week has proven that."

The smile faded from Jose's face, as he sat quietly thinking of the last few days of his life. It has been the worst days he had ever seen. Harder than his childhood growing up in the poorest towns in Mexico; worse than when he immigrated to the US with nothing but the clothes on his back and five dollars in his pocket. Worse still then the weeks and months he spent living on the streets before he was able to find a job. He had almost lost the greatest love of his life. His better half, as he liked to say. The previous week had changed the fabric of the man forever.

"Em, I've been meaning to talk to you about last weekend; about what you did for your mother."

Emily looked at her father's face, as tears began falling down his cheeks. She couldn't remember the last time she'd seen her father cry. Maybe never, come to think of it.

"It's ok Dad, you don't need to say anything." Emily replied softly.

Jose shook his head and continued, "I need you to hear this my darling. It's important to me."

Nodding, Emily sat quietly as her father spoke.

"Your whole life I've looked at you as someone who was capable Em. Even when you were very little, I never worried about you. Partly because I knew you always had Luca with you to keep you safe, but mostly because I knew you could handle anything that was thrown at you. You've always had such a cool head. When you moved away to university, so far from home, I knew you were brave and strong. You had to be to give up everything you had. You reminded me of myself a little; of my journey to this country. Not knowing anyone, not having anyone to rely on. I made my way alone, and so did you, I think. And then I met your mother and my life changed in the best way possible. Since the day I met your mother I've never spent more than a day without her. To think I might have lost her… I can't even think about it. Em, what I saw you do for your mother the other day, the way you took charge, was nothing short of incredible."

Emily smiled. She had never heard her father talk like this before.

"Emily you're a hero. My hero. I can't ever repay you for what you did."

Choking back more tears, Jose turned and put his arms around his daughter. He held on tight as they cried together. Luca, standing at the corner of the garden between his parents' house and Emily's, about to invite Jose over for a morning coffee, instead turned and headed back into his own parents' house to tell them he loved them.

Chapter 16

"And then he said the floors would be done by the end of the day and my house will be finally finished!" Emily said dramatically, throwing her hands up in a triumphant gesture as Luca sat on his bedroom floor, putting his shoes on.

It was 10am and Emily had walked over to collect him for their furniture shopping trip.

"I still don't know why you're making me come," Luca pretended to grumble unsuccessfully. "You know I'm giving up an important training session for this."

In response, Emily slid down off his bed onto her knees and landing right in front of him, leaning forward to kiss him suggestively.

"You're coming with me…because you're tough and strong," she said between kisses. "And you've got good taste in furniture," she finished, hoping he would buy what she was selling.

"Yeah, yeah," he replied as he wound his arms around her waist and began kissing her neck. "I know you just don't want to carry it all by yourself. You're just using me for my muscles."

Laughing, Emily said, "Well Mr Muscles, we really have to go if we want to get there before lunchtime."

Luca held on tighter, as she tried to pry herself from his grasp unsuccessfully.

"No way… you're not getting away that easily," he said lazily.

Realising protesting was futile, Emily relaxed into his arms and kissed him back.

"Oh for god's sake, get a room you two," remarked Mireya, as she turned the corner into Luca's room and found them on the floor.

Luca laughed as he replied, "we have one Mum… get out of it!"

Mireya reached out and clipped her son swiftly on the back of the head.

"With attitude like that my boy, you'll be sleeping out on the lawn."

She laughed and turned around, walking back down the hall. Taking advantage of the distraction, Emily quickly extricated herself from his tangle of arms and legs, stood and moved to the door.

"You've got five minutes," she said, smiling sweetly at Luca as she turned and followed in the same direction as Mireya.

"Women," Luca muttered to himself, as he stood, grabbed his wallet and keys, and headed towards the kitchen.

"Seriously Emily, how hard is it to pick a damn side table."

Frustration obvious on his tongue, Luca paced back and forth across the warehouse floor. The woman was completely hopeless, he thought to himself as he watched her look from one item to the other.

"It has to be perfect Luca," she replied, concentrating on picturing both the tables in her new bedroom.

"It will be Em, with either of these bloody tables," Luca retorted, as the saleswoman tried not to laugh.

They had been at the store for two hours already and had chosen a lounge set, dining table and chairs, white goods including a fridge and washing machine, and were currently looking at options for bedside tables.

"It won't matter anyway," Luca continued sarcastically, "you're only going to cover it up with all your crap. You won't even be able to see what colour it is."

Glaring at him, Emily said through pursed lips, "well how about you decide then Mr Perfect."

"That's Mr Muscles to you, thank you," Luca quipped, as he dodged the furniture brochure hurled in his direction.

"We'll take the wooden one with the black stand." Luca said, looking in the direction of the saleswoman.

Writing something on her piece of paper, the lady nodded and began moving towards the bedding section.

"Will you be needing a bed ensemble?" she asked Luca, as Emily followed behind them.

"Oh yes, we will definitely need one of those," Luca replied, as he glanced back at Emily and winked suggestively.

Turning a bright shade of red, Emily felt a mixture of extreme embarrassment and frustration. This wasn't how she'd pictured her shopping trip with Luca. She'd thought they would walk around, keeping to a particular order of items; carefully considering each piece and weighing up the pros and cons before agreeing on a suitable choice. As she watched him lay down on possibly the ugliest bed she had ever seen, she realised her shopping dream was not going to become a reality.

Luca was sure he was pissing Emily off, and he was thoroughly enjoying it. For as long as he could remember, he had enjoyed frustrating her. Seeing her brows knit together and frown lines appear on her forehead, reminded him of when they were much younger. She looked adorable.

"Come try this one Em, it's really comfy," he said, patting the space next to him on the bed.

The look of disgust on her face at the thought of lying on the ugliest bed in the whole shop, made him laugh aloud. The sales lady, sensing an argument about to begin, excused herself and walked to her computer to start ringing up the first of the purchases.

"Luca, I hate that one and you know it," Emily said under her breath, turning to walk away from him.

She could tell he was in a mood to annoy her. And it was working. He was lucky she was just too tired to keep biting back, she thought to herself. Walking to the opposite side of the bedding section, Emily's eyes settled on a masterpiece. The most beautiful queen size bed she had ever seen. With beautiful stained wooden posts in either corner, and a bed head with intricate Spanish inspired patterns carved into it, Emily knew she had found her bed. Arriving next to her, Luca noted the animated look on her face. This was the one all right.

"Its amazing Em," was all he said, as she walked to the side of the bed, turned, and flopped down onto it.

It was like heaven, she thought to herself. Just the right size; just the right softness in the mattress. She felt like goldilocks in the house of the bears. Smiling to herself, she looked over at Luca who had joined her on the display bed.

"I can see this one in your room you know," he said. "And I can definitely see us in it."

He winked and without warning rolled over, so that he was half on top of her.

"Luca seriously get off me," Emily said quickly and quietly, as she looked around to make sure no one was watching them.

Seeing her blush the colour of a tomato, Luca grinned and stayed exactly where he was.

"You know," he said with a cheeky smile, "We could give it the old once over… you know… to make sure its suitable."

Emily thought she was going to die of embarrassment. This was mortifying. They were grown adults for god's sake. Imagine if anyone saw them!

"Luca Mendes, you have exactly three seconds to get the hell off me before I scream, and they call the police," Emily said indignantly.

Luca began to laugh uncontrollably. She was such a drama queen, he thought as he rolled back over onto his side of the now creased and crumpled display bed.

"Come on Em," he said playfully, "stop being such a prude. Anyone would think you'd never messed around with anyone in public before."

Emily rolled her eyes dramatically and looked up at the roof. In actual fact, she *had* never messed around, or made out with anyone for that matter in public, but she wasn't going to tell him that. Michael had never really been interested in public displays of affection. He didn't consider them appropriate or classy. They had barely held hands outside of the house for most of their relationship. Emily considered this as she glanced over to Luca, laying askew on the bed, smiling his brazen, give no shits smile. She'd always admired his fearlessness and bold disregard for the opinions of others. As a teenager, she'd tried to learn how to be braver. She'd watched him intently, observing his every move in an effort to unlock the secret to his confidence. She'd even tried herself a few times to be louder; more opinionated. It had never really worked for her though.

Once she'd grown and left for North Carolina, she felt like she'd begun to find her voice. She had created a new persona with her new friends. One where she pretended to be confident and bold… like her best friend back at home. For the most part she'd pulled it off… but every now and again, she fell back into her old self-conscious, insecure thoughts and behaviours. It was her work life that had finally given her the opportunity to really practice and hone her assertiveness. As a doctor she'd worked extremely hard to balance the two sides. The sweet, caring, and thoughtful person, and the strong, decisive, and forward moving professional. Working had been her outlet, her excuse to say and do all the things she'd never been brave enough to say.

She recalled the time she'd yelled at an intern for forgetting to wear gloves to begin a procedure. It had felt good to be in-charge… for a moment. Until she saw the look on the girls' face, and instantly felt bad. Over her years in training and then working, Emily had developed an ability to be both firm and kind, and it had fared well for her in her profession. She missed her work. The sudden realisation that she had been avoiding for months dawned on her. Her work was the one thing that gave her balance in her life. The one thing that drove her forward and re-invigorated her passion for life. As much as she was tired from sleeping on her floor and emotionally exhausted from all that she'd been through with her mother, Emily recognised that hiding from her work had also made her tired and directionless.

"Earth to Emily, come in Emily," Luca's voice broke through her thoughts, as she realised she was still lying on the bed in the furniture warehouse. "I swear you're getting weirder by the day," he said jovially, as Emily picked up a throw cushion and socked him on the face with it.

"Careful with the merchandise," he joked, as he tried to dodge the blow. "I'm expensive remember… break it, you bought it… you sure you want all of this?" he said playfully, flexing his muscles and giving her his best supermodel impression.

Emily laughed loudly. What the hell was she going to do with him? Deciding to throw caution to the wind, Emily quickly and without warning rolled over towards Luca, taking him by total surprise. Landing half on his chest with her face directly in front of his, Emily smiled at his slightly dazed expression. For the first time in a long time, he wasn't in charge. Moving her hand up to his face and resting it on the side of his jaw, Emily leant down and kissed him gently. Luca, completely taken by surprise, instinctively moved his hand to rest on her lower back. She smelt like roses and cherries, he absently thought to himself. Swept up in the moment and feeling the surge of adrenaline that came with being in control, Emily kissed him again, more deeply this time. All thoughts of proper behaviour and class left her mind as she felt herself relax and stop thinking. Without warning, a familiar voice broke through the comfortable silence, stopping Luca in his tracks.

"Luca, is that you?"

Luca froze, his brain attempting to register the voice. Realisation dawned on him as he looked over at the person standing near them. Not knowing what to say, Luca took his arms from around Emily and sat up on the side of the bed.

"Hey Claud," he said flatly, contemplating whether to stay or run for his life.

Claudia stood with her arms crossed in front of her, a mixture of shock and confusion registering on her face. Never in a million years had she expected to run into Emily and Luca here. And she certainly hadn't expected to see them cuddled up on a bed playing tonsil hockey… in front of the entire world. Claudia felt her heart beating in her throat as she took a deep breath. Anger and resentment bubbled in her stomach as she looked at the father of her children. Her gaze shifted from Luca to Emily. After all this time, here was her oldest friend. Claudia didn't want to admit it, but Emily looked great. Like she always did, Claudia thought to herself bitterly. Perfect little Emily Rodrigues strikes again.

Realising the awkward silence was now lingering in the air, Luca stood and said as casually as he could manage, "So what brings you to the furniture place today?"

Claudia looked back at him incredulously and snapped. "Seriously? That's what you're going to ask me?" she said, with a build-up of venom on her tongue. "You really want to know why I'm here Luca? Maybe if you actually bothered to spend any time with your children you might know why I'm here. You might understand that your eldest son's been sleeping on the floor after his bed fell apart a few days ago. That I've just spent my entire paycheque on a new one for him. Maybe… if you weren't running around playing happy families with your new girlfriend," Claudia pointed at Emily without taking her eyes from Luca, "you might know what's happening with your *actual* family."

Luca was rendered speechless. He was completely blindsided by the ferocity in her voice, the look of rage on her face. It was something he'd definitely seen before, but not for a very long time.

Emily looked at Claudia intently. This wasn't the best friend she remembered. Claudia had always been passionate… always ready to give her opinion and put her two cents worth in. But this person standing in front of her was angry. Resentful. Of what though?

'What had happened in her friend's life to make her so bitter,' Emily thought to herself.

Rolling over to stand on the other side of the bed to Luca, Emily said in his direction, "I'm going to give you both some time."

She looked to Claudia and said, "It's great to see you Claud."

Claudia glared at Emily with disinterest and disdain. Turning, Emily walked towards the saleswomen who was entering the items into her computer and trying not to make it obvious that she was listening in to the drama unfolding in her shop. Nothing interesting like this ever happens in here, she thought as Emily approached her, looking clearly shaken.

"Is that the last of the items Ma'am?" she asked Emily politely.

"I'd like the Spanish print bed as well," Emily replied simply.

"A beautiful choice," the saleswoman continued, "And when would you like these delivered?"

Emily considered the question. Her floors were being laid as she stood there. There was no reason to delay it any longer.

"Any time you can," she replied, not really paying attention as the lady went into delivery dates and times.

She was more interested in the heated conversation that was occurring a little way away from her, between Luca and Claudia. Their body language spoke volumes. Her waving her hands around and pointing repeatedly at Luca like she wanted bullets to fly out her finger and strike him in the chest. Him standing with his hands by his side, head hunched over, looking at the floor as he spoke. Emily thought he looked like a naughty school kid being scolded by a teacher. As Claudia turned and marched towards the exit, Luca turned to Emily. The look he gave her was one of pure devastation.

Paying for her items and thanking the saleswoman, Emily walked over to Luca.

"Are you ok?" she said quietly.

"Let's just go," Luca said, sounding defeated.

They drove home in silence, gusting wind whipping wildly around the car as it moved along the quiet streets. Luca felt the same thing happening in his mind; like the wind was creating a tornado in his brain that he couldn't control. He was deflated; utterly destroyed. How could everything go from so amazing, to completely falling apart in an instant, he thought as he drove along. He couldn't think properly… couldn't process the information Claudia had thrown at him. In her rage, she'd told him he would never see his kids again; that he was out of their lives for good. The thought of not seeing his kids again, killed him inside. His heart beat heavily in his chest. He was doing all he could not to break down. To yell and scream and punch something.

Arriving at Emily's home, Luca saw all the work vans in the drive and in the surrounding streets. He couldn't be near people now. Couldn't handle any form of small talk. From anyone. Sensing he was upset, Emily sat quietly looking at him. She wanted to grab him and tell him it was all ok. But it wasn't. She hadn't heard what Claudia had said after she'd walked away, but the look on Luca's face told Emily it was nothing good. She suspected it had to do with his kids, but she wasn't sure. Emily felt guilt creep into her heart. She knew how much Luca loved his kids. If she'd caused problems for Luca, Emily would never forgive herself. This was all her fault.

The two sat in Luca's car in silence for what felt like an hour.

Finally, Emily cleared her throat and said quietly, "I'm sorry Luc."

Turning to look at her, the pain on Luca's face was obvious. He couldn't speak, so just nodded.

"We don't need to be here now," Emily continued. "We can just head back to your place and I'll grab my car."

Nodding again, Luca turned the car back on and pulled away from the curb, heading towards his parents' place. From the front room of Emily's house, Adam looked out the window and wondered what on earth Emily and Luca were doing as they drove away.

Arriving at his parents' place, Luca suddenly felt like being alone.

Looking over at Emily he said simply, "I need to go out for a bit."

Not wanting to push him to talk about what had happened, Emily nodded.

"Will I see you later?" she asked.

"I don't know," was all he replied.

Emily turned and opened her car door. Stepping onto the curb she watched as Luca pulled away and sped off down the road.

Chapter 17

Luca needed to hit something. Hard. Pulling into the car park at the Inner City Boxing Gym, he prayed he wouldn't come across anyone he didn't particularly like. He was bound to do something stupid if he did. Walking into the gym, no training gear, no workout clothes, he figured he'd just borrow a pair of gloves and bash a bag for a few hours until he felt better. Hitting stuff always made him feel better. His thoughts shifted to the gloves his trainer kept aside for his kids when they came to visit, and his heart instantly felt heavy. The pain sitting at his core made him feel physically unwell. Turning the corner into the main room, Luca found the space full. Men and women of all ages; all fitness levels, congregated in every corner of the room. People worked in the many boxing rings that were lined down the middle of the room, perfecting foot work and striking. Others stood to the back of the room, before floor length boxing bags, practicing technique, and building stamina. Still more patrons took to the weights room in the left-hand corner of the space, aiming to build muscle and strength. Glancing around the room, Luca took in the sights and smell of the space. The sounds of hard work; of people from all walks of life, all races, all creeds, coming together to work. Being here in this place, always helped to clear his mind.

It was early afternoon. Of course the place is full, Luca thought to himself. It was always the busiest time of the day for the gym. He'd lost track of time with Emily. Negative thoughts threatened to bubble over in his mind, as Luca worked hard to bury them… for now. John, Luca's coach, and long-time friend took one look at him and knew something was wrong. An old school traditional type, John was never someone who liked to pry. He figured his fighters had a right to their private lives, and what they did outside of the gym was none of his business… unless of course, it affected their work in the gym. Then all bets were off. He looked at Luca and wondered if whatever was bothering him was going to cause a problem in the gym today. He hoped not. Not now… when Luca was on the cusp of getting the biggest fight of his life; the fight he'd been training for since he first walked in the doors of the gym as a teenager.

John thought back to a conversation he'd had with Luca after one of his first training sessions. He'd asked him what his goal was… what he wanted to be when he was older.

Without missing a beat, Luca puffed out his chest and stuck out his jaw saying, "I'm gonna be the best fighter in the world. The World Champ."

John remembered looking at the kid, with his thin frame and gangly legs and thinking, 'this kid's got no idea.'

But to John's surprise, Luca had proven him wrong. He'd worked harder than any other student he'd ever had, practiced day and night, long after everyone else had gone home. His dream had never changed. Even when he'd grown up, started a family… the dream never changed. Luca watched John walk towards him and tried hard to keep his face expressionless. The last thing he needed was a pep talk from his long-time coach.

"Hey Luc, how's it going?" John said, extending his hand to shake Luca's.

"Good thanks. Just in the neighbourhood and thought I'd come down and get an extra session in," Luca replied unconvincingly.

He hated lying to John but had no intention of sharing the events of his morning with him.

"No dramas man, it just so happens I'm free for the next hour, so go grab some gloves from the back and jump in the ring."

Luca nodded and made his way to the office at the right of the gym to grab some gloves and hand wraps from the box of spares John kept for occasions just like this. It was never unusual for a fighter to show up to training missing at least one piece of his kit. Gloves were usually the main culprit. Strapping his hands methodically, left to right, one finger at a time, one hand after the other, Luca pulled on his gloves and climbed up into the ring.

"Let's start with five minutes of shadow boxing to warm up hey?"

Luca nodded in John's direction, and began pacing around the ring, counting out steps and combinations into thin air, as if he had an opponent standing across from him.

At the conclusion of his warmup, John climbed into the ring and tightened his own focus mitts. Flat round pads that covered his hands, they gave Luca something to aim at.

"You ready to work?" he said to Luca, as he held up one of the mitts.

Stepping forward and shifting quickly to his right, Luca's glove hit the mitt with a crisp thud, giving John the answer he needed. It felt satisfying to work. Sweating out all the drama, the emotions threatening to overwhelm him. He was strongest when he was fighting. He felt alive as he paced and jabbed; dodged and weaved around the ring. He couldn't imagine ever doing anything else in his life. This *was* his life. Always had been, always would be. His thoughts shifted out of the ring and to his kids. His breath caught in his chest. Swallowing deeply, he tried his hardest to forget how much it hurt to think he might not see his kids again. How much his chest ached. Without warning, a focus mitt hit Luca square in the back of the head.

"Concentrate or get out of my ring," John said simply.

Luca nodded and shifted his weight to his other foot to work on a new combination, blocking out any unhelpful thoughts. An hour later, covered in sweat and smelling like he'd crawled out of a dumpster, Luca finished off his session with 100 push ups.

"So you gonna tell me what's bugging you?" John asked, ignoring the voice in his head telling him to keep out of Luca's business.

"Nope," Luca replied sharply, removing his gloves, and beginning to unwrap his hands.

"How's Emily?" John continued, figuring Luca was pissed off about something to do with the girl.

She was all he'd talked about the past few weeks at training. How they'd been spending time together, fixing her house together. With no response from Luca, John tried one more time.

"Trouble in paradise then? Don't tell me she turned you down buddy?"

Luca launched himself in his coach's direction without thinking. John, a seasoned and experienced trainer who'd worked with his fair share of pissed off young men, anticipated his moves and with expert precision, had Luca flat on his back with almost no effort.

Hand firmly pressed on his chest, holding him to the canvas, John looked directly into Luca's fire filled eyes and said, in an unmistakably blunt voice, "Enough!"

The rage inside Luca began to fade. Realisation struck him like a hammer. He'd almost hit his coach. The one person truly in his corner; the one who believed in him more than anyone. He'd really fucked up this time.

Sensing him calm, John lightened his grip on Luca's chest and without moving, said "You good?"

Luca nodded, not able to speak. Standing up and taking a step back, John picked up the focus mitts and gloves now laying discarded at the side of the ring. Without looking at Luca, he abruptly climbed out of the ring and walked off into his office. Bypassing the showers, Luca stood and left the building without a single word to his coach, or to anyone else. The hum of quiet voices echoed through the gym, as every person in the centre wondered what had gotten into Luca.

Pulling into the driveway at his parents' home, Luca wondered absently how long Emily had stayed after he'd left. He knew he would need to apologise to her. For blowing her off; for the scene Claudia had made in the furniture shop. None of it was Emily's fault. Her only crime was returning home, to what was Luca's massive mess of a life. It was as if all his demons had finally caught up with him, all at once. Right when things seemed to be falling into place. He climbed out of his car and made his way to the house, questioning how he had stuffed everything up so royally.

'Maybe I do wish I could go back to when we were kids,' he thought, recalling the conversation he and Emily had had weeks earlier.

As he entered the front door, he heard voices coming from the kitchen. He wasn't in a mood to talk but knew that if he tried to avoid his mother, she had a way of seeking him out and prying even more. He figured he should get her nosiness out of the way as quickly as he could.

"Hey Ma," he said, as he entered the kitchen to find his mother alone at the kitchen table. "Who were you talking to just now," he asked, leaning over and kissing his mother on the cheek.

"I was on the phone to Carmen," Mireya replied. "She's sounding so much better every day. They're moving her out of the ICU tomorrow and into one of the general cardiac areas. She said they might let her come home in a week or two."

Luca looked at his mother's happy face and felt his mood lift slightly. This was great news. Emily would be so excited.

"Where is Miss Emily?" Mireya inquired, as she picked up a dish cloth and began drying the dishes on the sink.

"She went home earlier… had some stuff to do," Luca replied, trying his hardest to sound normal.

It didn't work. Mireya could always tell when her son was troubled, and today was no exception. It was like a 6th sense she had honed, and perfected over many years. Even now, standing with her back to her son, she sensed something was wrong. Turning to look at him, her suspicions were confirmed by the look on his face. Even as a child, Mireya could tell when Luca was lying to her. Like the time he broke the kitchen window throwing a baseball and tried to say it was the kids up the road. She could see right through him then… and now.

"I'm about to fix an afternoon snack, why don't you take a shower and come sit with me in the yard after," Mireya said smiling.

Luca, knowing there was no way he could get out of a discussion with his mother, nodded and turned to head towards the bathroom.

Feeling refreshed from the cold shower he'd forced himself to tolerate, Luca walked to the back door and out into the garden. The sun was starting to set, throwing pinks and oranges across the sky like an artist's canvas. His mother sat at the outdoor table near the grill, two beers and a plate of cheese and crackers set up in front of her. Smiling despite his foul mood, Luca walked to the table, grabbed his beer, and took a long, thoughtful sip. It certainly hit the spot.

"Take a seat my boy," Mireya said casually, as she looked up at the beautiful sky. "Tell me you've seen anything more beautiful," she continued wistfully. "We are so lucky to have everything we do. Our health, our home, our family."

Glancing over at Luca, Mireya continued, "You only have to look at what Carmen's been through these last few weeks. Doesn't it just make you appreciate every little thing?"

Mireya tried hard to look serious, hoping that her son got the message she was sending him. Luca took another drink of his beer and let out a sigh.

"I get it Mum, I do. I know how lucky I am to have you and Dad. And Emily."

He took a deep breath and continued as his voice broke ever so slightly, "And the boys…"

Mireya looked at her son.

Concern registered on her face as she sat forward in her seat, "What's wrong with the boys Luca?" she said seriously.

"Nothing's wrong with the boys Mum, they're as healthy as ever."

Mireya sat back in her seat, breathing a quiet sigh of relief.

"Tell me what's bothering you Luc," she said quietly, looking out into the darkening night.

Luca, realising it was futile to refuse, turned to his mother sitting across from him and told her about his day.

Mireya sat in silence taking in all she had heard from her son. His thoughts on seeing one of her greatest friends crying in his backyard; to his eventful shopping adventure with the girl who made his eyes brighter; to his run in with the mother of his children, and finally the altercation with his long time boxing coach. He had certainly had a day to forget. Luca finished talking and sat back in his seat. His beer, finished long ago, sat empty on the table in front of him. He had no appetite.

"I just don't know what to do Mum," he said, exasperation in his tone.

"Emily means the world to me. She always has. And the last couple of weeks have been amazing. The last few months with her have been better than I ever thought possible. But I know I haven't seen the kids as much as I've wanted to. As much as I needed to. I should have juggled everything more; should have made more effort. That's my fault."

Thoughts, regrets, and worries began swirling around his head, making it hard to think straight. He tried to continue, "I just don't know how to fix it all Mum… I don't know how to have it all at once. If that's even possible."

Mireya sat quietly. It was important that she let her son come to his own conclusions. Solve his own problems, as much as possible. Since he was little, she'd always let him fight his own battles, reluctant to be one of those mothers who swooped in to save their children from themselves. He was the strong, self-sufficient man that sat in front of her now, because he'd fought his own battles. He knew she was always there for him though, no matter what. For a shoulder to cry on or a listening ear.

"How can I be with Emily when it obviously makes Claudia so angry?" he continued, as if he was talking to himself. "I don't even get why she's so pissed! It's not like there's been anything between us for years now. Nothing. She's even seeing some new guy so what's her problem?"

Luca looked over to his mother, hoping she would help him fill in the blanks.

Mireya shrugged and said, "I don't know Luc. It could be lots of reasons. Obviously, it's something pretty important for her to react the way she did. I think only Claudia has an answer for that."

Luca sat back, thinking.

"And who the hell does she think she is telling me I can't see my own kids? She doesn't own them… any more than I do."

Feeling the tension and anger begin to bubble in his stomach again, Luca closed his eyes and took some deep breaths. He wouldn't get angry in front of his mother.

"And you should have seen Emily. In all of this she just wanted to make sure I was ok. And I kicked her out of my car and drove away."

He realised now, how much he regretted doing that.

"I'm sure she understands you needed some time to yourself honey," Mireya reassured him. "We've both known Emily for a long time, and she's always been an understanding person. Especially with you."

Mireya smiled, as she thought back to all the times Emily had sat at her kitchen bench as a teenager, worrying that Luca was home late from school, or missing from the house when he was meant to be doing chores. Emily had always cared deeply for Luca… always protected him in her own way.

Standing up and walking around the table to take her sons hand, Mireya led him to the middle of the patio.

"Let's dance hey?" she said smiling.

As they shuffled around the concrete, the sky darkened, causing the garden lights scattered throughout the flower beds to flicker on, looking like glow bugs in the night.

"Luca, I'm going to give you some advice that I hope you really think hard about." Mireya said, as she danced with her son.

She loved dancing, especially with Luca. It was something they'd done since he was little. She'd taught her son two especially important life skills, she mused. Vacuuming and dancing. Both of which served him well as an adult.

"Relationships of any kind are hard. They take time, and work. It's very rare to find someone who you can communicate with, without any effort."

Luca's thoughts instantly fell to Emily. He had that with her.

"Your father and I work every day on how we communicate with each other. We don't always get it right… and believe me, we've been through some rough times, when it had almost felt too much to hold together…"

Luca listened intently to his mother, surprised at what she was saying. He'd always thought his parents were solid. Nothing seemed to come between them.

"Luca, if you want your relationships to work… to be positive and enriching, you have to work on them. With Emily. And with Claudia. It's hard, and sometimes it feels like you can't possibly win. But it's worth it in the end. It will be worth it to have your children, their mother and the woman you love in your life." Luca nodded and sighed.

He was really going to have to do some work over the coming days.

Chapter 18

Walking back into the house with his arm around his mother, Luca heard his phone ringing from his room. Running to grab it, he answered just in time.

"Hello, is this Luca Mendes?" an unfamiliar voice asked.

"Yes, it is… who's this?" Luca replied.

"Hi Luca, my name is Randy Martin. I am the marketing manager for the American Boxing League. I've got someone here with me who would like to speak with you."

Surprise overcame Luca, as he stood in his bedroom, wondering what on earth this phone call could be about.

"Umm, sure," was all he managed, before a man with a very loud and very gritty voice took the phone.

"Luca, this is Brian Blackman, CEO of the American Boxing League. How are you my friend?"

Luca was completely caught off guard. He'd heard of the man for sure. But never in a million years did he think he'd ever speak to him. Brian Blackman had a reputation as a hard ass. He was a tough and unforgiving businessman. He largely kept out of the day to day running of the League, preferring to let his staff manage the booking and organising of the fight promotions. This call though, he had asked to make personally.

"Now listen Luca, I really like you kid. You've got grit and you're a damn good fighter. I've watched all your past tapes and seen your recent fights in the ABL."

Luca walked out of his room, down the hallway and back into the kitchen where his mother stood looking at him curiously. He pulled out a chair and sat down, concerned that he may pass out.

"I'm calling to offer you a fight Luca. A big one. One of my fighters tore his rotator cuff in training this morning. He can't fight… straight into surgery tomorrow and at least three months on the sideline. That's why I'm ringing buddy… I want to offer you a shot at the title."

Luca couldn't quite believe what he was hearing. Had he just seriously been offered a title fight? He was speechless… a mixture of elation and confusion clouding his mind.

"Luca are you there?" Brian called down the phone.

"Yes… yes sir I am," Luca replied. "I… I just don't know what to say," he continued, stuttering and stammering through his sentence.

"Well, all I need you to say is yes!" Brian said, with a deep belly laugh that startled Luca.

"Yes… yes, I will take the fight," Luca said more confidently. "It would be an honour to fight for the belt in your organisation Sir."

"Well now that's just fine," Brian said sincerely. "I'll need you to fly out to New York to sign your contracts and get all your pre-work done, and then we'll be good to go."

Luca tried hard to think about what to ask… what he should say… but his mind was pulling blanks.

"When do you need me to come out to NYC sir?" Luca asked, finally thinking of something remotely useful to say.

Brian murmured something to someone on the other end of the phone and then said clearly, "Can you be at LAX in two hours Luca? I can get you on a flight at 8pm sharp so you'll arrive in New York early tomorrow morning ready to get started."

Surprised and overwhelmed, Luca tried to work out how he could make it work in such a short amount of time.

"I'll be there Mr Blackman… and thank you again for giving me a chance," he said, trying to sound sure of himself.

"Not a problem Luca, I'll look forward to meeting you in person very soon."

With that the phone went dead and Luca, not sure what to do or what to say, sat staring incredulously at his mother who stood giving him an equally confused look.

"I'm going to fight for the belt," he said slowly to his mother.

"Are you serious?" she replied.

All Luca could do was nod… and smile. For the second time in the evening Mireya began to dance… a happy dance that made Luca laugh aloud. Maybe…just maybe, his life wasn't a complete mess, he thought to himself. But there were some things he needed to do, people he needed to speak to, before he flew out in two hours. The first thing involved packing an overnight bag and trying to find his only nice suit! 20 minutes later, with a bag packed and his parents waving goodbye, Luca reversed out of his drive and down the road, heading towards someone he needed to speak with urgently.

He knew the front door would be unlocked as he parked his car and made his way inside. The familiar smells of the place that had always calmed him and given him a sense of security, now made butterflies speed around in his stomach. He had some apologising to do.

"Luca what are you doing here?" John asked surprised.

He hadn't expected to see Luca for at least a few days after his little brain explosion earlier in the afternoon. Luca walked up to John and extended his hand. It was time to put his pride aside.

"I came to apologise for my behaviour this afternoon John. It was totally uncalled for and just wrong. I just wanted to tell you how much I appreciate all you've done for me over the years. It really means the world to me to have you in my corner… but I understand if you don't want me to come back to the gym anymore."

John was taken back by Luca's comments. He'd known the boy for many years and was used to his tantrums and angry outbursts, just as a father was used to the antics of a naughty child. But this man standing in front of him now, apologetic, and remorseful… this was someone new. John couldn't remember ever feeling prouder of Luca. Taking his outstretched hand, John lifted it up to mimic Luca smacking himself on the back of the head.

"Stop talking crazy talk," he said smiling. "You don't get out of the torture inflicted in this gym that easily. It's a lifetime deal buddy… like death and taxes. And anyway, from the stories I heard from the other boys in here this afternoon… I put you on your ass better than any other fighter in the ABL has so far… so I figure I probably owe you an apology too."

Laughing, John turned and walked towards his office.

"Come on," he said glancing behind him and gesturing for Luca to follow him.

Relief engulfing him, Luca let out a deep breath and followed John into his office.

"Take a seat and tell me what the hell is going on with you today," John said kindly.

Luca, mindful of the time, replied, "I'd love to John, but I've got some important news to tell you… and I'm on a bit of a deadline."

Intrigued, John took a seat behind his desk and listened to Luca as he filled him in on the phone call he'd received only half an hour earlier. As he relayed the bit about the other fighter being injured, John let out a low whistle and began smiling like a cheshire cat. He knew exactly what it meant, before Luca even got it out. This was it. His chance to make all his dreams come true, John thought. The kid was finally going to make it. Before Luca could finish what he was saying, John leapt up out of his chair and rushed around his desk, grabbing Luca and lifting him up into the air.

"This is amazing news," he said, excitement woven throughout his voice. "God man, this is it! The big test. Shit, we have to get training. I'll need to schedule your sessions for the next few weeks… get your diet sorted out for your weight cut…"

Placing Luca down, John walked swiftly back around his desk and lifted up a pen and paper, madly scribbling items on a to-do list.

"Do we know the date of the fight yet?" John asked, glancing up from his list to see Luca smiling from ear to ear.

John began laughing as he stood and put the pen down.

"I'm so damn proud of you Luca," he said sincerely.

Luca took another deep breath and nodded. John really was the best coach anyone could ask for. He knew how lucky he was to have him in his corner.

"I have to fly to New York tonight to sign all the paperwork and do some preliminary media stuff tomorrow… like photo shoots and stuff for the posters." Luca caught himself bragging a little and laughed.

"I can't believe I just said that," he said, "I'm going to be on posters!"

John smiled. "You sure are bud… plenty of them when you win that belt. What time do you fly out?"

Luca looked at his watch and realised he was running out of time to do all the things he needed to do before he left.

"I have to be at the airport in about an hour and I've got to stop and see someone on the way," he replied.

"Get your ass into gear then man," John said jovially.

Luca walked around the desk and embraced his coach in a bear hug.

"Thanks for everything John… I really mean it. Your support means everything to me."

"I know it does Luc," John replied, as he walked with Luca out onto the training floor.

Whistling as loud as he could muster, John yelled at the top of his voice…

"Ladies and gentlemen, may I introduce to you all… the next 145-pound American Boxing League World Champion."

Hoots and cheers rang out around the gym, as Luca shook hands with John, turned and made his way back to his car with one more stop to make before he got on the plane.

Emily lay in her sleeping bag, wondering what she was going to do about Luca. She hadn't heard from him all afternoon, since he'd dropped her off and left her out the front of his parents' place. She'd understood he needed to be alone for a bit. But now, six hours later… she wondered if it was more than that. Her mind wandered back to the last few weeks with him. They had been amazing. The two of them had spent almost every waking moment together.

'That's precisely the problem,' she thought to herself, as she turned onto her side to look out through the glass double doors that led to her garden.

From her vantage point on the floor she could see the night was overcast, the moon behind some ominous looking clouds. Luca had spent so much time with her recently and she loved it. But a niggling suspicion made her think that his time with her had meant that he hadn't seen his kids as much he was supposed to. And being completely selfish, Emily hadn't pushed him about it at all. She'd figured his kids were for him to worry about… he was an adult… he knew how to take care of his business. But now laying here alone, she wondered if she'd been too selfish… if maybe she'd tried to keep him all to herself too much. Could it have cost him his relationship with his kids? Surely not, she thought. Surely Claudia wasn't the kind of person to be so manipulative… so vindictive. Emily thought about the look Claudia had given her in the furniture shop; the way she'd spoken to Luca. She wondered how the kind, friendly person she'd known all those years ago had changed so dramatically. Or if maybe, that person was always there… just hidden under layers of teenage angst. A knock at the door startled Emily and had her jumping up and racing down the hallway in the dark. She just knew he'd come to see her. Knew he'd want to sit and talk with her after everything that had happened earlier in the day. And maybe after they'd talked, Emily could convince him to stay with her the night. The thought had her smiling as she opened her front door. Switching on the porch light, Emily clutched her chest in utter shock. Where she was sure Luca would have been standing… stood Michael.

Claudia sat alone in her lounge room cursing herself. She had really stuffed up. Completely taken by surprise at seeing Luca and Emily together, she'd totally overreacted. As she sat staring at the TV, not caring what show was on, regret welled up in her chest, making her feel sick to her stomach. She should never have said what she did to Luca. About his kids… his relationship. She knew it was none of her business what he did, or who he dated. She'd stopped looking at Luca like that a long time ago. She herself had a new boyfriend, and for the first time in a long time, she finally felt happy again. A lawyer at the firm she worked at, Jared had been a good friend of hers for a few years and had recently asked her to dinner. He was great with her kids… and great in bed.

'What more could a girl want,' Claudia thought with a smirk.

She thought back to the afternoon, to walking into the furniture store to find a bed for her son. The kid was growing up way too quickly. Guilt left a foul taste in her mouth as she thought about the lie she'd told Luca about Riley's bed. It hadn't broken at all… she'd just been paid a raise the week before, and decided it was time for her eldest son to have a bigger bed. She felt like the worst person in the world. She *was* the worst person in the world. Emily's face jumped into her head, as Claudia sat trying to find some reason to justify her actions… with no success.

Truth be told, it had hurt Claudia to see Luca and Emily together. Not because of what they were doing; but the fact that they were spending time together… without her. It was such a teenage thing to think… a ridiculous thought for a woman in her late 20's. But still, the thought lingered in her mind, and the pain she'd felt was as real as anything she'd experienced before. They had always done everything together. Always spent every waking moment together. The fearless four.

'It is ridiculous,' Claudia thought. 'We're grown bloody adults! What's wrong with me.'

Debating whether to pick up the phone and try to piece together some sort of apology, Claudia was surprised to hear a knock at her front door. Jared was out of town on business, and she hadn't been expecting anyone. She opened the door to find Luca standing there.

"Hey," he said with anticipation, not sure if he would end up with the door… or a fist, in his face for his troubles.

"Hey," she replied dryly, resigned to the realisation that she was going to have to apologise in person.

Opening the door wider, she moved out of the way to let Luca in. He hadn't expected this reaction, and so, cautiously, entered the house. He'd assumed she would still be angry with him; still wanting to enact some terrible form of vengeance for what she'd seen earlier in the day. He walked tentatively into the living room and sat himself down on the floor, bracing for the barrage of negativity.

Luca had known Claudia for a long time; had lived and loved the woman for many years. He knew her better than most. He knew her at her best, and he'd seen her at her worst. But nothing prepared him for the woman sitting before him now. Claudia was… different. Calm, remorseful; sadness etched on her face, as she offered Luca a heartfelt apology. He'd never seen this from her and wondered for a fleeting moment what might have been if she'd responded in this way more often… back when they were younger. That was a long time ago now, he thought to himself as she continued to explain how she had overreacted.

"You're a good dad Luca," she said sincerely. "I know I don't say it very often, but I see how the boys idolise you; how much they love you. I don't want them to miss out on that… because we can't get along."

Luca nodded. He didn't want to miss out on that either.

"I'm sorry I haven't been around much," Luca added. "I've just been so carried away with helping Emily… with her house and everything… you know her Mums been really sick and… no," he stopped himself, as he listened to his own excuses building up. He didn't want to be that person.

"No more excuses Claud. I haven't been around like I should and I'm just sorry. I'm going to make it up to the boys… as soon as I get back."

Claudia looked at Luca and saw the remorse in his eyes. She really had done a good job on him. Swallowing her pride, Claudia began the task of setting the man she'd once loved more than life itself, free.

"I need you to know that I'm happy for you and Emily, Luc. I really am. You guys should have been together from the very beginning. I think you probably would have been if she hadn't moved away. Don't get me wrong… you know I loved you… so much. And I love our boys and the life they've given me. I wouldn't change it for the world. But you and Emily… you're soul mates. You're meant to be together. Everyone that's met you knows it… and I think you do too."

Luca sat and listened to the words coming out of his ex's mouth. He would never have thought he would be sitting here, now, listening to her saying these things. The day really had been a strange one.

"And just while we're on the topic of relationships…" Claudia continued, "I want you to know I'm seeing someone. His name is Jared and he works where I work. He's a really nice guy and he really likes the kids. I want you to know about him, because I think he could be someone important to me."

Luca felt a mixture of emotions at hearing Claudia's news. He wasn't silly enough to think that she would never find anyone else… especially after all the time they'd been separated. She'd been on dates in the past but had never bothered to fill Luca in on who she was seeing.

'This must really be something important to her,' he thought.

A tinge of sadness sat in his heart at the realisation that, after all the years and experiences they'd shared, this really was the end for them. Sitting on the floor, looking at each other with a new sense of resolution, Luca realised his life was changing… whether he liked it or not. And he needed to get a move on if he was going to continue to chase all his dreams.

Chapter 19

"What the hell are you doing here?" Emily said, completely shocked by the man standing at her doorstep.

She hadn't seen him in months. Since they'd sold all their belongings and gone their separate ways.

"It's lovely to see you too Emily," Michael replied, obviously pleased with himself for making her react that way. "Are you going to ask me in darling?"

Emily stood in her door frame, wishing Luca had taught her how to punch… hard.

"Actually, I was in bed as a matter of fact," she said, trying to sound disinterested and unamused at this disruption to her life.

"Now now, don't be so insolent. Let me have a look at this friendly little place you've got yourself."

Ignoring the livid look on her face, Michael entered the house and began switching on lights as he walked down the hall. Taking a few deep breaths and trying her hardest to bury the acute anger that threatened to take over, Emily turned on her heels and followed him into her living area. He stood in the middle of the room, hands in his pockets taking in every detail of the space. Without a word, Emily watched him judge everything she had built.

'He's probably counting up how much everything is worth,' she thought sarcastically.

He really was a piece of work.

"No furniture then," Michael said in a tone that didn't even attempt to hide his arrogance.

"Not that it's any of your business, but the floors were only just finished, and the furniture should arrive in the next few days." Emily replied, cursing herself for feeling the need to justify her actions to him.

Shrugging his shoulders dismissively, Michael turned to Emily and surveyed her. In her pyjamas and without makeup, she looked rather casual. Still lovely though, he thought to himself; that would never change. Dating Emily had been a bold and risky move for him, he reflected. But one that he had enjoyed, for a while. Until she'd changed that is… become all 'save the world' on him. It really was a pity, he thought as he looked her up and down. She had been a fine addition to his lifestyle.

"Why are you here Michael?" Emily asked curtly, disrupting his thoughts.

He always hated when she did that.

Clearing his throat Michael replied, "I'm here to tell you about a big favour I've done you Emily, one that I think you will be very happy with."

Emily stood in front of her ex, trying her hardest to appear disinterested.

A thought struck Emily as she waited for him to continue, and knowing how much it annoyed him when she interrupted him, Emily said, "Before you continue with your important story, how did you find my home?"

Michael's eye twitched and Emily knew she had accomplished her goal. The knowledge was oddly satisfying.

"I spoke with your mother actually," Michael advised, causing Emily to take a sharp breath, and needing to steady herself.

"You've spoke to my mother?"

Confusion now obvious on Emily's face, Michael smiled his annoyingly aloof smile and continued, "Actually that's part of why I'm here to see you Emily. I was visiting Los Angeles General earlier in the week. I'm speaking at the hospitals yearly Gala Charity Benefit... but I'm sure you've heard about that."

She hadn't… and didn't particularly care.

He continued, "And while I was at the hospital touring the facility with the General Manager, he happened to mention that your mother was an inpatient."

Not stopping to notice the look of disgust on Emily's face, Michael continued, "And so I thought it was only right to go and pay my respects and wish her a speedy recovery."

Emily gritted her teeth. She began imagining him standing over her mother, all pretentious and arrogant. She hoped her Mum told him where to go.

"And once I'd visited your mother today, and she advised me that you had not worked since you left North Carolina, I took it upon myself to seek out the General Manager of Los Angeles General again and impress upon him the urgency of offering you a position. Skills like yours can't just sit on the shelf you know Emily. As I always say, you must use it, or you'll lose it."

Satisfied with himself, Michael crossed his arms and nodded happily. Emily took a deep breath, steadied herself and turned towards her front door.

"Michael, it was lovely to see you," she said in a tone that she hoped displayed the level of contempt she felt for the man standing in front of her. "Now I'd appreciate if you could get out of my house so I can go back to sleep."

Clearly insulted, Michael opened his mouth to tell her how rude she was being. Beating him to the chase, Emily continued, "I appreciate your concern for my career but as I've told you in the past, what I choose to do and where I choose to work is none of your business. I'll also be having a word with your friend the General Manager the next time I'm at the hospital as I'm quite sure it's against every policy known to man to divulge personal details of a current patient to anyone who is not a family member or does not officially work at the hospital."

Stunned into silence, Michael looked from Emily to the front door she was pointing towards. As he turned and marched towards the door Emily heard him mutter, "No appreciation for anyone… I deserve more respect after everything I've done."

Emily waited until he'd closed the door behind him and let out a huge breath.

'Thank god he's gone,' she thought to herself as she walked to the door and locked it.

And double checked it was locked. She definitely didn't want any repeat visits tonight. Switching off all the lights Michael had turned on earlier, Emily climbed back into her sleeping bag on the floor. She lay for hours, replaying their interaction in her head over and over, becoming increasingly comfortable with the fact that she never wanted to see the man again as long as she lived. And she hoped he hadn't upset her mother too much. The last thing she wanted was for her insufferable ex fiancé to cause her mother any harm.

'What the hell was I thinking dating someone like him,' she asked herself.

Her thoughts shifted to Luca. She'd hoped he would come and see her tonight, but after what had occurred with Michael, she was a little relieved that he hadn't been in the house to witness the show.

The next morning, Emily pulled up to Luca's parents' home and turned off her car. She hadn't heard from him in almost 24 hours, and she was getting concerned. In her mind she'd just assumed that Luca would come and find her to talk through everything that had happened the day before. It's what they always did; had always done since they were young. She hoped he wasn't avoiding her because she really needed to talk to him. About Michael, and what he'd said the night before. And about the job offer that he'd put on the table. She needed her best friend to talk to… to discuss with… to calm her overactive, overcautious mind. And she needed a hug. Emily knocked on the front door and was greeted by Luca's father, Carlos.

"Emily, come on in," he said, surprised to see her. "Mireya's in the kitchen so go on through. I'm off to see your Dad."

Smiling, Emily said, "Tell him I said hi and I'll be in to see him myself soon."

Carlos nodded and closed the door behind him as he left. Emily turned the corner into the kitchen and was greeted by Luca's mum, dancing around the kitchen, dishcloth in hand.

Turning to face Emily, she stopped and smiled a warm smile, "My beautiful girl, come and give me a hug."

Emily complied, and gave her pseudo mother a big hug. It was something she hadn't been able to do with her own mother since she'd been unwell, for fear of causing her pain. She missed her mother's warm, strong hugs. Mireya let her go and looked at her face curiously,

"What are you doing here today? Is everything ok?"

Emily smiled brightly. "Everything is fine, I was just looking for Luca?"

Confusion registered on Mireya's face as she walked to the kitchen table and sat down.

"Come and sit down lovely," she said. Emily did as she was told and sat waiting for a response.

"When was the last time you spoke to Luca?" Mireya asked.

Emily thought for a minute. "It was just after lunchtime yesterday," she replied. "He dropped me here and I picked up my car. He said he had some errands to run."

Mireya sat quietly, thinking.

"Is everything ok with him?" Emily asked, becoming increasingly concerned that she had missed something important. "Everything's fine love. In fact, everything is wonderful. Luca isn't here at the moment because he flew to New York on an overnight flight last night. He's been offered a title fight and needed to fly over to sign his contract and do some media and promotional things."

Emily sat quietly, letting this news sink in. Luca had left town… last night… and had been offered a title fight. Disappointment overwhelmed her at the thought of not being with him when he received that important call. She imagined how he would have reacted. How excited he must have been. And she'd missed it. As much as she tried to block it out, Emily hated that she felt like she'd missed out on something with him. She'd missed out on so much already… 10 years' worth of events and experiences.

'Add another to the list,' she thought to herself sadly.

Seeing the look of upset on her face, Mireya took Emily's hand and said, "It's ok Em, he'll be back in a couple of days. He isn't leaving town for good."

Emily smiled a sombre smile and nodded. "I know, I guess I'm just a bit disappointed that I wasn't here to see his reaction and celebrate with him."

Mireya smiled knowingly. She had suspected for a while that Emily's feelings for Luca were deeper than just an attraction… more than a friendship… more than a casual fling. Her reaction now, at missing out on sharing such an important moment in his life, not hers, confirmed this. Mireya wondered if Emily had realised yet, that she was in love with her son.

"I'm so happy for him," Emily said after a minute. "Do we know when his fight is? Or where it will be?"

Mireya thought back to the previous day, to the snippets of information she'd gathered listening to Luca on the phone.

"I don't Em. The only information I got from his side of the phone call was that they wanted him in New York ASAP. He only had enough time to pack a bag and he was out the door."

Mireya had assumed when Luca said he had some people to see before he flew out, he had meant Emily. Sitting here now, listening to the poor girl completely clueless, she realised he had meant someone else.

"He didn't even tell me when he would be back love. He might be a day or a week. And you know what he's like with keeping in touch. He doesn't even ring his poor mother."

Mireya smiled. She could see her reassuring words taking effect. Emily looked much more relaxed, now minus the frown lines covering her forehead. Mireya decided to change the topic.

"Have you seen your mother over the last few days?" she asked.

Carmen had been moved out of the ICU and into a cardiac ward a few days earlier. Each time Emily saw her she looked more like herself. She was even heard to sing a few tunes around the place while doing her chest physiotherapy exercises. If all was well and stayed on track, the doctors were predicting she could be home within a week. This was both exciting and terrifying for Emily's father, Jose. He had phoned Emily every night over the past week asking questions and querying things he'd read on the internet. Emily thought it was sweet. And she was glad he was so particular in this instance… like father, like daughter. Chatting to Mireya for a while longer, Emily said her goodbyes and made her way next door to catch up with her father before making her way back to her home to do some gardening… alone.

The furniture truck arrived at the front of Emily's home two days after Luca left for New York. She still hadn't heard from him; and wondered more than once, if she would.

'He's obviously busy', she thought, as she signed the paperwork to take possession of the entire décor of her house.

Four big, strong, burly men stood in her driveway preparing to unload the huge truck and fill her home with items. Excitement mixed itself with something else as Emily stood pensively on the front step and watched her beautiful bed head being unloaded. Next was her sofa and living room set; the one Luca had found hidden in a back corner of the warehouse and Emily had adored. Then came the bedside tables that Luca had chosen, and the fridge that had the specially added ice maker in the front. Luca had barracked for that too. Emily closed her eyes and took a deep breath. She had imagined he would be here for this. She wondered where he was at that moment; what he was doing.

Stepping back into the house, Emily busied herself unpacking smaller items that she'd picked up the day earlier. Kitchen items (including a glass vase), bathroom accessories, pillows, and sheets for her bedroom. She'd tried to keep to a general colour scheme and theme for everything she'd bought. Mostly sticking to greys and whites; with a few items in bright colours to create some feature pieces. Unpacking a bright blue set of glass jars for her bedside table, Emily was confident that everything would fit together just how she imagined it.

With the kitchen almost done: the fridge, microwave and coffee machine installed, and the utensils and cutlery drawers full, Emily moved onto the bedroom. Her bed had been delivered in pieces, and she worked diligently with the set of tools she'd borrowed from her father to put it together. Around 20 minutes into the project, with only one part of the bed fitting together how it was supposed to, Emily cursed the damn thing for ruining her life. She sat, defeated, in the middle of the bedroom, surrounded by random pieces of wood and a variety of different sized screws. Emily hated stereotypes, especially as a strong female in a largely male driven occupation. But secretly, never willing to admit it to anyone, she found herself wishing Luca were there to help.

"Looks like I'm sleeping on the floor again tonight," she muttered to herself, as she threw the instructions at the wall.

"You know, you're supposed to read those… not throw them."

Startled by the sound of the voice behind her, Emily whirled around and was greeted by the person she had least expected to ever see at her door. Standing, leaning against the door jamb with a large coffee in each hand and a hesitant smile, was Claudia Garcia.

"Want a hand?" she continued, as she walked into the room and handed Emily a coffee.

Completely lost for words, Emily just sat and looked at her old friend, perplexed. Other than at the furniture store, Emily hadn't seen or spoken to Claudia in over 10 years. And that hadn't gone well at all. Emily felt anxiety begin to churn in her stomach as she wondered what motive Claudia had for standing in her bedroom. She was sure there was one… Claudia never did anything for nothing.

"You're probably wondering why I'm here then?" Claudia asked, smiling at the look of shock and confusion on Emily's face.

"That… that would be one thing I'm wondering," Emily replied hesitantly.

Claudia laughed. "It's ok… I'm not here to murder you; or to yell at you," she added, pretty sure Emily was wondering if the crazy chick she'd seen a few days earlier was still around.

"Luca told me the other night that you might need some help with all this stuff, and I figured since he's still away, I'd come by and see if I could help."

Emily took in this information. Of course, Claudia had spoken to Luca before he left. Of course she knew where he was and what he was doing. Jealousy threatened to taint the words on Emily's lips.

Mustering all her will power, Emily replied politely, "I'll take all the help I can get at this point."

Taking a screwdriver and grabbing the instructions that sat neglected on the floor, Claudia surveyed the situation and decided it was time to take charge. It was the least she could do after all the problems she had caused lately.

"Right, I've put a few beds together in my time," she said simply, "So I need to tell you that you have all the pieces around the wrong way."

Emily sighed and put her head in her hands. Of course she did.

Claudia laughed and continued, "But its ok… we can fix this."

She stood and began rearranging the pieces into piles as Emily watched on. Smaller pieces on one side of the room, larger ones at the other.

"Aren't you meant to be a doctor Em? I'm pretty sure I remember you being more organised than this," Claudia joked lightly, not wanting her old friend to think she was criticising her.

"You'd think that, wouldn't you?" Emily replied, part sarcastically, part honestly. "I can't remember the last time I felt organised. I think I left that side of me in North Carolina."

Claudia smiled. "It must have been a big change coming home after so many years away?" she prodded gently, genuine interest in her voice.

"Yeah, yeah it was," Emily said, hearing the reluctance in her own voice as she spoke.

"Did you drive back? Or catch a flight?" Claudia continued, trying to engage Emily in any kind of conversation, as she began placing sections of the bed together in their right order.

Emily watched her old friend competently putting together her furniture. Surely, she wouldn't bother with all of this if she was just going to yell at me, Emily thought as she handed Claudia another screw. There was definitely something else going on here.

Chapter 20

Luca felt like all his Christmas's had come at once. He couldn't believe any of this was actually happening. All his hard work was finally starting to pay off. From the minute he landed in New York, he'd been treated like a king. From limousine rides, new clothes gifted to him by interested sponsors; to fancy dinners in five star restaurants, and a six star hotel with three pools, a swim up bar, saunas, and the most incredible gym with more equipment then he'd seen in his life. Luca felt a bit like a kid in a candy shop. A really, really big candy shop. He'd only been in NYC for a few days but had already been so many places and met so many people, his head was swimming. From agents to sponsors, to random people coming up to him in the street saying they were fans of his; Luca quickly realised he was a long way away from the poor neighbourhood he'd spent his whole life in.

Sitting in his hotel room overlooking Central Park, Luca thought how much his boys would enjoy being here with him. How amazing they would find all the sights and sounds of New York. From the craziness of traffic buzzing around the city, to the familiar sound of emergency vehicles battling their way through the chaos. From the Statue of Liberty, to the Empire State Building; Rockefeller Centre to Times Square… New York was a feast for the senses. He wondered if Emily had felt something similar when she'd left town all those years earlier; whether she'd been swept up by the new scenes and experiences of North Carolina, as he was being in New York. He would have to ask her when he got home, he thought.

Having arrived in NYC early the first morning, Luca had been greeted at the airport by Randy Martin, the marketing manager for the American Boxing League. A short, stocky man of about 5'4, Randy reminded Luca of a circus ringmaster, controlling, and commanding the next act and the last with precision and detail. With short dark hair and features that suggested Italian heritage, Randy was obviously a man who could talk the talk. The limousine ride from the airport to the hotel had certainly confirmed this. Randy talked the whole way, explaining his role in the company and his relationship with Brian Blackman, CEO of the American Boxing League. From what Luca gathered, Randy was the go-to guy behind the scenes; the brains of the operation. From booking and confirming fighters, to media enquiries, marketing offers and sponsorship, Randy was across it all. In the space of the short car ride, Luca had listened to him expertly broker three deals with companies looking for sponsorship opportunities and confirm a fight deal with a fighter on the other side of the planet. The guy knew how to wheel and deal.

Luca sat back in the car and took in the sites of New York. He'd been there once or twice before and loved it. The hustle and bustle of the city made him feel like a little fish in a very big pond. Back at home, everyone in a 10-block radius knew who Luca Mendes was, either from his younger days as a troublemaker, or his adult years as the best local fighting prospect to come out of the area. No matter where he went or what he did, someone would recognise him. It wasn't uncommon for a 10-minute outing to take over an hour because Luca ran into someone who knew him; someone who wanted to have a chat about this or that. He never usually minded; he appreciated the support of the local community. But it did make it hard to get things done in life. Luca figured he could enjoy some anonymity in the big city for a little while.

Thinking about home, Luca's thoughts shifted to Emily. He'd been meaning to call her when he landed. He'd been in such a rush to get to the airport, to try and smooth things over with John and Claudia before he flew out, that he'd run out of time to see Emily. He'd wanted to stop into her place on his way to the airport. To tell her about his trip and apologise for blowing her off. But after his talk with John, and his heart to heart with Claudia, he'd found he had 20 minutes left to be at the airport… and the trip took 15 minutes! He consoled himself with the knowledge that he would only be in NYC for a couple of days; that when he got home, he would drive straight to Emily's place and tell her that he was sorry. Tell her all about his trip and his title shot. She would be so excited. He tried to picture the enthusiasm on her face when he explained all the details and asked her to be there with him when he fought. He couldn't imagine fighting without her ring side, cheering him on.

"What's making you so happy hey?" Randy asked, noticing the smile on Luca's face.

Luca replied, "Just thinking about home."

Randy smiled and responded, "Tell me a bit about your home Luca. You fight out of Inner City Boxing Gym, don't you?"

Luca nodded. For the rest of the car ride, he sat chatting to Randy about his gym, the guys he trained with, and John his trainer. By the time they arrived at the hotel and Luca was set up with full access to all the amenities; gym, pool, sauna, he'd completely forgotten that he needed to call Emily.

By lunchtime Luca had met with three groups of sponsors and accumulated a new watch, shoes and three new outfits. He still couldn't get over the fact that it was all free. That even if he didn't agree to work with the sponsors, they wouldn't be coming back to take their stuff. It was his. He'd never experienced anything like this before. Getting something for nothing was as foreign to Luca as learning another language. Where he was from, there was always something for everything. Always a cost or a price to pay. His whole life he'd tried his best to weigh up the cost, consider the price before committing to something or another. Most times it hadn't worked… he would jump straight in headfirst, even when the odds were against him; when the price was high. It was part of the reason he'd been successful so far in the fight game. 'Feel the fear and do it anyway,' was a saying he loved and often lived by. Taking all his stuff up to his room, Luca decided to quickly check in at home. Dialling his mother's number, Luca smiled as Mireya's cheery voice lit up the other end of the line.

"Hi Mum, its Luca. How are you?"

Mireya laughed as she replied, "My famous boy… you didn't forget me!"

Luca laughed. He lay back on his plush, king sized bed and chatted to Mireya for around 20 minutes. He described New York and all the sites he'd seen while travelling to events earlier in the day. He told her about the hotel and promised to take some photos to show her when he got home. He also filled her in on the people he'd met; the sponsors and the agents.

"It sounds like you're having a wonderful time honey," Mireya said. "When do you think you'll be home?"

Luca thought back to the conversation he'd had with Randy earlier in the morning. Randy had asked him to stay in NYC until the end of the week, when the media day and photo shoots had been booked for the original fight card. Randy had hoped they could still rescue the original date for the fight night and all the press events, regardless of the fact that Luca was only now stepping in for the other injured fighter. It meant Luca's next few days would be ridiculously busy, fitting in a months' worth of work into just a few days. Then he would need to get back to LA for three weeks of intense training. It was a much shorter time frame then Luca had ever worked with. All his other fights had involved a six to eight week training camp, but he would make three weeks work. He had to. This was the opportunity of a lifetime; a chance to take the belt home. If everything ran to plan, Luca would fight on the main card for the American Boxing League 145-pound world title belt in just under a month. 28 days to be exact.

"That's so exciting honey," Mireya remarked, as she sat in her garden reading a book. "And do you know where the fight will be? Will we need to travel to see it?"

Luca smiled. He could always count on his mum to support him, no matter where in the world he was. He was sure she would jump on a plane at a minute's notice if he asked her to.

"That's the best bit Mum…" Luca replied, "The fight was originally planned for LA! I get to fight for the belt at home."

Mireya was so pleased for her son. So thrilled for this opportunity that he had in front of him. He sounded so animated on the phone, so full of excitement. It was well overdue, she thought. And well deserved. Mireya saw how much Luca had struggled in his life. How he had been written off as a teenager by most in the town. A troublemaker; good for nothing but jail. She'd heard time and time again, teachers advising her to send him away; to get him out of the neighbourhood and away from the older kids he was so heavily influenced by. But she could never do it. She could never send away her only child; her beautiful son. Mireya saw the potential in him for greatness, before anyone else. She saw the grit and determination. The fire in his eyes and in his belly.

As he got older, she saw the drive in him to do better, to be better. She had always encouraged him at every turn. Had always been there to fix his cuts and scrapes; his bruised and battered ego when it had taken a hit. The day Luca met John Graham, his boxing coach, Mireya had thanked the lord for answering her prayers. For so long, she'd prayed for someone to take Luca under their wing, to guide and direct him in a way neither she nor Luca's father could manage. John had been this person, and was still to this day, one of the greatest positive influences on Luca's life. Alongside Emily of course. Emily.

"Luc, before I forget, Emily was around here looking for you the other day," Mireya advised.

Luca cursed, and instantly regretted it as Mireya gave him an earful for his trouble. She hated cursing and made sure he received a swift slap on the back of the head anytime she was near him and overheard it.

"Sorry Mum, what did she say? Was she ok?"

Mireya relayed the conversation that occurred in her kitchen. How Emily had looked sad and disappointed when she'd heard that Luca was out of town. How her disappointment had turned into excitement when she'd heard about the opportunity for Luca to fight. Luca smiled. He really did need to give her a ring and talk. About his fight; about Claudia; about what was happening between them. He just wasn't sure where to start. He was no good at that sort of thing. Relationship talk stuff. Or that's what he was telling himself anyway. Plus, he really wanted to be there in person. To see her reaction when he told her the details of his fight. He always loved watching Emily react to good news. Seeing her face light up with excitement. No, he would hold off on calling her. He knew he was being selfish, but he thought she'd understand. She always understood him; better than anyone else.

 "It's all good Mum, I'll make sure to go see her on my way home from the airport." Luca said.

Saying his goodbyes, Luca hung up the phone and stayed lying on his bed thinking about Emily. Something told him he should really call her. At least to say hello; to see if her furniture had arrived, and to hear what she'd been doing since he'd left town. As he began dialling her number, a knock on the door had him cancelling the call. Standing and walking down the hall to the front of the hotel room, Luca opened the door to find Randy standing waiting.

 "Ready to go sign your life away buddy?" he asked enthusiastically.

 Luca shoved his phone in his pocket and grabbed the door key. He would definitely call Emily later.

Arriving at the World Boxing League's US Headquarters, Luca stepped out of the limo and instantly felt overwhelmed by the size of the building. 12 stories high, it cut an imposing figure into the skyline above him. Tall dark glass windows stretched the length of the building, creating a sense of corporate officialdom and power. An American flag flew at the front of the building, defining the patriotism that was so obvious within the premier boxing organisation. Entering the doors at the front of the building, Luca was greeted by a large symbol of the ABL set into the faux marble floor at the entrance. To enter the offices and spaces within the building, a person had to walk directly over this symbol, sitting proudly in place. No one entering ever had any illusions of where they might be.

Luca was blown away by the air of professionalism that radiated from every angle of the facility. From the corporate style furnishings; sleek and sophisticated, to the staff members dressed in business suits and ties. For a business that sold sweaty, messy, bloody boxing tournaments, they knew how to put on a professional show.

'Emily would love this place,' Luca thought to himself, as Randy motioned for him to follow on.

Stepping into a glass lift, Luca was whisked to the 8th floor and stepped out to be welcomed by none other than Brian Blackman.

"Luca, you made it my boy," Brian roared, with a huge grin covering his large, rotund face. The two men shook hands.

Slapping an enormous hand on Luca's back, Brian led him down the corridor and into an office… the size of his whole house. Luca was overwhelmed by the sheer size of the space. In the centre stood a large mahogany desk. Its detailed carvings and features were more intricate than anything Luca had ever seen. Couches, coffee tables and statues, probably worth more than Luca, were scattered around the space in an attempt to fill it. The room was surrounded by large glass windows at three sides, making it appear even larger. With so much to take in, Luca didn't know which way to look.

"Come and have a seat my friend," Brian said jovially, pointing to an armchair next to the desk.

Luca took a seat in the large and extremely comfortable chair. He instantly felt more at ease. Brian took a seat on the other side of the table and shuffled a few papers out of the way to give Luca has full attention.

"Now listen kid, like I said on the phone the other day, I like you. You've got spunk. And grit. I like both those things in my fighters. I've watched all your tapes and I can tell you've got talent. That's important. I don't offer title fights to just any old mug you know." Luca nodded, not sure if he was meant to reply or not.

"So, here's the deal. I'm offering you this title fight in a few weeks on the same conditions offered to the last guy. He had surgery this morning by the way and is out for a few months. Anyway, here's what I need from you Luca. To be a champion in my company, it's not just about winning fights. It's about much, much more. Champions in the ABL present themselves a certain way; follow certain core values that are particularly important to my organisation. These include honesty, integrity, and respect. They attend events dressed a certain way, and behave at all times, a certain way. We don't do scandal or drama of any kind in this team Luca. No disrespect, no trash talking… it's not how we run our business. Do you think you can live with that?"

Luca answered without hesitation, "Of course Mr Blackman. I understand completely."

Brian nodded and sat back.

"Good, good," he gestured to Randy who presented him with a black document wallet.

"Let's get to business then," he said smiling. "Here is your contract. Its terms are as outlined in the document and include a title fight at the end of this month, on the 27th. Should you win the fight, the ABL will pay you a sum of $80,000 to your nominated bank account. Following your fight, should you win, you'll be expected to undertake a number of press events and fan events both in New York, and in other parts of the US. This will involve you travelling regularly with all travel costs paid for by the company. Does that sound ok?"

Luca was dumfounded. He was sure he'd heard the man wrong. $80,000? That was more money then he'd earnt in all of his previous fights combined.

"Luca… you with us buddy?"

Luca glanced up and realised he hadn't responded to the previous question.

"Sorry… yes, yes I… that sounds great," he replied.

Brian laughed; a belly laugh that made his chin wobble.

"It's a lot of money isn't it son," he said warmly.

Luca smiled, a little embarrassed.

"Yes sir it is," he replied.

"Well, now all you have to do is earn it buddy."

Luca nodded as Brian slid the contract across the table towards him. After a quick read and clarification on a couple of points listed, Luca signed on the dotted line. With one swipe of an expensive looking pen, his fate was sealed. He was fighting for the world title.

Chapter 21

With the bed finally built, mattress down and covered with the new pale grey sheets Emily had purchased the day before, the two women stood back to admire their handywork.

"You should feel really proud of what you've done here Em," Claudia send genuinely, "Luca told me what a mess the house was when you bought it. He said, and I quote, I told her she was nuts for even thinking about buying it… the place was such a dump."

Emily smiled, imagining Luca overexaggerating the state of the house in the beginning. In his defence, it really was in a terrible state when she first fell in love with it. Just like I was, she thought to herself. Emily did feel proud of what she was doing with her little home. At every turn, every change, she'd seen something growing; felt a strength of place and time; a sense of belonging growing inside her. One that she had been missing for such a long time. She felt like she was home. Like she finally had her own place in the world. Turning and walking into the kitchen, Emily placed her father's tools down on the bench carefully. The awkward silence returned as Claudia stood looking at her.

"Can I have a look at what you've done in your backyard?" she asked tentatively. "Luca said it looks really great."

Emily nodded, wondering how much time Luca and Claudia actually spent talking about her. She walked across the room and opened the glass folding doors out onto the deck. A warm, early summer breeze flowed into the house, bringing with it the perfume of all the beautiful flowers that were thriving back there.

"Em this is amazing," Claudia remarked, as she took in the garden beds with their random explosions of colour; their organised chaos.

Towards the back of the yard she saw trellises and realised Emily had put in a vegetable garden just like her parents. Memories of her teenage years, hours and hours spent sitting in Jose and Carmen's garden with

Emily, Luca and Ricky made Claudia feel strangely nostalgic. She hadn't expected that.

Walking over to the wooden steps leading down into the garden, Claudia sat down at the edge of the deck, resting her feet on the steps. Hesitantly, Emily followed. Sitting there together, reassured by the calmness of the space, Emily decided it was time to set the record straight; to put all the cards out on the table.

"Why are you here?" she said simply, trying to sound curious, but instead managed indignation.

Claudia had been waiting for it and turned to face her old friend.

"I came to apologise Em," she said, with eyes that held onto great sadness. "What I said the other day; the way I behaved; it was completely out of line."

Claudia took a deep breath and dove in bravely. "Not coming to visit you sooner… when I knew you were home, has been really selfish of me. I know that."

Claudia abruptly stood and walked down the steps into the garden. She turned and looked at Emily with tears in her eyes.

"You have no idea how much I've missed having you around Em. After you left all those years ago, I felt lost for so long. Like I had no one; just me against the world. I spent so much time telling everyone I was ok… convincing them that I didn't even notice that you were gone, that after a while I think I talked myself into it too."

Leaning up against the old oak tree growing stoically in the yard, Claudia continued, "When Luca said you were coming home, I was so excited. I even came to your parents' house for the party, the night you got home."

Emily looked at Claudia with surprise. She hadn't seen her or heard from anyone that she was planning on attending.

Claudia continued, "I pulled up out the front, heard the music coming from Luca's parents' yard… and I wimped out. I drove away Em. Drove home and felt shit about myself for days after."

Emily sat quietly, taking in the information.

"I spent 10 years of my life wishing you would come home so I'd have my best friend back… and when you do come home, I avoid you. Go figure hey."

Claudia walked slowly back up the stairs and sat down next to Emily.

"I don't understand," Emily said bemused, "Why would you avoid me? Why haven't you wanted to see me?"

Claudia looked down at her hands and spoke; so quietly that Emily had to lean in to hear her response, "Why do you think? Because of Luca."

Realisation shook Emily's mind. For months now she'd wondered about Luca and Claudia's relationship. About how it would affect all their friendships. And as much as she didn't want to admit it, she felt the jealously of knowing that Claudia and Luca had something together. That they had shared a life together, children together… loved together. Sitting looking at her friend, she could see that this weighed heavily on Claudia as well.

"Em I want you to know that what Luca and I had was over a really long time ago. He filled my life with so much joy and love. He gave me the most wonderful children anyone could ask for."

Emily listened on.

"But we weren't right for each other and we both knew it. When Luca and I began dating, I told myself that it was the right thing. That you were gone, and he was available. And for a while it was great."

Emily took a deep breath and dared to ask what she had been wondering for months, "So what happened then? Why aren't you together now?"

Claudia smiled and joked, "Because he drove me god damn crazy."

Emily smiled knowingly.

"Seriously though," Claudia said, "after a while the gloss wore off. The fun became hard work. All the things that I found cute, became things that made me mad. I'd get mad, and he'd get mad. We'd say things both of us regretted. We were fireworks. And TNT. And when we went off, people in the middle got hurt. Words travel, and our kids were always there. Always hearing the nasty things we'd say to each other. They were both so little that I don't think they ever understood, but we did. We knew what we were saying, how much we were hurting each other. It got too much and we had to stop. Go our own ways."

Claudia stopped talking and closed her eyes.

"It was the best and worst thing that's ever happened to me," she said simply.

Emily sat quietly, thinking about her own relationship; her own experiences during her time away. She wished she had experienced at least a little of the feelings Claudia described. Passion; desire; need. She lived instead with apathy and professional regard. How boring. Emily sighed deeply.

Turning to face Claudia, she said honestly, "I was at university when I heard that you and Luca were together. That you were pregnant."

She thought back to the phone conversation and the strange sensation she had felt hearing the news.

"To be honest, I was really confused." Emily chose her words carefully, "I didn't even think you liked him like that?"

Claudia laughed loudly and covered her mouth.

"I'm sorry," she said trying to compose herself. "I shouldn't be laughing but I have to tell you… I knew you'd think that! I remember sitting in my house with the positive pregnancy test, before I'd even told Luca, and thinking, Emily is going to be so confused by all of this!"

Emily smiled herself, imagining the scene.

"At first I didn't like him Em. And definitely not while you were still living in LA. We just started hanging out more, since we were the only two left. You'd gone to the other side of the country, Ricky moved away not long after. It was just me and Luca. And the more time we spent together, the more I got used to having him around; used to having him there, you know?"

Emily nodded, realising she'd felt the same over the past few weeks.

"And so we got together, and before we knew it, I found out I was pregnant. It wasn't planned. It just happened. We had Riley, and it was great at first. And then we had Joey and life got hard. Two kids, me working and Luca training… it just got too hard. We stopped having fun, started yelling at each other… and the writing was on the wall."

Claudia felt so relieved. She'd been holding onto all of this for so long. It felt good to finally be honest. To finally tell her best friend how she felt. To let it all out. Almost.

"Em, I need to tell you something. And I understand if you hate me after, but I have to say this."

Emily looked at Claudia, anticipation clear on her face.

"I knew he loved you, you know, even before he knew it. We all knew it… even if you both were completely oblivious. I think he's always loved you, even when he was with me. Sometimes he'd look at me, and I knew he was thinking about you."

Claudia sighed. "He gets this look on his face when he thinks about you. And I tried to pretend I didn't notice; that I was just being silly; overreacting. I tried to ignore his feelings for you, to keep him with me. I knew what I was doing, and I did it anyway… and I have to live with that. I've been living with that for 10 years."

Claudia looked down at her hands again, now covered in red marks from where she'd been clasping them together; wringing them out like they were a dishcloth.

"I think," Emily said honestly, hoping she wouldn't cry, "that you're being too hard on yourself. You've always been hard on yourself. Even when we were teenagers you compared yourself to everyone else. And always thought you came out second best. But you didn't."

The tears began to fall as Emily continued, "You're blaming yourself for something that's no one's fault. You fell in love. You had beautiful children. You made a life with someone who loved you very much. You don't realise how lucky you really are…"

Emily wiped tears away with the backs of her hands, thinking about how much she had once craved what Claudia had.

"It sounds like we have a lot of catching up to do after all," Claudia said, as she leant over and squeezed Emily's hand.

A hot breeze flowed through the backyard and up towards the house, causing both women to shift uncomfortably.

"I think we should probably move this inside," Emily said, standing up and moving towards the doors.

"Sounds good to me," Claudia replied as she followed, "I'd love a cold drink if you have anything?"

Emily glanced back smiling, as she told Claudia about the ice machine in the front of the fridge and how Luca had insisted on getting it. Claudia rolled her eyes dramatically.

"Anyone would think he was moving in here," she said sarcastically, then stopped herself.

"*Is he* moving in here?" she inquired.

Emily shook her head quickly, "No, of course not. Why would you think that?"

Claudia shrugged. "I don't know, I guess I just thought… after I saw you at the furniture store the other day… you know!"

Emily looked at Claudia with confusion on her face.

"Well… I'm assuming you've… you know." Claudia said, winking.

Emily blushed bright red and looked immediately at her feet.

"Oh my god Em, you're still the biggest prude!" Claudia said, laughing aloud and holding her stomach.

"Shut up, I am not," Emily replied despondently.

"Well for what it's worth…" Claudia continued, "when you do, you won't be disappointed,"

Emily rolled her eyes, thinking how ridiculous it was that they were having this conversation at all.

Attempting to divert the conversation away from the topic, Emily asked Claudia about her kids. Claudia described Riley and Joey; their personalities, their likes, and dislikes; their funniest moments, and all the things they were great at. There were a lot.

"Sounds like they are just as competitive as their Dad," Emily said smiling, as she sat at her kitchen bench.

"You have no idea," Claudia replied from the other side as she sipped her ice-cold water. "Sometimes I wonder what I did to deserve two crazy, energy filled boys. And then I count my blessings that they are healthy and happy kids."

Emily nodded. "I've looked after a lot of kids who haven't been that lucky," she said thoughtfully.

"I can imagine," Claudia replied. "So, tell me about your work. Where are you working at the moment?"

Emily paused, not sure what to say. Could she talk to Claudia about her fears for her work? About her reservations at diving back into emergency medicine. The last thing she wanted was for Claudia to think she was being ungrateful, or selfish. Especially after they'd only just literally begun talking again. But she also recognised she needed someone to talk to about it all; that she couldn't sort it out herself, as much as she'd tried over the past few weeks.

"I'm actually not working at the moment." Emily said simply, causing Claudia to look at her with surprise.

"But if we're going to talk about my work… I should probably fill you in on the other bits too."

Intrigued, Claudia stood and walked over to the newly purchased couch in the middle of the living area.

Gesturing for Emily to follow her, Claudia said simply, "Fire away."

Emily began at the start; opening up about her life in North Carolina. About university and college life. Study, exams, assignments. She talked about her excitement at being offered an internship; about her passion for helping others and how much she loved her training. About meeting Michael, and their dysfunctional relationship. About the sadness she felt that their relationship had been so clinical; loveless. Claudia sat listening in awe. Never in a million years would she have guessed that Emily would live with someone like Michael. Someone who sounded so… boring! Claudia had always imagined Emily's life in North Carolina to be some exciting party life. Some incredibly fantastic adventure that she herself had missed out on experiencing. She realised that she had judged her friend's life unfairly.

"Have you told Luca about Michael?" Claudia asked.

"Not yet," Emily replied seriously.

"I'm… I think I'm scared that he won't understand. That he will think differently of me," she said gloomily.

"I didn't," Claudia said honestly. "And I don't think Luca will think any differently of you at all. Em, the guy is crazy about you. Has been since we were kids. You could tell him you were married to a pirate, and I don't think he would look at you with anything less than love."

Emily looked at Claudia and burst out laughing. It was so good to laugh; to have someone to laugh with.

"So, tell me about what you've been doing since you got home," Claudia said, settling back into the comfortable lounge cushions.

Emily replayed her road trip adventure home, describing her stop overs and adventures in Nashville, Memphis, and Oklahoma on her way.

Claudia sighed wistfully, "I can't imagine what it must be like to feel that free," she said to no one in particular. "No responsibilities, no time frames, no one to complain at you… or demand snacks from you."

Emily smiled. She hadn't really thought about her trip home like that, but Claudia was right, she had been lucky to experience what she had.

"Tell me then," Claudia said, "what's the plan? You've finished your house. What now?"

Emily shrugged. She had no idea what she was going to do next.

"To be honest," Emily said, "I haven't really thought that far ahead. I was so caught up in doing the house, in making it exactly how I wanted it… that I stopped looking ahead. It's been really nice actually. To not have a five year plan; to not have every element of my life planned out perfectly. But now I feel like I'm lost… or like I'm being left behind."

Emily closed her eyes. She realised she'd just been more honest than she had been in a long time.

"You want to know what I think?" Claudia replied.

Emily opened her eyes and looked at Claudia as she continued,

"You bloody think too much. You've always thought too much… since we were kids. Everything had to be planned out… organised. You used to drive me crazy woman! With your lists and your plans and your goals. I have to say though, look where that's gotten you. And look where I am."

Claudia smiled, "Maybe I needed a little more planning in my life, and you need a little less?"

Emily nodded. "Probably," she replied smiling.

"You know…" Claudia started, then thought better of it.

"I know what?" Emily continued encouragingly.

"Well… just hearing you talking about your work, or lack of work, reminded me of the old doctors' surgery in my office complex. It went up for sale earlier in the year after the old GP who ran it got sick and had to retire. It's sat vacant for months and I know lots of his patients are struggling to find another doctor to see around the area. I hear all about it when they come in to complain to me that it's not open… like I have any say in it!" Claudia laughed.

Emily smiled, considering the idea. And just as quickly discounting it. She couldn't be a GP, she thought to herself. Not after she'd lived for so many years with the excitement and complexity of emergency medicine. General practice seemed like a demotion in Emily's brain.

'Snob,' she heard Luca say in the back of her mind.

It was a good idea, but it just wouldn't work for her.

"I appreciate the thought Claud," Emily said. "But I don't think general medicine is my thing."

Claudia shrugged, not really knowing what the difference was… they were all doctors weren't they?

"Well… maybe you can start an interior design business?" Claudia said, looking around the room, "This place looks seriously amazing!"

Emily smiled, "it does look great doesn't it. It's exactly how I imagined it in my head so many months ago. I just knew it was the place for me… the minute we saw it."

Emily caught herself thinking of Luca and felt uncomfortable.

"You know it's ok to talk about him," Claudia said, recognising the look on Emily face. "I told him the other night that I'm really happy for you both Em. Everyone knows you guys are meant for each other. You shouldn't hide that."

Emily smiled. Claudia was right, she shouldn't have to hide how she felt. She'd already done that for far too many years.

"Crap is that the time," Claudia said, glancing at her watch. "I've got to run and get the kids from school."

She stood and grabbed her handbag from the new dining table.

"I'm so glad I came over today," Claudia said, looking at her friend with a smile.

"I am too," Emily replied, relief and contentment settling comfortably in her chest. "I really missed you…"

Emily continued, "I have for a really long time."

The two women embraced. A hug that was well overdue and spanned a distance of 10 years.

"I'll give you a call later," Claudia said, as she made her way down the hall and to the front door.

"I'd love that," Emily said, waving to her friend as she walked down the drive towards her car.

Leaning against the door jam, watching Claudia drive away, Emily wondered how her life had become so messy and complicated… and wonderful.

Chapter 22

Stepping off the plane in the early hours of the morning, Luca took a long, deep breath, taking in the warm LA air, and stretched his aching muscles. He needed to train… badly. Collecting his bags, he made his way to the airport parking lot where his car had been sitting since the beginning of the week. Throwing his bags in the back, he climbed in the driver's side, fired up the Ford Ranger and headed onto the highway towards home. As he drove along, he thought about all the amazing experiences he'd had in New York. He'd barely had any time to himself for the whole week. From media sessions with reporters from boxing TV shows to online bloggers from every country in the world, Luca was asked every question known to man. The questions around his fighting he'd been able to answer easily. How long had he been fighting; how long had he wanted to be world champion; where did he train; who was his coach.

He answered each and every question honestly and respectfully. But when it came to personal questions, about his family, his childhood, his children, if he was seeing anyone… Luca found himself answering with vague responses. It wasn't that he was afraid or ashamed of his personal life; it was that he hadn't asked any of them if they wanted to be caught up in his whirlwind. His parents hadn't asked to be named on TV, Claudia certainly hadn't expected to have her name, or their children's names plastered online. And Emily… how could he talk to reporters about what he and Emily had, when he wasn't even quite sure what that was himself? Best friends; partners; lovers? It was much easier to stay mysterious and not give away too much information.

As Luca pulled into his parents' street, he thought back to the phone call he'd made to them the night before. They'd been so happy to hear from him, and to hear all about his contract signing, media interviews and sponsorship deals. Mireya was particularly excited to hear that her son would be in the local newspaper before the end of the week, after an LA based journalist flew over the NYC to interview him. Luca joked with the guy that he could have just come around to his home for a beer and a chat any time he liked. While Luca spoke to his parents, Mireya told him that Carmen was finally being discharged from the hospital. She had met all her rehabilitation goals and was ready to head home. Luca imagined Emily's reaction when she'd heard the news. He wished he'd been there to see it. Mireya told him that Carmen would be home later the next afternoon, and if she felt well enough Emily was planning a housewarming party and a welcome home party as an all in one, at her new place. Luca was really looking forward to seeing Emily. He'd been thinking about her more and more while he was away. Every day he saw something or thought about something that reminded him of her. It was exactly like when she'd first moved away… everything reminded him of her, even things that weren't things. Only this time, he wasn't planning on letting her out of his sight.

Pulling into the driveway at his parents' place, and killing the engine, Luca was pleasantly surprised by the two little boys sitting on his parents' front steps. Riley and Joey stood and cheered when they saw their dad pull up. They'd woken up especially early to welcome him home. As he climbed out of his truck, they both ran as fast as their feet would take them and launched at Luca. He caught them both mid-flight and swung them around while they squealed.

"I think I've caught myself a couple of little pigs here," he said to his mother, who stood in the frame of the front door.

Joey began giggling, saying "No Dad it's us, Riley and Joey!"

Luca smiled at Riley and winked. "Phew Jo, lucky you told me that… I was just about to sell you to the butchers for bacon!"

Joey pretended to scream and try to get away, as Riley climbed down and put his arms around his dad's waist to walk with him into the house. Putting down the wriggling Joey, Luca gave his mum a big hug.

"Welcome home baby," Mireya said warmly.

"Thanks Mum," Luca replied, "It's good to be home." He meant it too.

"So," Luca said, turning to Riley and Joey who both stood in the living room together, "what trouble have you two caused while I've been away?"

The boys glanced at each other suspiciously. Riley, much older and wiser, muttered to his little brother, "don't say anything."

Joey, who missed the subtlety in the gesture, turned to his father and said in a matter of fact tone, "we didn't do anything naughty… except we broke Mum's boyfriends' phone."

Luca stifled a laugh as his father walked into the house.

"Luca, welcome home," he said, shaking his son's hand.

"Hey Dad, good to see you. How have you been?"

Carlos nodded and said abruptly, "Good, real good."

Luca smiled at his father. It used to bother him that he never really talked to him when he was younger. Luca would ask him for advice, for direction and he would receive a one or two word response. For a long time, Luca felt cheated by it. Now that he was older, a man himself, he understood that his father was a man of few words. He was an honourable and honest man who worked hard every day of his life. He just didn't like to talk about it, and that was fine. Luca told Carlos all about his trip and all the amazing things he'd seen. He sat quietly listening and occasionally nodding. As Luca finished describing his media day, Carlos stood up and said,

"Great son, I'll be outside," and proceeded to leave the house.

Luca smiled and shook his head.

"You know he's very proud of you don't you," Mireya said to her son. Luca smiled and nodded.

Luca spent the morning just hanging around with his boys. They threw a football in the yard, had a few rounds of hide and seek, and made a pillow fort in his room. All the while, Luca listened intently to his sons talking about things that they loved; things they were interested in. From cartoons they'd watched the day before, to toys they'd seen on TV commercials. Luca made a point of listening carefully to both boys, making mental notes for each. He'd made a promise to himself in New York; that once he fought, and came home with his paycheque, he was going to spoil them both rotten. To make up for all the birthdays and Christmas's he'd only been able to buy them something small. To make up for all the nights he wasn't there to tuck them in and read them a bedtime story. He was going to make it all up to them… and then some.

"Ok Dad, it's your turn to find us," Riley called, as both boys got ready to hide in the yard.

Turning to face the wall, Luca began counting. "1, 2, 3… 22, 23, 24…" when he reached 30, he turned and began scouting the yard for his little people.

After a few minutes, he came across Riley wedged between the BBQ and the wall.

"Got ya bud," he said laughing, as Riley wiggled out of the tiny space.

"Lucky you're not claustrophobic," he remarked, as Riley turned to help look for Joey.

They both walked around and around the yard for what felt like 20 minutes, looking in every conceivable hiding space in the yard. The kid's good at this game, Luca thought as they looked. It was at the point when they'd done their 3rd lap of the yard, that panic set in for Luca. Joey wasn't hiding in the yard; he was sure of it. They'd literally looked in every corner of the place and he wasn't there. Trying to sound calm and not scare Riley, who also looked worried at that point, Luca called out,

"Joey… you win buddy. Time to come out now."

Both Luca and Riley stood perfectly still listening for a response; a noise… anything. Luca was about to run inside and alert his mother to the fact that he'd probably lost his youngest son, when a faint sound triggered recognition in the back of Luca's mind. It was a very quiet squeaking noise. A noise he'd heard probably a million times before. But it wasn't coming from his yard. It was coming from the yard next door… from Carmen and Jose's garden.

"Come on Ry, I know where the little troublemaker's gone," Luca said, jogging towards the back gate that separated the two properties.

Luca felt a mixture of relief and enthusiasm. Relief that he hadn't lost his five year old, and enthusiasm at the potential of seeing Emily for the first time in a week. He wasn't sure if she'd be there, now that her own place had been completed. He'd thought a lot on the plane ride home, about heading straight to her place after he flew in, and he almost had. But after he'd spoken to his parents the night before and heard that Carmen was being discharged and was heading home at some point that day, Luca decided to give Emily some space. To give her time to help her mother settle in and feel comfortable at home. He didn't want to interrupt her family time or make her choose to see him, over her mother. That didn't sit right with him. He knew how important her family was to her. And anyway, he'd see her tonight at her housewarming party if it went ahead.

Arriving in Carmen and Jose's yard, Luca and Riley made a beeline for the old tree standing in the corner of the yard where Joey sat swinging back and forth.

Seeing his father and brother approach, Joey said simply, "Did I win?"

Luca, only mildly irritated at the scare his youngest son had given him, replied, "You're lucky I don't whoop your butt for taking off out of the yard like that."

Realising he sounded very much like his own father, and seeing the deflated look on his son's face, Luca continued, "But you got us buddy… you won the game."

Joey's face lit up as he realised he'd beaten his father... and his big brother.

"Dad, can you push us on the swing?" Riley asked, as he walked over and sat down next to Joey.

Luca hesitated. He thought they should probably get moving, since Carmen would need some rest if she was home, and the squeak from the swing was definitely not conducive to peaceful rest.

But seeing the hopeful look on the boys faces, Luca replied, "Well… maybe just for a few minutes. We don't want to interrupt Mr and Mrs Rodrigues."

As he stood pushing his boys on the same swing that he'd spent his childhood playing on, he heard the sliding door behind him open. Turning towards the sound, he found himself looking up at the one person he was looking forward to seeing more than anyone. Emily was home. Behind her, Carmen walked slowly out onto the back-deck area, smiling her fabulous, warm, kind smile. Luca looked at Emily and saw the joy on her face, the sheer happiness that emanated from her.

"Luca Mendes… fancy finding you here," Carmen said smiling.

"You know it's my favourite place in the entire world," Luca replied, walking up to Carmen and giving her a kiss on the cheek.

In reply, Carmen wrapped her arms around him and gave him a gentle squeeze.

"I see you have some off siders with you today," Carmen continued, as she looked down to the swing that had hung in her yard for as long as they had lived there.

Jose had put it up the very first weekend after they'd moved in… and it had hung there proudly ever since.

"Your yard is really cool Mrs Rodrigues," Riley said happily,

"Yeah it's like an awesome jungle," Joey contributed, "Can we go exploring?"

Joey looked hopefully from Luca to Carmen.

Carmen replied, "Sure can boys… I hear the gremlins that used to live in the vegetable patch still lurk around in the shadows sometimes, so make sure you keep your eyes peeled."

Riley and Joey looked at each other incredulously and high fived. As they ran off to explore the yard, Luca heard Riley say to his little brother,

"Stay close to me bro, I'll protect you."

He couldn't remember ever feeling prouder of his eldest son.

Laughing at the sweet boys as they ran off, Carmen looked around her yard. It was a jungle indeed, she thought to herself. Only a few weeks earlier, she remembered standing in the exact same spot, feeling frustrated at the look of the space. Now, after everything she'd been through, everything that had occurred, she couldn't imagine wanting it looking any differently. It was her favourite place. She took a deep, cleansing breath, taking in all the pungent perfumes; the gorgeous smell of summer. The beautiful flowers, varieties of fruit and vegetables almost ready to be picked. It was a stark contrast to the white walls and clinical smell of the hospital wards she'd been sitting in for weeks. Carmen couldn't wait to get down into the gardens and get her hands dirty. She had thought about it, dreamt about it for the entire time she'd been away.

'It's the small things we take for granted,' she thought to herself, as she looked at her daughter.

Standing there next to her, Emily's attention was certainly not with her mother. Carmen noticed the exchange of smiles between the Luca and Emily.

"I might head inside and have a rest," Carmen said, sensing Emily and Luca might need some time alone. "Luca, can you let your Mum know I'm home and ready for visitors whenever she'd like to walk next door."

Luca nodded, as Carmen smiled and turned slowly, walking back into the house, and closing the door behind her. Luca stood looking at Emily, not sure what move to make.

"Hi," was all he managed to get out.

Emily smiled and replied, "Hi to you too."

An awkward silence overtook the space, as the sound of the Luca's boys exploring the yard floated up towards them.

"They sound like they're having fun," Emily said smiling.

Luca nodded, not taking his eyes off her.

"They seem pretty happy to have you home too," she continued.

Luca replied abruptly, "What about you Em, are you happy to see me?"

Emily looked at him standing at the other end of the deck. She didn't need to think before she responded, "Of course I missed you Luc. It's been driving me nuts not seeing you or talking to you these past few days. Which is ridiculous when you think about it… I mean, it's only been a week. We went without talking for 10 years… and I've been crazy over seven days!"

Emily laughed at the absurdity of what she was saying. Luca smiled too; a feeling of satisfaction overcoming him at the realisation that she had missed him just as much as he'd missed her.

"I can't wait to hear all about your trip," Emily said, "Your Mum said you were signing a fight contract?"

Satisfaction quickly turned to remorse, as Luca realised he hadn't told Emily anything about where he'd been and what he'd done.

Taking a deep breath, he turned and walked to the swing. Gesturing for Emily to join him, he waited for her to walk down the steps and settle next to him. Instinctively, Luca leant over and kissed her on the top of the head, a gesture he'd done a hundred times before, but one that gave Emily an instant sense of calm and peace. He was home.

"Em, before you say anything… I really need to apologise to you," Luca said, placing his hand under her chin and lifting her face to look at his.

Looking into her eyes, he continued, "I've been really unfair to you lately. I should never have driven off on you the other weekend. I should have talked to you, explained everything to you. I owed you that. Instead, I left you standing there all alone. That was wrong of me and I feel like complete shit for it."

Emily listened to Luca talk, wanting to tell him that it was ok; that she didn't mind, but he went on,

"When I got the call to fly to New York the first person I wanted to tell was you. I knew how excited you'd be… how happy you'd be for me. I was planning to come by to see you on my way to the airport. I went to see John to apologise to him for being an idiot, and I went to see Claudia to try and smooth things over with her…"

Emily smiled as she realised that Luca didn't know that Claudia had filled her in on the conversation herself.

"And then before I knew it, I had 20 minutes to be at the airport or I'd miss my plane. But I need you to know I was coming to see you Em… I didn't forget about you."

Emily nodded, wishing she'd known this all a week ago to save herself the worry.

"Then in New York, I'd planned to call you so many times. I dialled your number so many times… but things just kept getting in the way. Meetings, events… my own stupid thoughts. I wanted to talk to you so badly… but I wanted to tell you everything in person, not over the phone. I wanted to see your face when I told you I signed a contract to fight for the world title… in three weeks."

Surprise took hold of Emily's face as she grinned and grabbed Luca's hand.

"Are you serious?" she said incredulously, hardly able to control her happiness.

Luca nodded and smiled. Her reaction was exactly why he'd waited to tell her in person.

"You are so important to me Em. The most important person in my whole world; you and the boys mean everything to me. I should have told you a long time ago. I need you to hear it now. I don't want us to dance around each other anymore. I don't want us to be sort of anything, or kind of something. I know what I want now; I've wanted it for a while."

Emily looked at Luca, as he said the words she'd been waiting to hear,

"I want to be with you Em. Just you. And not as friends… I want more for us. I want everything. I love you Emily."

Emily smiled and placing her hand on his cheek, replied simply, "I love you too."

As Luca leant over to kiss the girl of his dreams, the sound of two little voices echoed from the bushes behind them, "Eww."

Chapter 23

The party was in full swing when Luca arrived with his boys. Emily had left him and the kids in the early afternoon to head home and get ready for the party. She'd needed to do a final clean-up of the house, cook a few dishes, and set everything up exactly how she wanted it. Not only would Luca be seeing the place completed for the first time, furniture and all, but so would his parents, and her own parents. Emily hadn't wanted to show the place to her father while her mother had been hospitalised; she'd wanted them both to see it together. As well as her family, Emily had invited Ricky and his wife Rachael, and Claudia. She'd hesitated at first about inviting her, since she hadn't spoken to Luca yet about seeing Claudia earlier in the week. She hadn't mentioned it today either. She'd been meaning to bring it up… but he was so excited about his New York trip, so enthusiastic about his fight, that she hadn't wanted to drag drama into the conversation. Even now, as she stood in her kitchen putting together the final pieces on her plates of nibbles, she was nervous about how Luca would react to Claudia's attendance. She hoped they would all get along ok. It was the first time they would all be in the same house since Emily left for university, all those years before. It's time, Emily thought to herself, time long overdue.

The first knock at the door came around 6pm. Ricky and Rachael walked down the hall and into the living area at the back of the house as Emily finished putting food on the dining table.

"Emily, this place is amazing," Rachael said, the two ladies embracing.

"Thank you, I'm so happy you guys could make it," Emily replied happily.

"Any excuse for a night out and away from the little muffins," Rachael said laughing.

"Got any alcohol?" Ricky asked, heading for the fridge.

Rachael rolled her eyes dramatically. "Anyone would think he hadn't had a beer in 20 years or something," she said laughing.

Emily smiled as Ricky took a beer from the fridge and cracked it open.

"So, who else are we expecting at this fancy gathering then?" Ricky said, taking a seat on the new couch.

"Well," Emily replied, "my parents, Luca's parents, Luca and his boys…" she paused, "and Claudia."

Ricky's eyebrows instantly headed north as the look of surprise overcame him.

"Claudia? Really?" he said, with an inquisitive tone.

He nodded thoughtfully as he took another sip of his beer.

"Don't pay any attention to him," Rachael said, casting her husband an exasperated look. "I think it's great that you're all catching up again after so many years. Ricky talks all the time about the adventures you all had together."

As if on cue, the sound of footprints echoed down the hallway as Claudia appeared in the living area. Smiling and holding a bottle of champagne, she walked over the Emily and gave her a big hug.

"A little housewarming gift," she said warmly.

"Oooooh, let's get this party started," Rachael said with obvious enthusiasm, as she walked to the kitchen and started looking through cupboards for glasses.

"Dear god, my wife's going to get plastered," Ricky said sarcastically, as he got up to hug Claudia.

Emily and Luca's parents arrived together shortly after, travelling in the same car. Walking carefully into the house, Carmen took her time, walking from room to room as she made her way down the hall. She looked at each space and admired the furnishings and finishes. As she entered the living area, she was pleasantly surprised by the amount of work Emily had obviously put into the room. Not having visited for over a month due to her hospital stay, Carmen could really see the changes that had taken place. From the walls that were removed in the kitchen to open up the space, to the extension of the living room and inclusion of the glass sliding doors that opened up to extend the space out onto the deck and into the yard. She especially loved the choices Emily had made with her furniture. Crisp and clean lines; small pops of colour throughout the rooms. Carmen couldn't imagine a space that epitomised her daughter better than this one. Emily walked towards her mother with arms outstretched.

Giving her a gently hug, Carmen said, "Em, this place is beautiful. You've done such a wonderful job."

Mireya, Carlos, and her father Jose agreeing that the house was perfect for Emily.

Without warning, a thunderous sound came hurtling down the hallway as two little boys with boundless energy appeared in the living area.

"Holy moly," Emily said as they entered, "I thought you two were a herd of elephants coming to trample my house!"

Riley and Joey laughed and stopped in their tracks. With a look of great surprise, both boys raced over to the other side of the room. Claudia, standing talking to Rachael about the beautiful floors in Emily's home, put down her wine glass to embrace her boys.

"Mum! What are you doing here?" Riley asked, looking both perplexed and immensely happy.

He turned to look hesitantly at his father, who had just appeared at the end of the hallway. Surprise also overcame Luca as he saw his ex-partner standing in his girlfriend's house.

"Hi Claud," he said, looking first at Claudia and then to Emily. "I didn't expect to see you here."

Emily held her breath, wondering what on earth had gotten into her, inviting both Claudia and Luca to a party without telling each one the other would be present.

"I couldn't let you have all the fun, could I?" Claudia replied happily, "And anyway, Emily was *my* best friend more than she ever was yours."

Surprised by her response, Luca opened his mouth to reply, but seeing the look of apprehension on Emily's face, he decided against the sarcastic response sitting on the tip of his tongue.

"Well… the more the merrier I say," he replied instead, smiling at Emily and giving her a look that he hoped she read as 'it's all good.'

Emily turned and walked into the kitchen, busying herself with preparing everything for dinner. She felt so nervous; so overwhelmed; she wasn't sure how she was possibly going to manage to have a good time. Luca walked into the kitchen behind her and seeing the look of terror on her face, took her by the hand, leading her into the hallway. Turning and looking up into his eyes, Emily searched for a sign that everything was going to be ok.

Sensing the tension in her body language, Luca kissed her on the forehead and said quietly, "I'm glad you invited her Em. It makes sense."

Emily closed her eyes and exhaled. Instantly she felt a little better. Placing her arms around his neck, she leant up on her toes to kiss him lightly. His arms tightened around her waist as the world spun around her. She was so glad he was home; glad that he was here with her.

"Emily, where do I find the…"

Turning into the hallway, searching for the host, Mireya found Luca and Emily instead. She laughed, turned on her heels and disappeared back into the kitchen.

"Don't worry, I'll find it myself," she quipped.

Emily looked up at Luca and said quietly, "I feel so out of my depth. Like at any minute everything is about to go to shit. I so want everyone to have fun. I want our family and friends to love this place as much as I do. It's really important to me Luc."

Luca smiled and stroked her cheek.

"Nothing is going to go to shit; you've got everything under control. *We've* got everything under control. I'm here to help Em. And anyway, you've run whole emergency departments… you can organise a dinner party with our families. I believe in you."

He smiled and kissed her again. She believed him. She could do this. As laughter and conversation echoed down the hallway, Emily took Luca by the hand and led him into the kitchen to help cut up some hors d'oeuvres.

Long after Emily and Luca's parents had left for home, and the kids had been set up in front of the TV in the spare room, Emily sat at the table on her outdoor deck, surrounded by Luca, Claudia, Ricky and Rachael. Listening to Rachael describe her shock and exasperation at finding her three year old twins covered in nappy rash cream after working out how to open the jar earlier in the day, Emily smiled, enjoying the atmosphere and company of friends. The dinner had been an enormous success; all the food was delicious, and her first attempt at cooking in her new kitchen had been victorious. Nothing had burnt, or under cooked. The kids even seemed to enjoy the food, which Emily discovered was apparently a big deal. Sitting now, after all the work was done, Emily thought back to old times.

"How long's it been since we did this?" Ricky asked, as if reading Emily's mind.

The friends looked around at each other and shrugged.

"The last time I remember us all together was the night before Emily left," Claudia said.

"That's right," Ricky replied, "We spent the night sitting in her parent's backyard, taking turns on that damn swing."

Emily smiled and looked at Luca. That damn swing was still well and truly in use.

"God that was such a long time ago," Luca said, reflecting on all the time that had passed since.

"Hey Luc, do you remember the time you and Ricky tried to jump that BMX off old man Johnsons roof? We would have been about 14, I think?" Claudia said, a huge smile plastered on her face.

"Yeah, and I remember the time you and Ricky put firecrackers in his mailbox and blew the whole thing to pieces," Luca laughed as he thought back.

"It sounds to me," Rachael said, trying to sound stern, "that the common denominator in all of these stories… is my husband."

Everyone laughed as Ricky pretended to be offended.

"Whatever happened to Mr Johnson?" Emily asked.

"He died Em. A few years back." Luca replied sombrely. "A nice young family bought the house. I think they have about five kids?"

Claudia nodded, adding, "Their eldest is in Riley's class at school."

Silence fell over the group as memories swirled around all their minds.

"So much has changed around the place," Emily said, thinking about all the shops and spaces that had been knocked down, built, or replaced.

"But there's so much that's still the same," Claudia replied, smiling at Emily. "Do you remember that ice cream place near the pier?" she asked.

Emily nodded, remembering all the summers they'd ridden their bikes to buy ice-cream.

"Well it's still there, and the old guy who owned it is still working there."

"But he was old when we were young! Or at least he seemed old," Emily said laughing.

"Although I guess now, we're probably looking old to any teenagers we walk past."

Ricky, Rachael, Claudia, and Luca all smiled knowingly.

"The gym's still the same too isn't it Luca," Ricky asked, looking at his friend.

"It sure is," Luca replied. "Other than a few new pieces of equipment and an extra boxing ring, the old girl is exactly the same as the time you came to training and nearly died of exhaustion."

Luca laughed, as Ricky rolled his eyes. Turning to his wife he remarked,

"He's lying. He's just jealous because I was better than him at boxing."

Everyone laughed as Ricky again pretended to be insulted by their reaction.

"How is your boxing going Luc?" Claudia asked. "What happened in New York?"

Luca sat up straight in his chair and began describing his trip and what he'd done. He talked about the hotel and the limousines and all the expensive stuff he'd experienced. As he spoke, Emily was reminded of her time in North Carolina. Of the expensive dinners and parties she'd attended. She found herself smiling as she recognised again just how different Luca was from her ex Michael. Luca marvelled at the gold lettering he'd seen on cutlery at the restaurant he'd been taken to, and the feel of the expensive towels in the hotel; things that Michael wouldn't have batted an eyelid at. Noticing the smile on Emily face, Luca leaned over and took her hand, giving it a squeeze. From the other side of the table, Claudia pretended to make a vomiting noise as she laughed.

"Very mature," Luca said sarcastically, trying not to laugh himself.

"Well, on that note, I'd better hit the road," Claudia said, standing up and straightening her skirt. "When did you want me to grab the boy's tomorrow?" she asked Luca.

"Anytime Claud, I really don't mind," he replied.

As if utilising ESP, both Riley and Joey came running out onto the deck to their mother.

"Dad can we go home with Mum tonight?" Riley asked sweetly.

"Why's that bud?" Luca replied.

"The kids next door, they have a new puppy…" Riley continued, "and they said we could go and pat it when we got home… and play with it tomorrow morning."

Luca looked at Claudia and shrugged his shoulders.

"It's up to your Mum boys," he said. "Maybe she wants a night off?"

Claudia smiled, impressed that Luca had considered that she might like some time to herself.

"Its fine with me," Claudia responded.

Her boys certainly drove her crazy sometimes, and she loved that they were spending time with their dad, but she missed them when they were away and she was always happy to have them home, tucked into bed where she knew they were safe.

"Well let's hit the road then troops. Give your Dad a hug and make sure you say thank you to Emily for having us."

Hugs and thank you's were exchanged between all parties as Claudia stopped to give Emily the biggest one of all.

"Thanks for tonight Em. I really had a wonderful time."

Emily smiled and replied, "Me too. Can we do coffee next week?"

Claudia nodded and promised to call Emily in a few days. Waving the whole way down the hall, the boys left with their mother, off home to bed.

"We should probably head off too," Ricky said, looking at his wife regretfully.

"I think we can stay for a little while longer," Rachael replied, "Since we don't get out very often."

Ricky smiled and took his wife's hand, kissing it lightly.

"Did anyone want another drink?" Emily asked, as she stood and made her way into the house.

A resounding yes came from all three friends sitting at the table. Returning with some beers and the other half of the champagne bottle, Emily sat back down next to Luca and poured herself and Rachael a drink.

"What are your plans now that you've finished the house Em," Rachael said, as she sipped her champagne.

"To be honest, I have no idea," Emily replied honestly. "I've done everything I wanted to do when I arrived home. I'm sort of feeling a bit lost now."

Rachael nodded. "What about work? Have you thought anymore about what you might do?"

Emily recalled chatting to Rachael at the beach months ago about not knowing what to do for work. How nice of her to remember, Emily thought.

"Not really," Emily replied. "When I first moved home, I got some calls from local hospitals with job offers; but I just wasn't in the right head space to even consider them. And they're all filled now."

Emily had made some inquiries after Michael had visited; just to double check. She couldn't reconcile taking a pity job that her ex had organised for her; no matter how good it might be. She needed to stand on her own two feet and find her own path.

"Claudia was talking the other day about an old GP practice near her work," Emily continued. "Apparently it shut down after the Doctor who owned it retired. But I'm not sure it's right for me."

Rachael nodded. "I know the one you mean. I used to take the kids there. And my parents used to see the doctor there. It was a great practice. Really busy, and a real community feel about it. It was sad when it closed down."

Rachael paused, thinking. "There are still some elderly neighbours of ours who have no doctor. They've tried to find someone else, but there aren't any other doctors in the area for about half an hour. They all just end up going to the emergency department. It's sad really."

Emily knew what she meant. Working in emergency departments, it wasn't uncommon for elderly patients to present with minor issues. When asked, they would say they either couldn't afford to see their doctor, or there wasn't one in town. It was a real problem.

"She'll work something out," Luca chimed in, smiling at Emily, "she always finds a way."

He winked at her, as he took a sip of his beer.

"Of all the people I've ever known," Ricky agreed, "you've always been the one that I knew would do amazing things, Em. We all knew you would. Luca, remember that time you fell off the roof of that old abandoned house we were trying to… visit?"

Ricky looked at his wife apprehensively as she shook her head.

Luca laughed, "Yeah I remember. I thought I broke my damn arm and limped home crying."

Ricky glanced at Emily, "and who fixed you up, and told you to stop being a moron?"

Luca smiled at Emily as he said, "My best friend; the super doctor."

Emily smiled. She hadn't realised how good it would feel to be with her friends again. Now that she knew, she wasn't going to leave it so long to do it again.

"So… no kids hey?" Luca said, as Emily put away the last of the dishes into the kitchen cupboards after Ricky and Rachael had left for home.

Emily smiled, having been thinking the exact same thing as she'd washed up.

"I guess we'll get a good night's rest then," Emily replied innocently, trying not to give away a laugh.

"Oh hell no," Luca responded, as he grabbed her around the waist and turned her to face him.

Kissing her passionately as they stood in the centre of the kitchen, Luca drew away long enough to whisper in her ear, "There will definitely be no sleeping in this house tonight."

Emily stifled a giggle, as Luca picked her up over his shoulder, as if she were light as a feather, and carried her towards the bedroom.

Chapter 24

Emily woke to the sounds of birds calling in the oak tree outside her room. Light pierced through the blinds, creating patterns on her wall as she rolled onto her back and stretched out, her hand resting on Luca's bare back. She smiled as she thought about him sleeping next to her last night. Next to her; on top of her, she smirked. It had been a night she would never forget for the rest of her life. Luca had shown her love; tenderness; passion, like she had never experienced before, but was looking forward to experiencing again. She closed her eyes and sighed happily. Laying there in her room, in the incredible house that she'd created, next to a man that she'd loved for as long as she could remember, Emily felt centred; calm. For the first time in 10 years, she felt completely at peace.

'If only I could bottle this feeling,' she thought to herself.

Luca began to stir. Rolling onto his back, he looked over at Emily and smiled; a smile she'd never seen before.

"Hi," he said lazily, stretching out and rolling over towards her, wrapping his arms and legs around her.

"Good morning," she replied smiling.

"It is isn't it?" Luca said, kissing her on the forehead.

"How did you sleep?" he asked, kissing her cheek, her neck.

Emily found it difficult to concentrate on what he was asking her, as his hands slowly stroked up and down her back.

"What was the question again?" she asked laughing.

Smiling, Luca pulled away and looked into her eyes. "I asked how you slept?"

Emily nodded, thinking back to the hours they had spent not sleeping.

"I slept just fine," she replied, "when I finally went to sleep."

Luca laughed and said, "Would you rather we had slept all night then?"

Emily shook her head and wrapped her arms around his waist.

"Hell no," she said as she kissed his collarbone.

He felt so strong beneath her touch.

"We should probably get up and have some breakfast," Emily said, looking at her watch. "Or maybe some lunch," she said laughing.

"Or…" Luca replied with a glint in his eye, "we could just stay here all day and work up an appetite."

Smiling, Luca rolled over until he was on top of Emily. As she kissed him, she felt the need to satisfy a different appetite.

Laying together hours later, Emily thought she felt brave enough to tell him about Michael. Even though it terrified her.

"Luc, I need to talk to you about something. About someone."

Luca lay next to her, still marvelling at how good she smelled, how good her skin felt against his. Nuzzling into her neck he began kissing her slowly, not really paying attention to what she was saying.

"Luca!" Emily said more assertively, catching his attention this time.

"Sorry… go ahead, I'm listening," he said, noticing the serious look on her face.

Emily took a deep breath. She so desperately wanted him to understand, wanted him to be ok with her past. Sensing the mood change, Luca leant back and rested his head on the pillow, looking at her face intently.

"I know we've talked about North Carolina, about my work and my studies while I was there," Emily began.

Luca nodded. "But there was something else I need to tell you about, something I haven't mentioned before."

She looked into his eyes, searching.

"Em… just spit it out," Luca said, now mildly concerned.

"I need to tell you about someone I was seeing when I lived in North Carolina; someone I was living with."

Luca raised his eyebrows in surprise. This was something new. He'd always assumed that Emily had dated while she'd lived in North Carolina. During that same period of time he himself had lived with Claudia and had two children. He wasn't naïve enough to hope that she'd spent 10 years away without seeing anyone.

"You've never mentioned anyone," he said simply.

Emily nodded, saying, "I know. And I'm sorry I didn't say anything. I wanted to, believe me. I don't want you to think I was keeping anything from you or being deceitful."

Luca smiled. "Em, of all the people I've ever met in my life, you would be the last person I would ever call deceitful."

Emily smiled with relief, as she started at the beginning and told her story. From meeting Michael, to dating and eventually living together. She told Luca about her engagement, about how he made her feel insignificant; about their cool and calm dynamic. While she talked Luca lay quietly listening. Emily noticed he wasn't really showing any sort of emotion as she talked and wondered what he was thinking.

Luca *was* thinking. About what sort of an idiot would let the most beautiful girl in the world walk away. What kind of moron made Emily feel unloved, unimportant. What kind of man made an independent, confident, and exceptionally intelligent woman feel like she wasn't good enough; wasn't capable of making her way in the world the way she wanted. At that moment, Luca understood Emily's hesitation at finding work; at working in the medical profession again. From where he lay,

Luca could see that Michael had damaged Emily's self-confidence; her self-belief. It made him furious. What I wouldn't give for five minutes in a room with that guy, Luca thought to himself.

Emily finished talking and looked at him with anticipation. He hadn't said a word since she'd started talking. What if he was angry at her? What if telling him about Michael had altered his impression of her? What if he didn't want her anymore? Panic began welling up inside her as Luca lay quietly, putting together his thoughts.

"You can say something now," Emily said tentatively, not really sure if she was ready for what he was going to say.

"I'm just thinking," Luca replied, "about what kind of drop kick loser would ever let you go."

Emily was surprised by his response. She was sure he was going to tell her he didn't want to be with her anymore. Luca noticed her surprise and laughed. "Were you waiting for me to jump up and run out of the room screaming?"

Emily smiled, a timid smile and nodded.

"Sorry to disappoint you honey," Luca continued, "but you can't get rid of me that easily."

Emily closed her eyes. When she opened them again Luca was looking at her intently.

"Emily, I love you. You know that. There's nothing you could ever tell me that would change how I feel about you. No skeletons from your past that would make me think any differently about you. I know you. I've known you all my life. And I know your character. The way that guy treated you makes me want to beat his head in. How he could let you feel like you weren't good enough for him, not good enough to be a doctor… it just makes me so damn angry. You are an incredible, loving, giving person. You've been a doctor since we were little, whether you had the piece of paper or not. Remember that time I broke my ankle, and our parents were away? You picked me up off the ground, wrapped me up and called 911 while I sat thinking I was dying. You took care of your mother when she had her heart attack. You were incredible Em. I've never seen anything like it."

Emily snuggled into Luca's shoulder as she pondered how much she wished she'd heard those words a few months ago. How hearing them now meant so much to her. How Luca meant so much to her. She felt stronger with him; braver. Like no matter what the world threw at her, she could face it.

"Thank you," she whispered.

Taking her head in his hands, Luca looked into Emily's eyes.

"Don't ever doubt how much you mean to me Em," he said honestly.

"You deserve everything in the world that you've ever wanted. Don't ever think any different."

Emily smiled and replied, "you do too Luc. I can't wait to see you fight in a couple of weeks. I can't wait to cheer you on."

Luca looked at Emily with a cheeky grin.

"You know," he said, "I could use some help with my cardio…"

Giggling, Emily leaned over and kissed him as her stomach grumbled loudly.

"But on second thought, we should probably go get something to eat," Luca said as he felt the sudden lurch in his own stomach.

He hadn't eaten in over 12 hours and knew he needed to keep fuelling his body leading up to his fight. Luca stood and began hunting around the room for his clothes. Sitting up and reaching for her shirt, Emily was about to get out of bed when her phone rang.

"Hey Em," Carmen said, as Emily struggled to concentrate on the voice at the other end of the phone.

Her attention was diverted to the good-looking man dressing in front of her.

"Hi Mum, how are you?" Emily said distracted, rolling over onto her stomach so she wasn't looking at Luca.

"I'm great honey. I just wanted to say how much your father and I enjoyed your party last night. And how much I appreciate you getting everyone together. It was such a fun night."

Emily smiled. "It was, wasn't it," she replied, thinking back to dinner, everyone chatting and laughing around her dining table.

"What are you up to today?" Emily asked her mum.

"Actually, I'm heading back to the hospital soon," Carmen said lightly.

Concern replaced Emily's good mood as she began to worry that something had happened to her mother.

"Why? What's wrong?" she asked, sitting up straight.

Luca, seeing Emily's body language change, lay back down on the bed next to her, listening in on the conversation.

"There's nothing wrong Em, please don't stress," Carmen replied. "I just have some check-ups to get done."

Emily looked to Luca, confused.

"But why don't you just get them done with your doctor? Why the need to go to the hospital?"

"Well I would have done that," Carmen said, "except my doctor retired and the medical practice closed down so now I go to the emergency department for my check-ups. They don't mind Em. We just have to wait for a few hours, so I always take a good book to read."

Emily frowned and sat up. This GP thing was becoming a regular topic in her life; a consistent theme since she'd decided not to take the job

Michael had organised for her. In the back of her mind, she wondered if the universe might be giving her a sign.

"Well can I come and sit with you at the hospital then?" Emily asked, still processing things in her mind.

Surely there was another doctor's surgery in the area? She needed to do some investigating.

"No, no its fine. Your father has taken the day off work to come with me. We're going to do some shopping afterwards. Speaking of your father, he's calling out to me now, so I'll have to go. I'll see you soon my beautiful girl. Enjoy your day,"

As an afterthought, Emily heard her say, "And tell Luca I said hi," as she laughed, and ended the call.

"What are you thinking in that beautiful head?" Luca asked, catching Emily deep in thought.

She smiled and said, "Do you ever find certain things keep coming up in your life… and no matter what you do, it just keeps appearing?"

Luca nodded in agreement. "Absolutely. That's happened to me a few times. I find, ignoring it or pretending it's not there, sometimes makes it worse."

Emily nodded. "You know the other weekend when you were in New York and Claudia came around?" Luca nodded.

Emily continued, "So we were talking about my work… or lack of work, and Claudia mentioned a doctor's surgery that closed down in her office block. She said lots of people were left without a GP and have to go to the emergency department and wait hours for simple things that a GP could fix."

Luca started to see the wheels turning in Emily's head.

"That's really sad for those people," he said.

"I know," she replied, "That's what I thought. It's really unfair that people in our community don't have a local doctor that they can see. In an emergency department, you can end up seeing a different doctor every time you go in. They don't know the persons history or what happened to them in the past. It's one of the things that used to frustrate me the most working in North Carolina. It didn't matter what we did, we never had enough information about our patients from their actual lives outside of the hospital."

Luca nodded, understanding.

"So… then at dinner last night Rachael mentioned that she used to take her kids there and her parents went there, but they don't have anywhere to go anymore."

Luca raised his eyebrows, "that is a coincidence, but it makes sense Em… there aren't many doctors working in this part of town. You have to admit, it's not really attractive for doctors to come and work in one of the poorest areas in LA. No one really has any money to pay their bills and you can bet most people who see a doctor around here have some pretty bad issues."

Emily nodded, realising there wouldn't be a single person from her graduating class at medical school who would have taken on the task.

"Well it gets even stranger. That was my mother on the phone," Emily said. "She just told me that has to go sit at the hospital today because she also doesn't have a doctor, because the same GP practice closed down. Now what are the chances of three different people in my life all going to the same doctor, and all having to go to the hospital because it closed?"

Luca paused. "I'd say it's pretty high Em. I'd say almost all of the people you know in this area were going to that doctor. He was one of the only doctors around who didn't charge stupid high rates for visits. I remember my parents took me there a few times when I was younger for different things."

Emily said, "It's just so unfair Luc. Imagine if a doctor had closed down in some of the better off neighbourhoods in LA. If there were no doctors for people who lived in areas where they made lots of money. There would be public outcry. And yet around here, people just have to do without. Put up with it. It's just not fair."

Emily crossed her arms and pursed her lips, reminding Luca of the time she found out that the high school wasn't recycling, and led a three month crusade to save the earth. He loved seeing her like this.

"Well…" Luca said after a minute, "I guess the only questions is what are you going to do about it?"

Emily looked at him knowingly. She'd been thinking the exact same thing. What *was* she going to do about it? She'd never considered working in any other field than emergency medicine. She wasn't even sure if she could be a good GP. What if she took on the task and failed? What if she let people down?

"You know, whatever you decide to do, I'll be there to support you," Luca said smiling.

Emily nodded. She did know that. She also knew that she needed a challenge, now that she'd finished her house. She also wanted to help the community where she grew up; where she became the person she was today. She needed to do some research.

Chapter 25

A week later, resting lazily on Emily's couch channel surfing, following the end of a great replay of an old boxing match, Luca heard a knock on the door. Emily was out, so Luca stood and made his way down the hall to open the front door. Standing there, was a polished, well-dressed man in an expensive looking suit and tie. He looked to Luca to be a travelling salesman.

Not really interested in buying whatever he was selling, Luca said politely, "Sorry buddy, not interested today."

To his surprise, the man replied with an obvious air of authority, "My name is Dr Michael Matthews. I'm here to see Dr Emily Rodrigues."

Luca was taken aback. This was the guy Emily had dated in North Carolina. The amazing ED consultant. The guy who'd treated her like a possession. Who'd given her up because she didn't match his idea of the perfect wife. Luca instantly disliked him. Tall, dark, and handsome was how many would describe him. Luca thought he better resembled entitled and cocky. With an air about him that reeked expensive. The complete opposite to himself, Luca thought as he looked the guy up and down.

Definitely not Emily's type, he decided as he responded, "Sorry, she's not here at the moment."

Michael didn't move. Instead, he stood with a look of mild irritation on his face and replied, "I'm happy to wait."

Luca, now more than annoyed responded sharply, "I wouldn't bother hey. She's going to be out for another few hours. And to be honest, there's nothing for you to talk to her about. You might as well crawl back under whatever rock you came from, and just leave her the hell alone."

Raising his eyebrows in a look that made Luca want to smack them into the back of his skull, Michael responded without any sign of emotion, "I'm sorry… who were you?"

Luca gritted his teeth and responded, "Not that it's your business but I'm Luca. Luca Mendes."

Recognition dawned on Michael's face as he put two and two together.

"So, you're her little friend from school. She talked about you once or twice when she lived with me. You know we were engaged, don't you?"

Michael said with a sneer. Luca took a deep breath and buried his anger and overwhelming sudden urge to kill the guy. He was sure Emily wouldn't be impressed if he did.

He responded, "Yeah I heard all about it. Now like I said, you can leave now."

Luca turned to slam the door in Michael's face when he heard him reply, "What makes you think you can speak for her? What gives you the right to do her bidding?"

Luca turned and without a second thought, fired back. "What? Like you did? Telling her how to dress, who to speak to, where to work? What makes you think you can walk up to this house and make demands on her? Who the hell do you think you are?"

He continued, "She doesn't want to speak to you. I know that because she's told me that. She doesn't want you in her house. I know that because she's told me that too. I can speak on her behalf because I know what she wants… because she's told me herself. Unlike you, who only ever told her what to do, spoke on her behalf without any consideration of who she was or what she wanted. You stand in my neighbourhood, thinking you're top shit but you're nothing here buddy. A no one. I love Emily, and she loves me. Whatever hold you thought you had over her is gone. Whatever purpose you had for coming here today is no longer important. Because you aren't important to her anymore. I am. So, get the hell off her property before I knock you out. And if you ever come back again; ever come near her again, the same thing will happen."

And with that, Luca slammed the door in Michael's face.

Luca listened to the footsteps grow fainter, the car starting and moving away before he leant against the wall taking deep breaths. His whole body shook with anger. It had taken all his will power and restraint not to knock the dude into next week. He hated people like that. Hated self-righteous, self-serving morons like that. What on earth was Emily thinking dating him? Agreeing to marry him? Luca's thoughts scanned back to the conversation they'd had the week before. Lying in bed, Emily had tried to explain her relationship to Luca. Now that he'd met the guy, he thought it might be a good idea to revisit that conversation with her. If nothing else, then to find out what on earth she was thinking! Sure, the guy was probably rich, but he was also obviously a few other things that Luca couldn't really say aloud. In the back of his mind Luca remembered travelling to New York a couple of weeks earlier. He thought about how he'd felt when he was there. How he'd been dazzled by the money and the fancy life. How he'd enjoyed the cars, the dinners, and the recognition he got when he was with other well-known fighters and promoters.

As he sat back down on the couch he and Emily had bought together, and the red haze of anger subsided, he thought maybe he did understand a little. Understand some of what she had experienced living the high life. Some of the reason it was so important to her to create this house exactly as she envisioned it; the reason she was so reluctant to work again in a role that was so heavily shaped by him. Luca imagined Emily didn't get much opportunity to do things how she wanted or think much for herself when she was with Michael. Even thinking about his name made Luca want to throw something. The guy may have had all the money, the status, and the lifestyle. He might have been able to talk the talk; live the fancy life. But Luca realised, as an idea began to take shape in his mind, that he had something more important than all that stuff. He had her memories, her history… and hopefully he had all of her heart. Grabbing his keys and locking the door behind him, Luca jumped into his car and headed off down the road with a plan to show Emily just how much she meant to him.

"Ok keep your eyes closed," Luca said, as he walked Emily from her car towards the house.

Having spent the afternoon having coffee and wandering through the local shopping centre with Claudia, Emily was surprised by the welcome she'd received from Luca when she'd arrived back home. There he stood on the front step, as the sun set in the sky behind the house, smiling from ear to ear like he'd just won the lotto. She'd left him at home earlier that day, watching an old boxing match on TV, so she knew he'd definitely not won the lotto. She was starting to feel like she had though. Having been pleasantly surprised earlier that morning, when Claudia had called unexpected and invited her to a girl's day at the mall, Emily had spent a fantastic day with her friend. She honestly couldn't remember the last time she'd been clothes shopping, let alone had coffee and lunch with a friend. Luca, coming into the last week of his training camp, had decided to stay at home, lazing around and watching TV. He'd been training nonstop for weeks and it was his rest day.

"I love you Em, but the last thing I want to do on my day off is walk around a mall with two women all day," he'd said.

She hadn't minded but pretended to be highly offended at his lack of passion for shopping. It was nice to spend time with Claudia; trying on clothes, chatting about life. She'd even bought herself a couple of new tops and a dress. Overall, it had been a successful day out.

"What's going on?" Emily asked, as Luca covered her eyes and led her down the hallway towards the living area.

Not a fan of surprises, Emily became increasingly nervous with every step she took.

"Just trust me, you'll love this," Luca said smiling.

Emily did trust him. More than she trusted anyone else in her life. Curiosity took the place of concern as she was led towards the backyard.

"Luca, it's almost dark out. I'm not going to be able to see whatever you're trying to show me," Emily said.

Luca lead her out the glass sliding doors and onto the back deck.

"Don't worry Em, you'll definitely see this."

Uncovering her eyes, Emily blinked a couple of times, letting her eyes adjust to the fading light. Looking around her yard she saw what he had done and gasped. It was the most incredible thing she'd ever seen. The most thoughtful, sweet thing anyone had ever done for her. In that exact moment, Emily knew without doubt that Luca was the person she would spend the rest of her life with. In that moment all her trials and troubles faded, as she stood with tears falling down her cheeks, looking at the wooden swing he had built her. An exact replica of the one her parents had hanging in their yard, it swung from one of the bigger branches of the old oak tree in her yard. Wrapped around the other branches, were small strings of twinkling fairy lights. In the fading afternoon light they gave the impression that the tree was covered in glow bugs, or little tiny stars.

Emily was speechless. All she could do was turn to Luca and stare at him. He stood proudly, enjoying watching her react to his handy work. This was exactly the response he'd hoped for. As he'd driven to the hardware store and purchased the items, he'd pictured here reaction at seeing the finished product. Then as he built and put up the swing, he'd pictured all the times they would spend here, talking, laughing, and dreaming new dreams.

Finding her voice, Emily said quietly, "This is the most thoughtful, beautiful gift anyone has ever given me."

Walking up to Luca, Emily placed her hand on his chest and said, between sniffles, "You are the most wonderful person I've ever met."

Luca smiled, pride filling his chest and his heart.

"Em, I wanted you to have this because I know how much the one at your parents place means to you. I know how many memories that place holds for you. I want you to have your own one here; your own memories in this new place. In your place."

Emily smiled, knowing exactly what she needed to say next.

"Luc, the swing at my parents place is special because of everything it represents. My childhood, my past, our friendship. I want to build memories like that here… with you."

As the lights twinkled brightly and the swing moved gently in the breeze, Luca and Emily walked down the steps into the yard and sat for the first time on the handmade wooden swing, creating a new memory together.

Laying together in bed later that night, Emily tried hard not to burst into laughter as Luca relayed the story of his unwelcome visitor earlier that day.

"You didn't seriously tell him you'd punch his lights out if he ever came back, did you?" Emily said, a fake look of shock on her face.

"Yeah I did," Luca replied, "and I meant it to."

He laughed and pulled her closer to him, as she tried to get her head around the information she'd just received. She imagined the look on Michael's face, and the reaction he would have had to being told where to go. Unable to contain herself, Emily let out a belly laugh that had Luca laughing along with her.

Composing herself, Emily looked at Luca and said, "Thank you for sticking up for me."

Luca kissed her on the forehead and wrapped his arms around her, pulling her closer.

Emily continued, "Luc… I was thinking," Luca leant back and rolled his eyes. "Oh god, please don't tell me we're starting some new crazy project of yours," he said sarcastically.

Emily punched him playfully in the chest and continued, "No… just shut up and listen to me for a minute. I was thinking, that with all the time you're spending here, and all the times your parents have hinted that they want their house back… that you might like to come and live here… with me?"

Luca was taken by surprise. It hadn't crossed his mind that Emily would want him here fulltime.

Seeing the hesitant look on his face she continued, "There's enough room for your boys to stay, on the weekends you have them. And it's not that much further from your training to travel. I know it probably seems fast, and I understand if you don't think it would be a good…"

Luca cut off her random ramblings with a kiss that sent shivers up her spine.

"Emily… you don't need to sell the idea to me… I'd love to move in with you."

Emily let out a squeal and covered her mouth. She was just so happy.

Chapter 26

As the days flew by, Luca trained for the world title with a new intensity. One he'd never experienced before. He wanted it so much. Wanted the belt around his waist more than he'd ever wanted anything. His training had increased in intensity day by day. He would arrive at the Inner City Boxing Gym early in the morning and find John setting up for the session. No matter how early Luca arrived, John would beat him there. As Luca laced up his gloves, he thought about how much he owed John. How different his path might have been if he hadn't had the mentorship and support of his coach.

"Ok Luc, today we're working on hand speed. Get you ready for some fast combinations on the weekend."

Luca nodded and climbed into the ring. He had been working on his footwork for weeks, his stamina and cardio in case the fight went the full 12 rounds. He had run so many miles over the past few weeks; lifted so many weights; completed so many sit ups and thrown so many medicine balls at the gym wall, he'd lost count. But each activity, each rep he'd completed, made him feel stronger. In his final week before the fight, he'd completed all his media requirements: interviews, photo shoots and fan signings. Now it just him, and John. Finalising preparations and perfecting their plan. They'd watched hours of tapes of Luca's opponent. Looking for weaknesses, and opportunities. Watching for patterns and movements they could take advantage of. They had a solid plan; both knowing that plans can come off perfectly or be thrown out the window in five minutes. They hoped theirs was good enough to be perfect.

As Luca trained, he thought about where he'd come from. All the times he'd failed and fallen. He thought about his family, his friends, Emily. They'd all been there from day one and had never given up on him, even when times were the toughest. He owed them more than they'd ever realise. He thought about his kids, about all the time he'd spent with them over the last couple of weeks. He'd made such an effort to fit everything in, and Emily had helped. So had Claudia. Dropping them off after school at the gym to watch him train and play around with John; dropping them at Emily and his house for dinner. Claudia had even joined them a few times. Luca saw how much Emily enjoyed it when she stayed. The boys would sit in the house playing video games on the TV, with Emily and Claudia enjoying a glass of wine out on the deck. Luca smiled. He still couldn't quite believe he was living with Emily. That his boys had their own rooms, and he had a home that was theirs. Sometimes he lay in bed watching her sleep, not wanting to close his eyes in case he woke up and it was all a dream. He knew it was silly to think that way but having fought his whole life for what he wanted; he didn't quite know how to sit comfortably in his normal life yet. He hoped he would keep learning after he won the world title.

John, sensing Luca was distracted, ended the training early. After packing down and cleaning up, the two men sat together in his office as John handed Luca a photo album.

"What's this?" Luca asked.

"Have a look why don't you," John replied with a laugh.

Luca opened the album at the first page and saw a newspaper clipping dated 13 years earlier. It was a picture of a young Luca holding up his first boxing trophy. He remembered the day like it was yesterday. His first match; first win. John had been there in his corner, supporting him and pushing him to be better.

"Seriously?" Luca said looking at his coach, trying not to tear up.

He turned page after page and found more photos, more articles. John had kept every picture and every clipping he'd found over the years.

"I knew from the first day you walked into this gym that you were special Luca. I kept that album from day one because I knew one day, I'd be giving it back to you. I knew one day you'd be the world champion."

Luca put down the album and walked around the desk to his mentor.

Standing, the two men embraced as John said, "No matter what happens on the weekend, everyone who knows you is so proud of you; loves you so much Luca."

And he meant every word.

The day of the fight arrived as Luca woke early. He'd been to the venue and weighed in the previous day, so had enjoyed spending the night before his fight eating and drinking normally again. He hadn't needed to cut too much weight, only a few pounds, so his body was feeling ready to go. Careful not to wake Emily, Luca slipped out of bed and made his way into the kitchen to get his breakfast started. He wanted to eat early so he had fuel in his body well before he had to leave for the fight. The last thing he wanted was to fight on a full stomach. It was never a good feeling. Opening the fridge, he took out the eggs to make himself an omelette. Opening the carton, he found a note wedged in beside a couple of the eggs.

'Luc, I love you so much and am so proud of you. You will be amazing today and I'll be right there beside you, Em.'

Luca smiled as he tucked the note into his pocket and started cooking his breakfast. He was a lucky man, he thought to himself, as Emily arrived beside him in the kitchen.

"Good morning," she said, as she grabbed him around the waist and squeezed. "I'm so excited for today Luc… I can't wait to finally see you fight!"

Luca smiled and turned to kiss her on the forehead. With expert precision, he flipped his omelette and it landed back in the pan.

"Tell me again what's happening today," Emily said, as she sat herself up on the kitchen bench.

Luca went over his schedule again, including the time he needed to arrive, the work out before the fight, hand wrapping, run down with the ref and finally walking out to the waiting crowd. Emily felt nervous just listening to him talk about it all. It sounded terrifying!

"Brian Blackman has seats reserved for you, my parents, Ricky, Claudia and the boys when we get there. John and a couple of the boys from the gym will be cornering for me so they'll stand ring side."

Emily could hear in Luca's voice that he was nervous. She'd never seen him really nervous before, and it intrigued her.

"What do you do to pass the time while you're waiting for the other fights to finish?" she asked.

Luca replied, "It depends on where I am and how I feel. Sometimes I'll listen to music. Sometimes I'll just sit and chat to the boys in my corner. Sometimes I'll watch the other fights on the screen in the warmup room. It just depends."

Emily nodded. This was all so foreign to her. Like another world. A knock at the door revealed a serious but smiling John, ready to collect Luca and Emily for the long day ahead of them. They had to be at the venue in an hour and with a 30-minute drive from their place, John was keen to get moving. Collecting up all the bags they'd packed the night before, Emily headed out to the car with John. Luca, hanging back for a second to finish off the last mouthful of his breakfast, grabbed a pen and paper and quickly scribbled down a note for Emily. He tucked in under her pillow and ran out the door to join the others in the car.

Arriving at the venue, the three were ushered into an area specifically set up for the fighters. They were given their own prep room and inside it contained all the gear Luca was expected to wear for the fight including shorts with sponsors logos on them. The set of gloves put aside especially for him had his name painted on them in gold lettering. They looked amazing. He picked them up and checked out every little detail on them before a loud, gruff voice interrupted him.

"Luca, my boy, welcome to the first day of the rest of your life!" Brian Blackman said jovially, standing at the door to the room beaming.

He was obviously happy this day had arrived and took the time to shake Luca and John's hand and introduce himself to Emily. Smiling politely, Emily wondered if he was always that loud and excitable.

"Now Luca, I want you to know I'm rooting for you today. I can't say that publicly, as you can imagine how it would look, but I'm definitely in your corner. Good luck my boy. See you in there."

With that, Brian turned and walked out of the room.

Luca smiled at Emily as John said quietly, "I bet he's on his way to the other guys room to tell him he's behind him too."

They all laughed, realising it was probably the truth.

Hours passed as the crowd began filling the arena for the fight card. Luca's parents, Claudia and the kids arrived and were ushered into the training room where Luca was warming up on the bag. Seeing his parents and his boys walk into the room almost made Luca break down. He wanted so badly to make them all proud of him. To prove to all of them that he was the best. He didn't care about the other 35,000 people in the arena. He just wanted his family to be proud of him. Shaking his father's hand, Luca was surprised when Carlos pulled him to the side. Luca was instantly concerned. "Is everything ok Dad?" he asked, worry obvious in his tone.

"Everything's fine Luc, everything's all good," Carlos replied. "I just need to tell you… I… I'm proud of you son. I need you to know that."

Luca was completely blindsided by his father. A man of very few words, Luca had never in his whole life heard his father tell anyone he loved them or was proud of them… especially him. It really meant so much to hear it now. Luca nodded to his father, suddenly the one without the words.

"Thanks Dad," was all he managed, before John called out to the room,

"All right everyone, it's time to head in and take your seats."

Luca gave his Dad a hug and turned to everyone in the room. Standing there looking at his family and friends, he realised how lucky he was. Now he just had to win for them all.

The fight got closer and closer; as did Luca's anxiety. His mind began racing as he sat getting his hands wrapped. He tried his hardest to take deep breaths, to talk himself through it. As he sat waiting to be called for his fight, the fear of failure sat firmly in his thoughts. What if he lost? What if he wasn't good enough? What if he embarrassed himself in front of his family and friends? At one point, he considered getting up and leaving. Just walking out, saying thanks for the experience, and getting a taxi home. He knew he couldn't possibly do that, but he thought about it. To keep himself busy, he paced back and forth; he shadowboxed; he practiced his footwork. When all of that didn't work, he decided to do something he never thought he'd find himself doing. He began cleaning up the room. As he packed his clothes and gear from earlier in the day into his training bag, a small scrap of paper fell from the pocket of the shorts he'd worn into the venue. Bending down and picking it up he remembered the note Emily had left him in the egg carton earlier that morning and opened it to re-read the message.

'Luc, I love you so much and am so proud of you. You will be amazing today and I'll be right there beside you, Em.'

Just like that, Luca felt a calm come over him. He felt the love of his family and friends wash over him. He took a deep breath and tuned out all the negative thoughts. This was his time. This was his belt. As the ring announcer called his opponent to the ring, Luca placed the note in his bag, and turning to face the door, walked out to meet his destiny.

Walking out into the arena, hearing the crown screaming, the lights flooding the space, Luca felt a hundred feet tall. The adrenaline began pumping, as he walked with his coach and corner crew down the long walk towards the ring. Arriving at the centre of the arena, Luca climbed into the ring and was greeted by his opponent standing on the other side of the space. A tall guy with a shaved head and mean looking face, Luca was instantly reminded of a kid he'd gone to school with. Always picking on kids smaller than him. The guy was a bully. Luca had caught him taking money from a little kid once… and given him a black eye for his trouble. He hoped he'd do the same to this guy today. Luca glanced down into the crowd and spotted his parents, Ricky and Rachael, Claudia, and the kids… and Emily. He could tell she was nervous, the stress obvious on her face. He smiled as he wondered how it was possible that she felt nervous and he, about to fight for a world title, felt pretty calm. The referee called the two fighters together and went through the usual rules. Fight clean, listen to my commands, protect yourself at all times. It was a spiel he'd heard many, many times but one he listened to just the same. Turning and walking back to his corner, John had one last piece of advice for Luca.

"I need you to remember, his weakness is his left side. We know that. Use it… and go get that belt." Luca nodded to his coach and turned to face his opponent as the bell rang for round one.

Luca quickly went to work as he moved around the ring with a fluidity that many in the crowd had never seen before. Tuning out the cheers and jeers of the crowd, Luca ducked and weaved around his opponents' shots, finding his own range, and launching with some body shots to his left side. The guy lurched forward as Luca caught him with a left hook. He could tell he was winning, as he pushed forward and had his opponent hard up against the ropes. The guy, realising he was cornered, faked, and hit Luca with a good right hook, cracking him on the jaw. It felt like he'd been hit by a sledgehammer, but it didn't stop him. Nothing and no one was going to stop him from getting that world title belt, he thought to himself.

The bell rang as the round finished and Luca made his way back to his corner. Listening to the instructions from John, Luca nodded and took a drink. He felt fresh; felt good. His jaw began to throb a little, but he ignored it. John gave him some new instructions and Luca listened intently. He'd won the first, now he needed to win the next few. Standing and facing his opponent, the bell rang for the second round. Luca moved around the ring again, faking left and right; throwing shots as he saw them. Towards the end of the round, he launched and hit the guy with a left jab and right hook. Instantly, he felt the bones in his right hand break as he connected. The pain was excruciating. Dropping his hands for just a second, his opponent took advantage and hit Luca with a hard right to the temple. Blood spurted from the cut that had opened on his head as Luca wobbled on his feet. He looked down at the canvas and saw his own blood falling around him. He was going to lose. The bell rang for the end of the round as Luca, a little confused and disorientated, made his way back to his corner.

"Luc, look at me," John said, as Luca sat on the stool clutching his broken right hand.

"What's going on with you?" he said seriously.

Quietly, Luca replied, "My right hands broken man. I can't hit with it."

John thought quickly.

"What do you want to do? Do you want me to throw in the towel?"

Luca looked at his coach as if he were mad. No way was he giving up this opportunity. They would need to drag his dead body out of the ring before he'd throw in the towel.

"No way, I'm not giving up. This means too much."

John nodded, knowing Luca would never give up, but needing him to say it aloud.

"OK then, lets fight hard. Lead with your left. It's his weak side. Use some of that footwork we've been training and keep your broken hand up around your face. If you can't hit with it, at least use it to protect yourself."

Luca nodded and stood, the cut on his head no longer bleeding, after being treated by his corner to stop it temporarily. It wouldn't be long before it started again, dripping, and oozing claret in his eye, making it difficult to see his opponents' hands.

As the bell rang for the start of the next round, Luca bit down on his mouthpiece and went to war.

Chapter 27

Emily stood in the front row next to Claudia holding her hand like her life depended on it. She felt sick. She'd just watched Luca being punched in the face, bleeding all over the ring. She'd seen him shake his head like he wasn't sure where he was. This was terrifying. Any thought of being excited for him turned to terror as she prayed he wouldn't get hurt anymore then he already was. Watching a loved one being stalked, attacked, was not something she found she enjoyed. All she wanted was for him to come home to her safely. To be ok. The bloody belt could get stuffed. She just wanted Luca to be ok.

"He's gonna be fine Em," Claudia said, seeing the frightened look on Emily's face.

Claudia had been to plenty of these events before; seen Luca get bashed and bruised in the ring more times than she could count. But it never got any easier. It never felt good to watch a loved one being hurt. Riley and Joey stood near Claudia, playing around and pretending to hide under the seats in front of them. Completely ignoring what was going on in front of them, the two boys were having a ball playing together.

'At least they won't see their dad get beaten,' Claudia thought sombrely.

She clasped Emily's hand more firmly and said a silent prayer as the bell rang for the next round.

Luca stood tall in his corner, ready to make up for the last round. He had to. In his mind the score card was even. He needed to turn it in his favour, and quickly. His hand hurt to move. He could tell it had already started to swell in his glove, making it hurt even more. He couldn't throw it; couldn't use it to punch or even block. All he could do was plaster it to his face, protecting one side of his jaw. Moving around to the left, Luca watched the realisation register on the face of his opponent, when he worked out Luca had hurt his right hand. He saw the guys eyes light up and his lips curl into a satisfied grin. Luca watched the smile turn to a smirk, right before he launched an attack on Luca's right side that left him staggering and gasping for breath.

At one point, he had Luca pinned up against the ropes, throwing body blows that made Luca feel like his ribs were being broken. They possibly were. Completely narrow visioned in on Luca's right hand, his right ribs, Luca saw his opening and let fly with a left jab that took the guy by surprise. Staggering backwards, Luca quickly leapt forward and followed with another two jabs and with strength that he didn't realise he had, launched his right hand into the face of his opponent as hard as he could. Broken or not, he wasn't going to let this guy get the better of him. He wasn't going to let his family watch him lose today. Stunned, the guy swayed for a second before he hit the canvas. As he lay clutching his head, unable to get up, the referee counted to ten. Luca, gasping for breath and not able to even feel his right hand any longer, let alone lift it, looked over to Emily standing in the crowd sobbing, and held up his left hand in triumph.

Luca felt invincible in that moment; the entire world at his feet. But god his body hurt. As the adrenaline began to subside, acute and extreme pain replaced it. In his head, his arms, his hand. It was the worst of all. Luca felt like he'd gone 12 rounds with a semi-trailer. But he'd won. He'd won! The realisation that the world title belt was about to be hung around his waist set in, as Brian Blackman entered the ring and walked over to Luca.

Placing his hand on his shoulder, Brian said, "Real gutsy show tonight kid. You've got a long and successful career with the American Boxing League ahead of you. Mark my words."

Luca smiled and nodded, unable to speak from the pain shooting up his arm and into his chest.

As Brian placed the golden belt around Luca's waist, he looked around at the people in his support corner. His parents, always there for him no matter what trouble he'd caused them; his friends, Ricky, and Claudia, two of the best people he could ever hope to know. He saw his boys, messing around on the seats, completely oblivious to what their father had just accomplished. A poor kid from a bad neighbourhood; a kid who was written off his whole life as a no one; a nobody, had just won the American Boxing League World Title. One day they'll get it, he thought to himself as he grimaced in pain. He saw John and his teammates from Inner City Boxing. John, he owed the most. From a scared, angry teenager, John had shaped Luca into the man that stood in the centre of the ring, triumphant. A world champion. No words would ever describe the respect and love Luca had for John.

And then he saw Emily. The greatest love of his life. His soulmate. The girl who built sandcastles and mud pies with him as a child; helped him with his homework and fixed up his many injuries as a teen; loved him and supported him as an adult. She was more than his lover, just as he was more than just a fighter. They were equals in every way, and he knew then and there that he never wanted to lose her again.

Chapter 28

Three months had passed in the blink of an eye, as Luca stood at the front of the newly painted building holding his world title belt. His hand had been repaired with a number of surgeries and was now free of the casts and plasters he'd put up with for months. His cuts and bruises had faded long ago, and he now stood looking healthy and happy. The photographer took her shots as Luca stood proudly displaying his achievement. Next to him, Emily stood equally as proud, in front of her new doctors' offices. She'd spent all her time after Luca's win, refitting and refurbishing the old GP surgery she'd purchased, to make it look brand new. Clean. Appealing to people who might need to sit in the waiting room for a period of time. Luca had been there to offer his help, working with only one hand for most of it. She'd put him to work painting left-handed, fixing holes in walls left-handed and generally being helpful… left-handed. She'd been there for him too, helping him with daily tasks at home, like opening bottles and cans; getting dressed (which she didn't mind at all) and putting up his hair into the signature man bun he'd become synonymous for.

Since winning the world title, both their lives had changed so much. Luca had become a household name, especially around the LA area. It wasn't unusual for him to spend six hours each day doing interviews and events in LA and around the US. He travelled often, but always came home to Emily at the end of his trips. After his fight, Claudia agreed to let the boys stay over more often, and Emily now had two bedrooms permanently set up for Luca's two boys. They even stayed over when Luca was away, which Emily loved. They played video games and video called their Dad to talk before they went to bed each night. Emily had purchased the doctor's surgery the week after Luca had won the world title. She'd made some enquiries leading up to his fight, and was happily surprised when the local realter just happened to be Martin, the young guy who'd sold her the house she and Luca lived in. He was happy to see Emily again, within such a brief period of time and was genuinely pleased when she showed him pictures of her renovated home. Martin sold the office space to Emily for a great deal, helped along by the fact that the World champion, Luca Mendes happened to attend the appointment with Emily, knowing full well that Martin was a huge fan of boxing.

Emily had done an amazing job with the old space, replacing the front of the building with a bright, light façade. It now matched the other shop fronts in the complex and made the whole space look new and fresh. The other shop owners loved Emily for it. They'd been asking the previous owner to fix up the front of the building for years before he'd retired. Now, standing in the front reception space, with Claudia, her best friend sitting behind the desk ready to take in the first patient, Emily felt like she might burst with happiness. Luca walked up to her and picked her up, swinging her around.

"Hey, hands off the boss," Claudia called out, laughing.

The door swung open as Emily's first patient made her way into the medical office. Standing at the door with a huge smile on her face, was Emily's mother Carmen.

"Can anyone here take a blood pressure?" she asked with a smile.

"I imagined this a long time ago," he told her, as they danced together on the deck, with the fairy lights from the tree giving off just enough light for Luca to see the expressions on her face. "When you first began fixing this place up, I pictured us out here dancing together," he said.

Emily smiled, believing every word.

"You know I've loved you since before I could walk," he whispered, smiling as he gazed into her eyes. Eyes full of love for him. Only him.

"I know," she replied. "Luca, I don't ever want to imagine my life without you. You're everything I need in my life. I love you so much."

Standing there, under the warm, starry night, a soft breeze rustling through the flower garden they'd planted so many months before; her long hair softly waving in the breeze, Luca knew it was the right moment. He led her down the steps to the swing he'd built her with his own hands; the replica of the one they'd spent their childhood on; laughed on; dreamed on. Turning to face her, he took her hand in his and kissed it gently.

'She has no idea,' he thought smiling.

He'd always loved to surprise her. The fairy lights twinkled brightly in the old oak tree above them, as Luca got down on one knee. Reciting her favourite Shakespearian sonnet like a pro, he asked his best friend, the women he loved more than life itself, to marry him.

The End